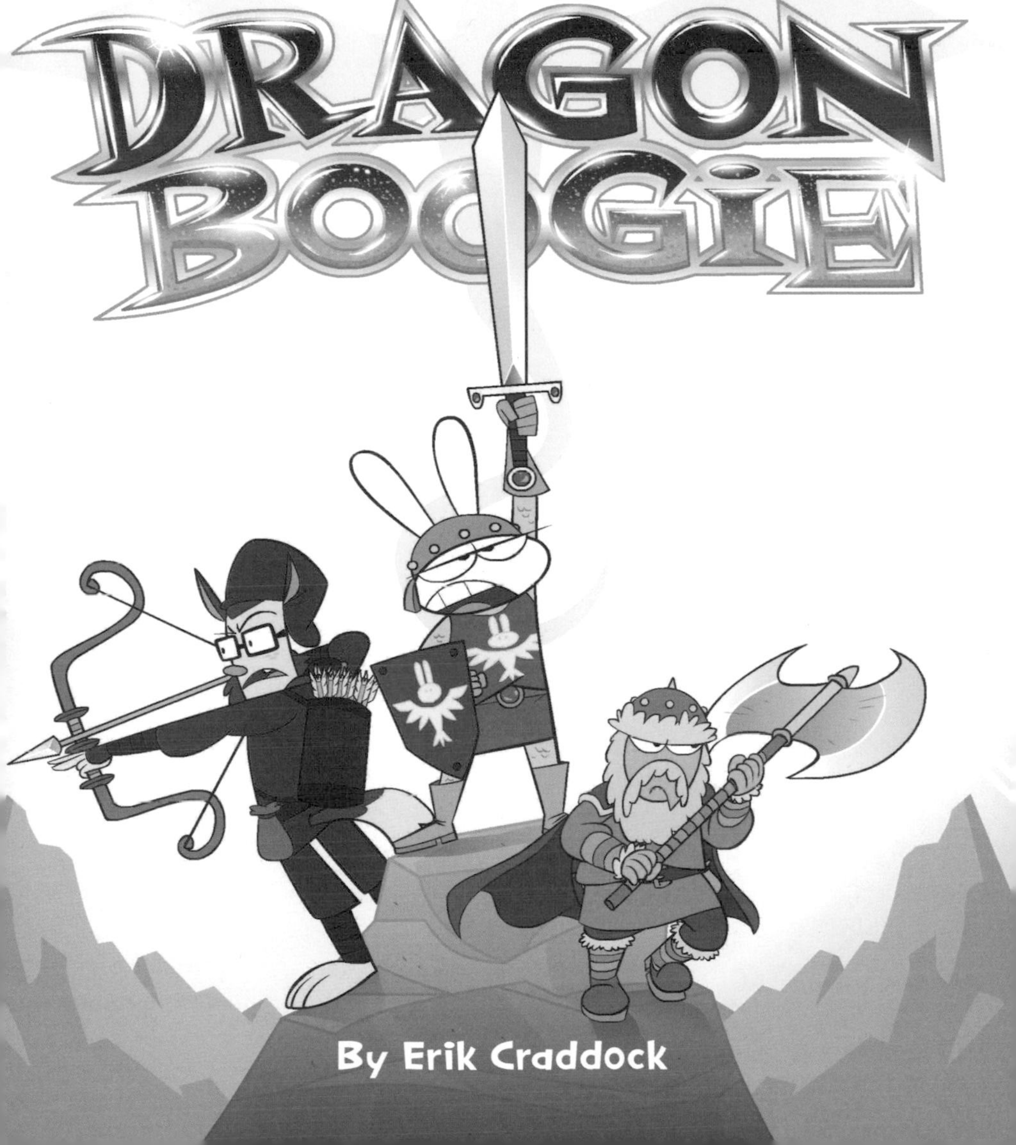

DRAGON BOOGIE
By Erik Craddock

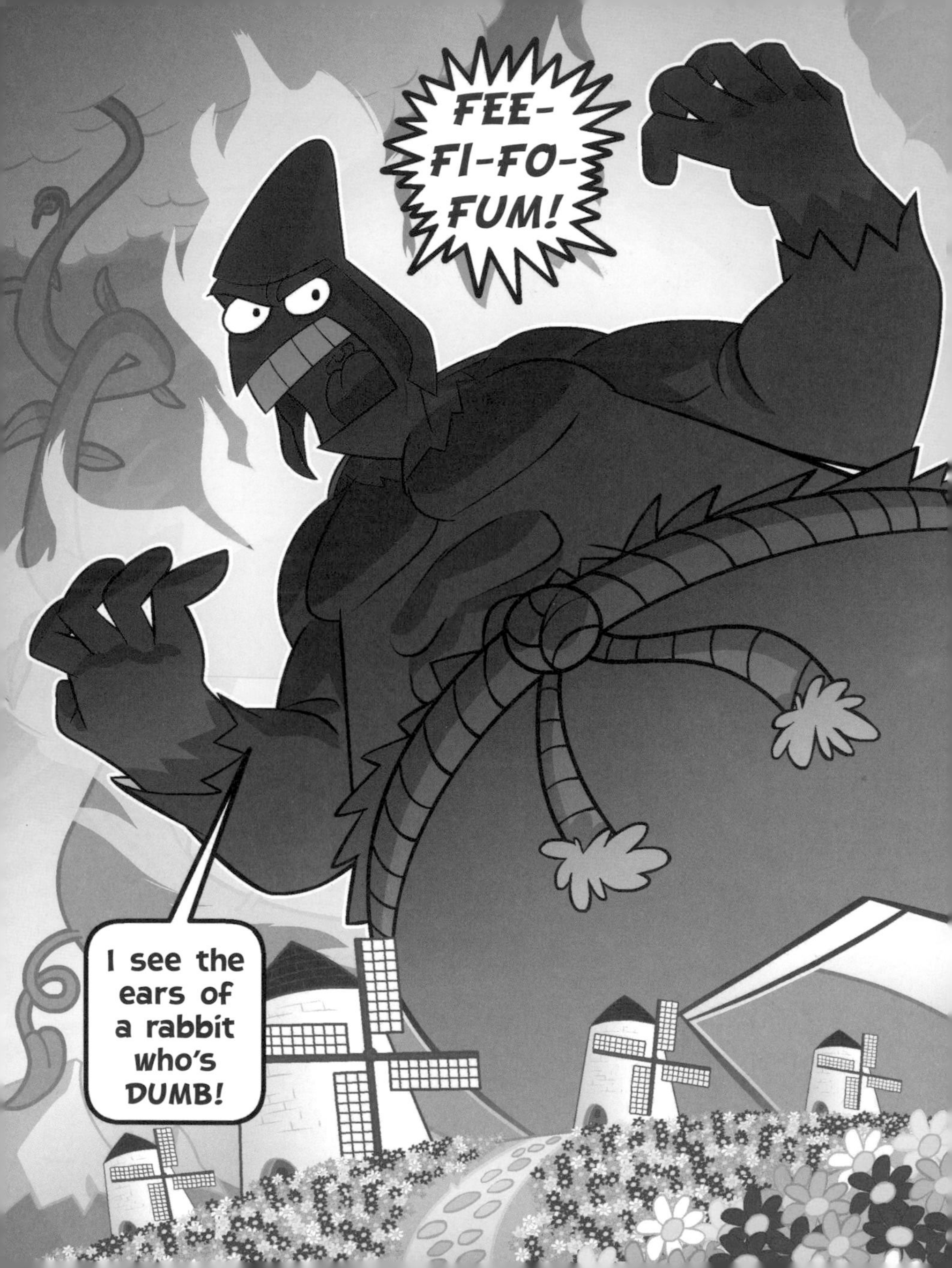
FEE-FI-FO-FUM!
I see the ears of a rabbit who's DUMB!

Published in the United States by Random House Children's Books, a division of Random House, Inc., New York.

Random House and the colophon are registered trademarks of Random House, Inc.

Visit us on the Web! randomhouse.com/kids

Educators and librarians, for a variety of teaching tools, visit us at randomhouse.com/teachers

stonerabbit.com

Library of Congress Cataloging-in-Publication Data

Craddock, Erik.

Dragon boogie / Erik Craddock.

p. cm.

Summary: When a storm cuts off the electricity, Stone Rabbit, Henri, and Andy start playing a board game using strange dice that Henri "found," and soon they are trapped in the game and must defeat an evil Dark Lord in order to get home.

ISBN 978-0-375-86912-9 (pbk.) — ISBN 978-0-375-96012-0 (lib. bdg.) — ISBN 978-0-307-97872-1 (ebook)

1. Graphic novels. [1. Graphic novels. 2. Board games—Fiction. 3. Games—Fiction. 4. Supernatural—Fiction. 5. Rabbits—Fiction. 6. Animals—Fiction. 7. Humorous stories.] I. Title.

PZ7.7.C73Dr 2012 741.5'973—dc23 2011009434

MANUFACTURED IN MALAYSIA 10 9 8 7 6 5 4 3 2 1 First Edition

Random House Children's Books supports the First Amendment and celebrates the right to read.

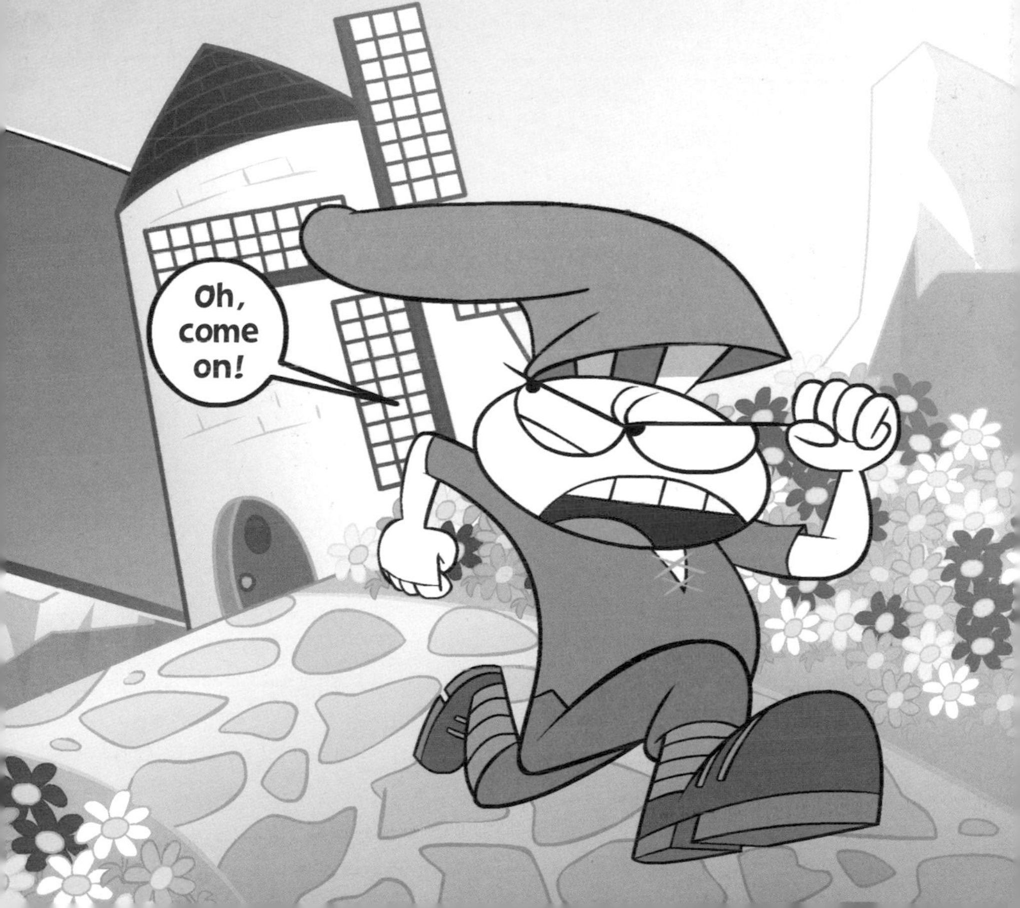
Oh, come on!

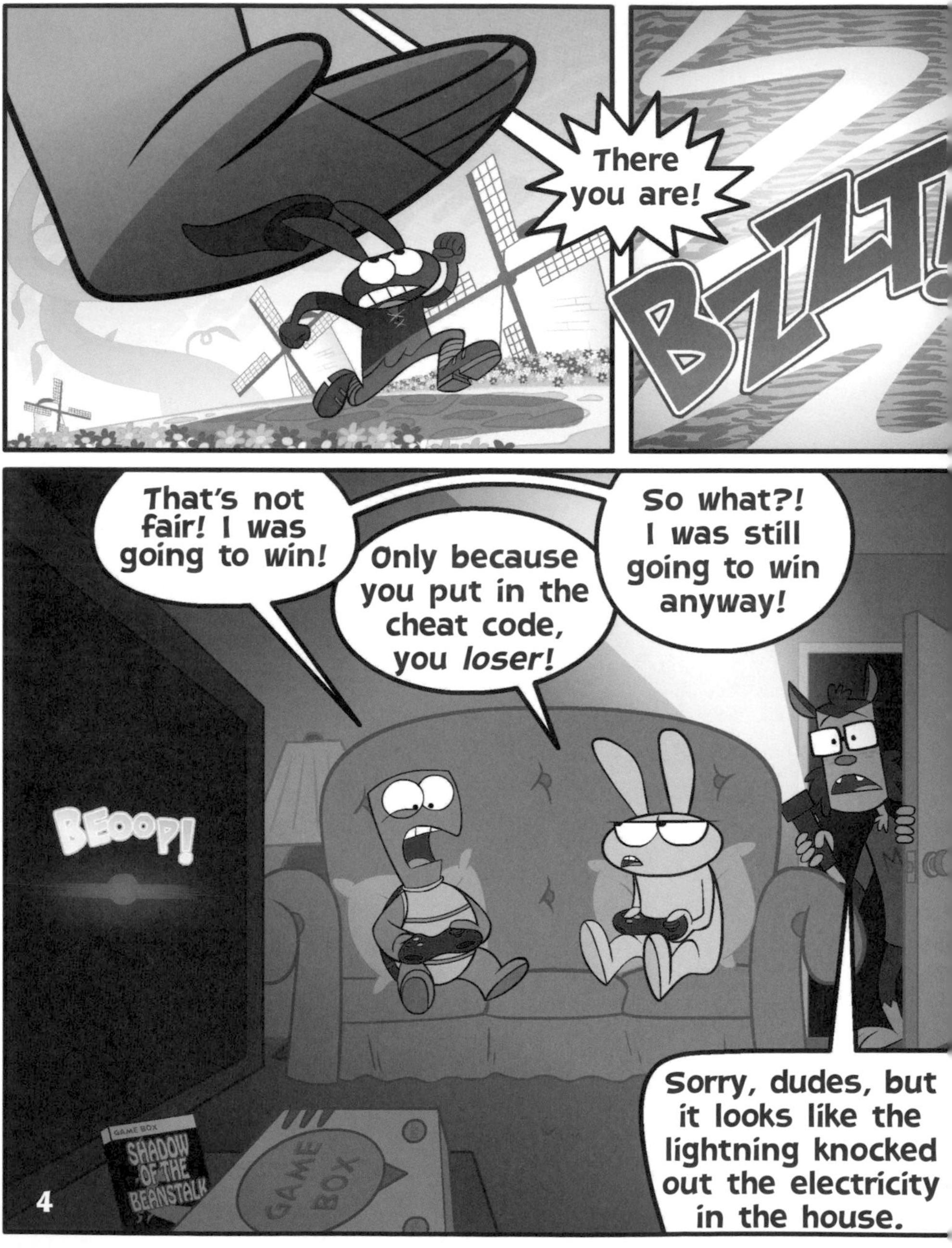

There you are!
BZZZT!
That's not fair! I was going to win!
Only because you put in the cheat code, you *loser*!
So what?! I was still going to win anyway!
BEOOP!
Sorry, dudes, but it looks like the lightning knocked out the electricity in the house.
GAME BOX
SHADOW OF THE BEANSTALK
GAME BOX

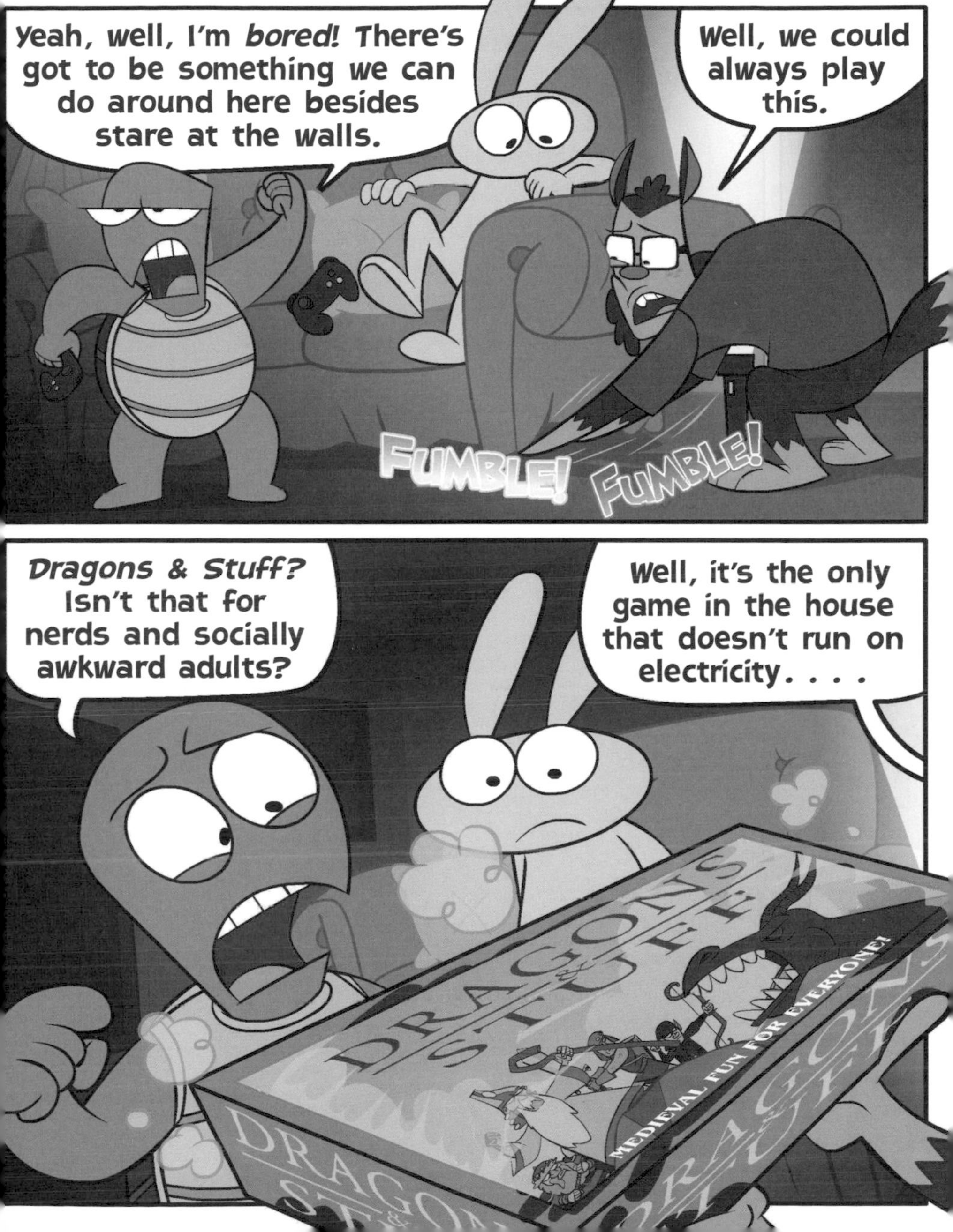
Yeah, well, I'm *bored!* There's got to be something we can do around here besides stare at the walls.
Well, we could always play this.
FUMBLE! FUMBLE!
Dragons & Stuff? Isn't that for nerds and socially awkward adults?
Well, it's the only game in the house that doesn't run on electricity. . . .
DRAGONS & STUFF
MEDIEVAL FUN FOR EVERYONE!

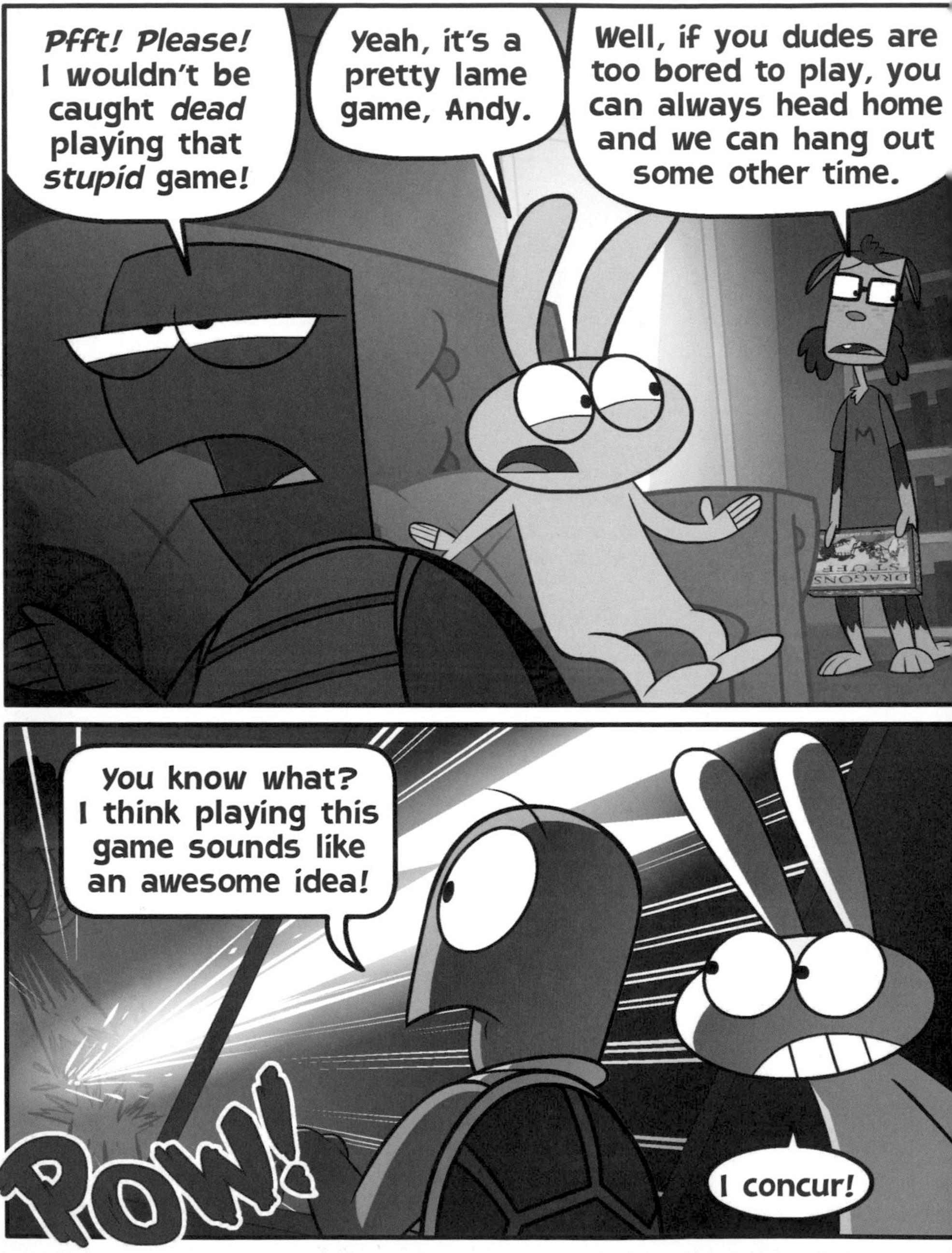
Pfft! Please! I wouldn't be caught *dead* playing that *stupid* game!
Yeah, it's a pretty lame game, Andy.
Well, if you dudes are too bored to play, you can always head home and we can hang out some other time.
You know what? I think playing this game sounds like an awesome idea!
POW!
I concur!

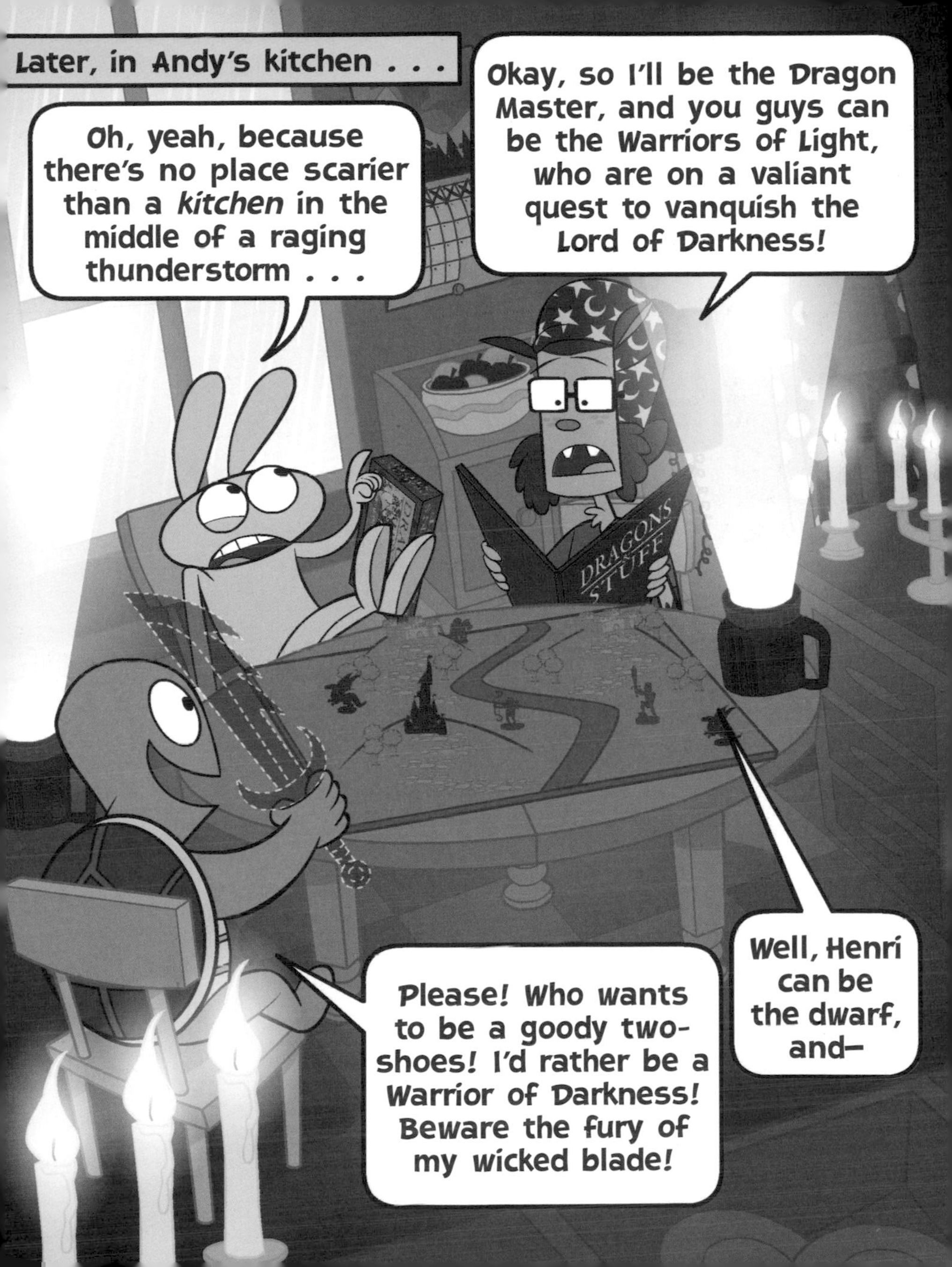
Later, in Andy's kitchen . . .
Oh, yeah, because there's no place scarier than a *kitchen* in the middle of a raging thunderstorm . . .
Okay, so I'll be the Dragon Master, and you guys can be the Warriors of Light, who are on a valiant quest to vanquish the Lord of Darkness!
DRAGONS STUFF
Please! Who wants to be a goody two-shoes! I'd rather be a Warrior of Darkness! Beware the fury of my wicked blade!
Well, Henri can be the dwarf, and—

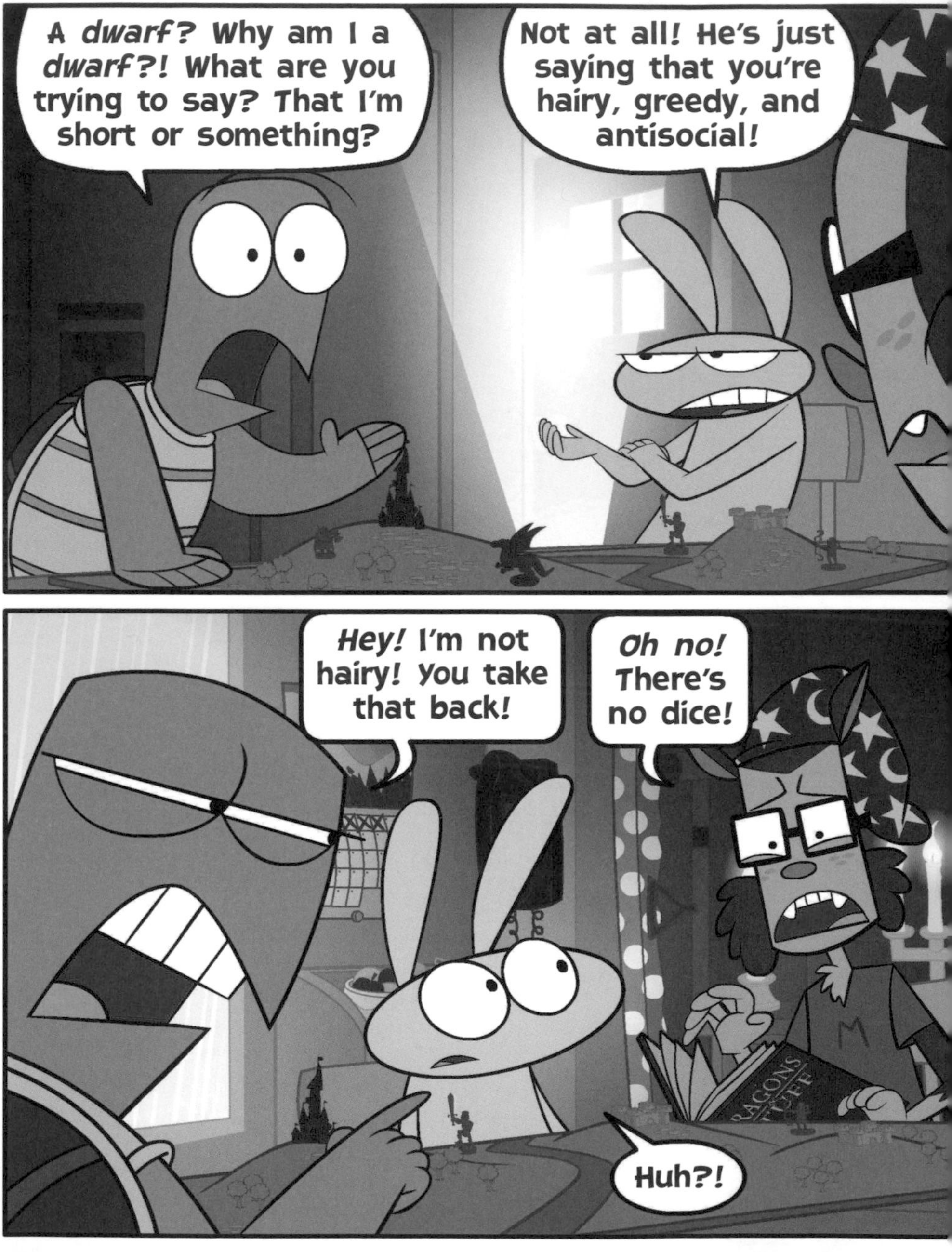
A *dwarf?* Why am I a *dwarf?!* What are you trying to say? That I'm short or something?
Not at all! He's just saying that you're hairy, greedy, and antisocial!
Hey! I'm not hairy! You take that back!
Oh no! There's no dice!
Huh?!

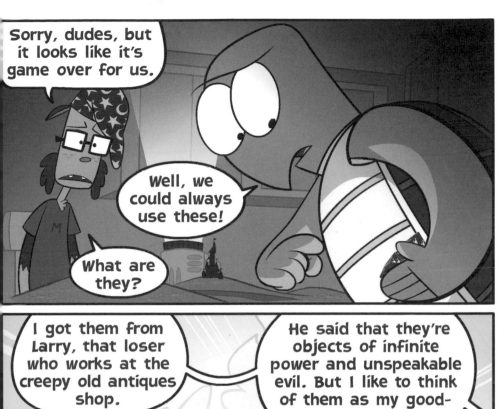

Sorry, dudes, but it looks like it's game over for us.

Well, we could always use these!

What are they?

I got them from Larry, that loser who works at the creepy old antiques shop.

He said that they're objects of infinite power and unspeakable evil. But I like to think of them as my good-luck charms!

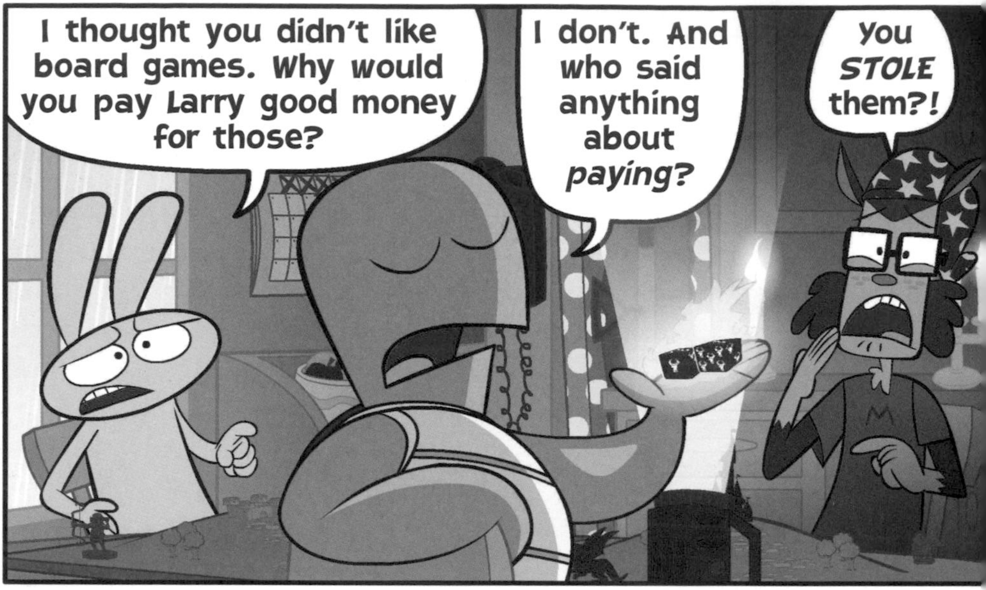
I thought you didn't like board games. Why would you pay Larry good money for those?
I don't. And who said anything about *paying*?
You *STOLE* them?!

Of *course* not! They fell out of his pocket when he was reaching for his Mister Freezy ice cream cone. As far as I'm concerned, "Finders keepers, losers weepers!"

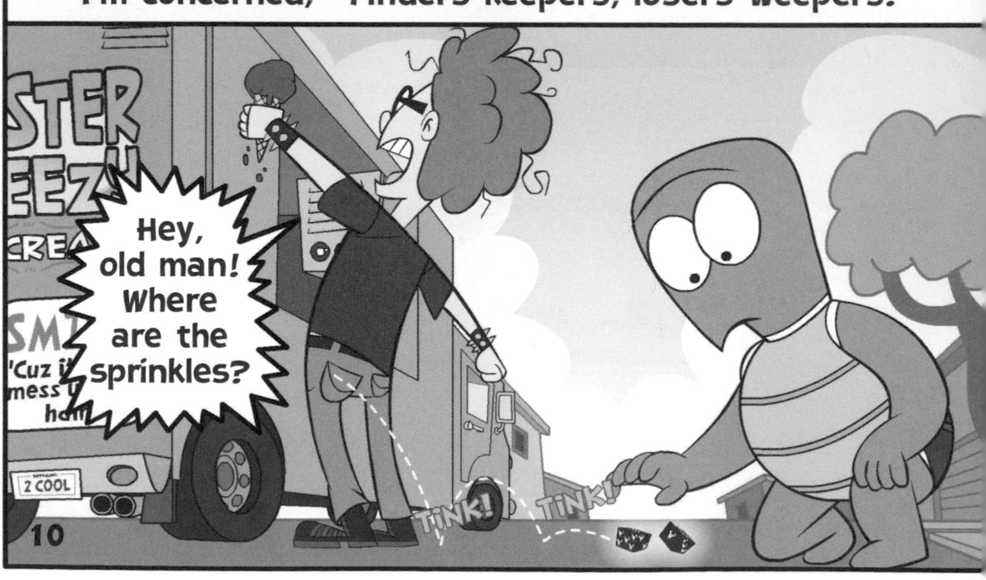
Hey, old man! Where are the sprinkles?
2 COOL
TINK!
TINK!

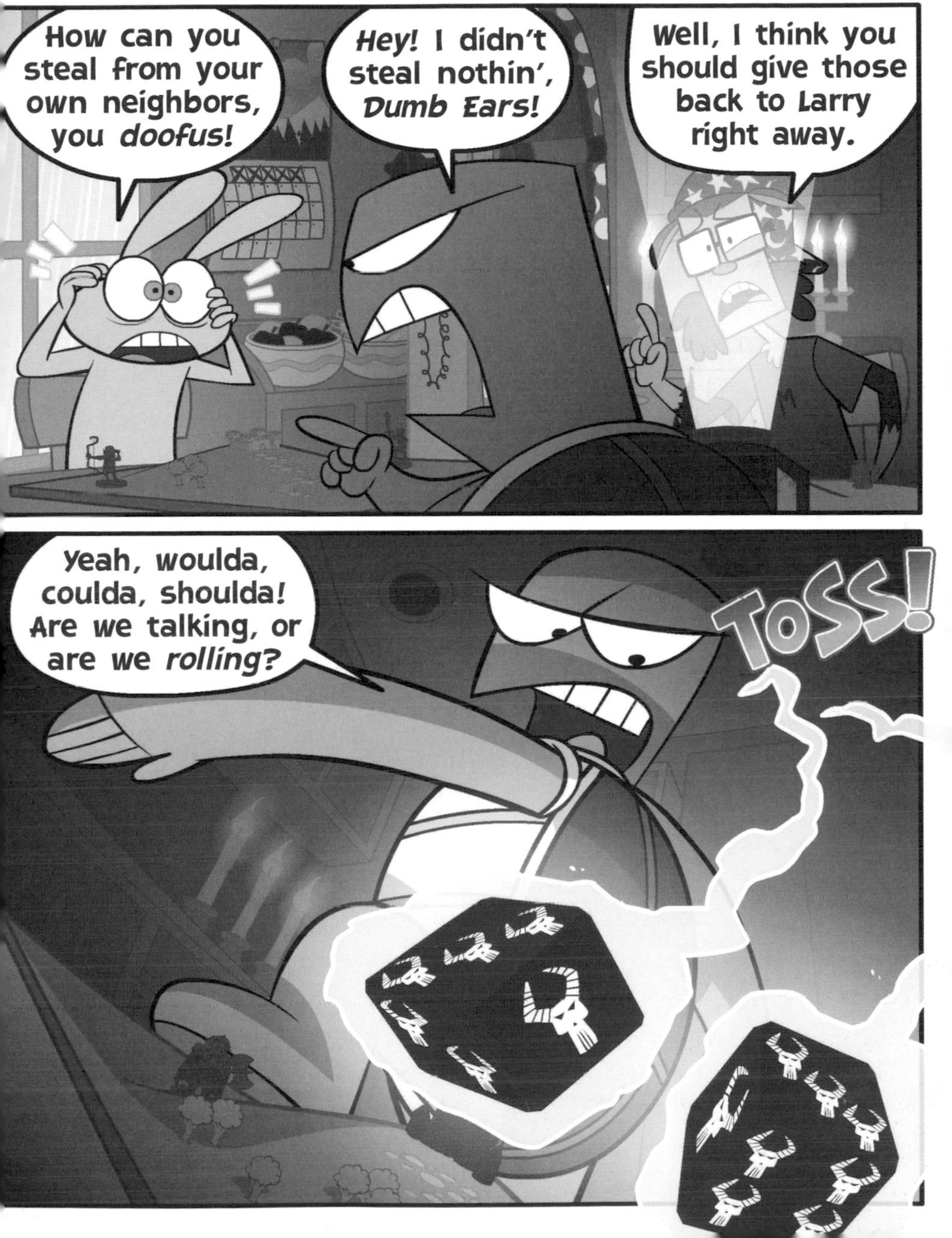
How can you steal from your own neighbors, you *doofus*!
Hey! I didn't steal nothin', *Dumb Ears*!
Well, I think you should give those back to Larry right away.
Yeah, woulda, coulda, shoulda! Are we talking, or are we *rolling*?
TOSS!

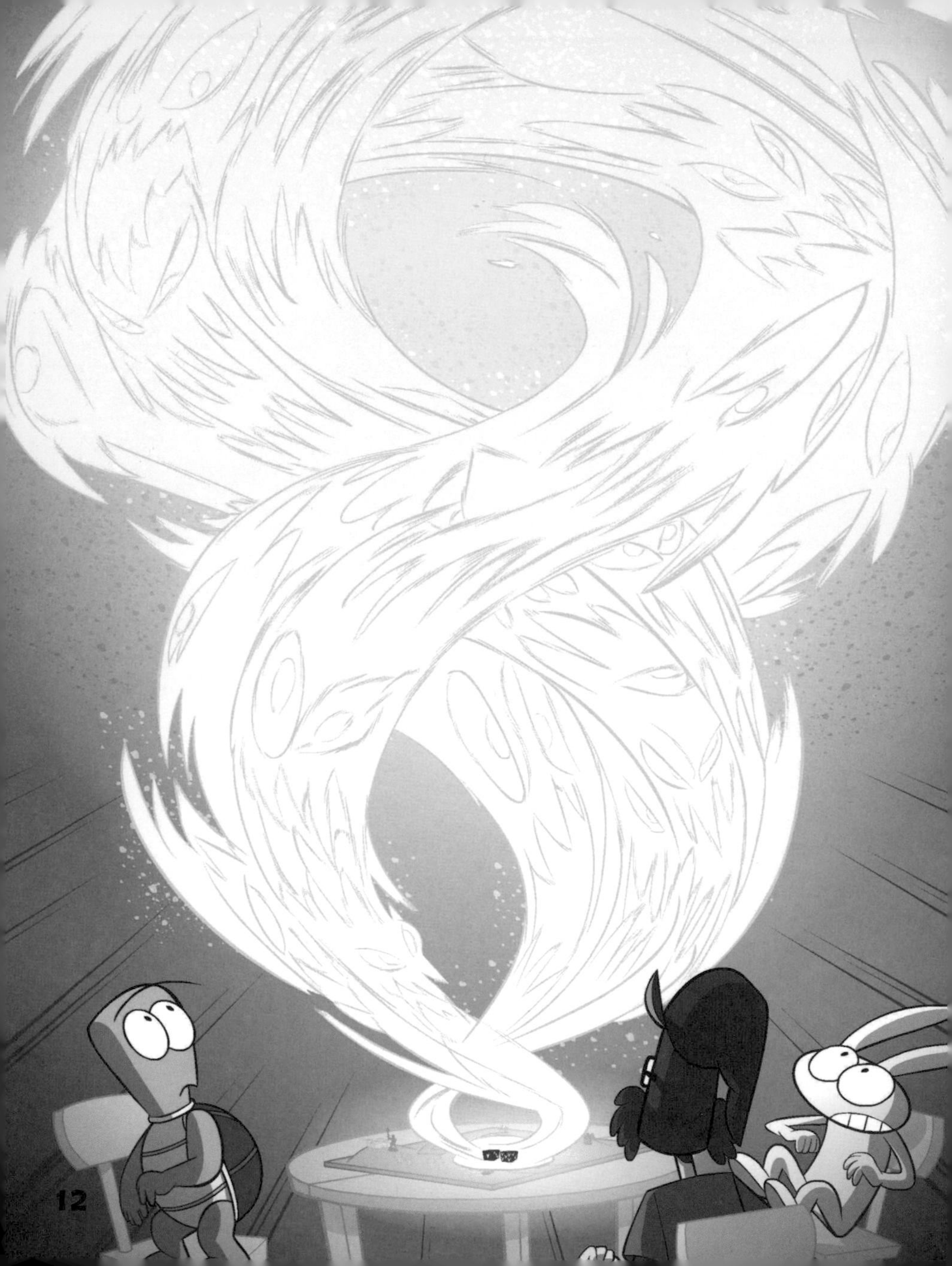

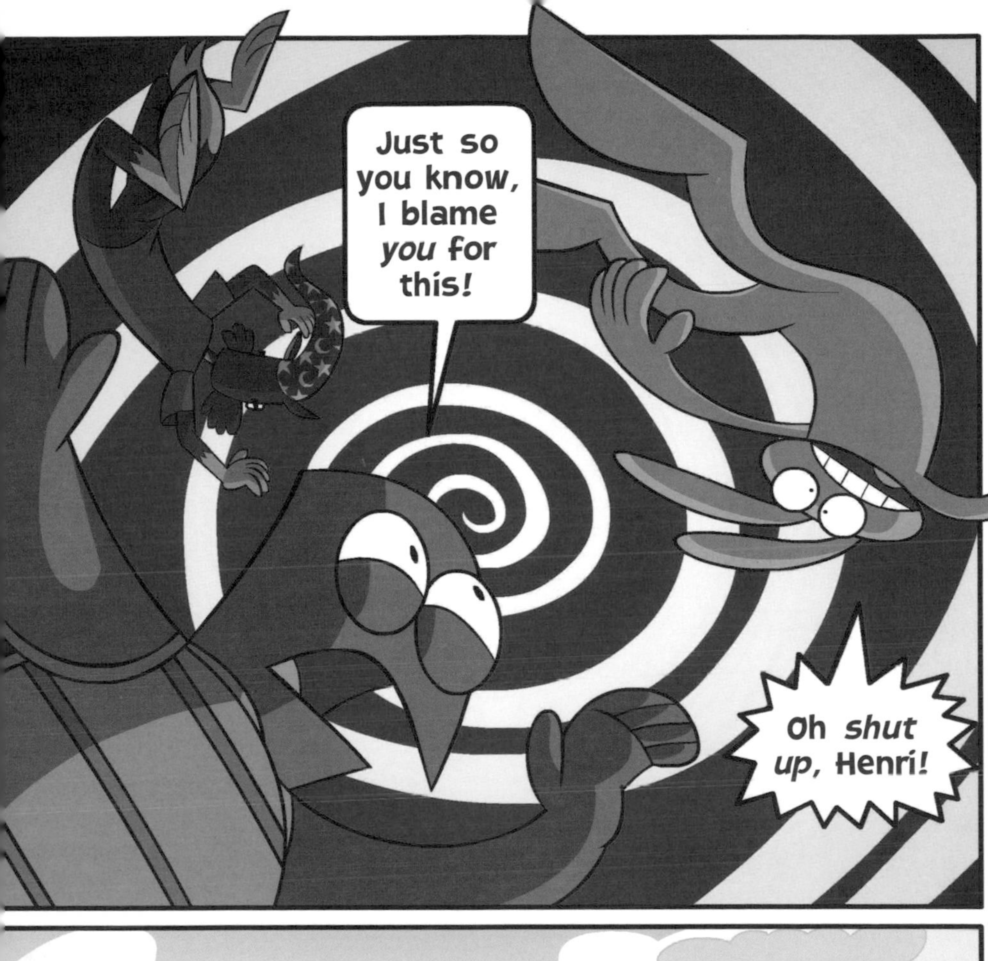
Just so you know, I blame *you* for this!
Oh *shut up*, Henri!

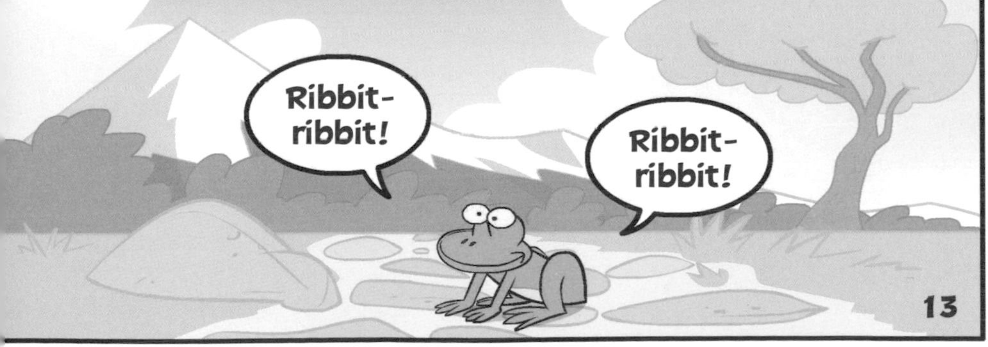
Ribbit-ribbit!
Ribbit-ribbit!

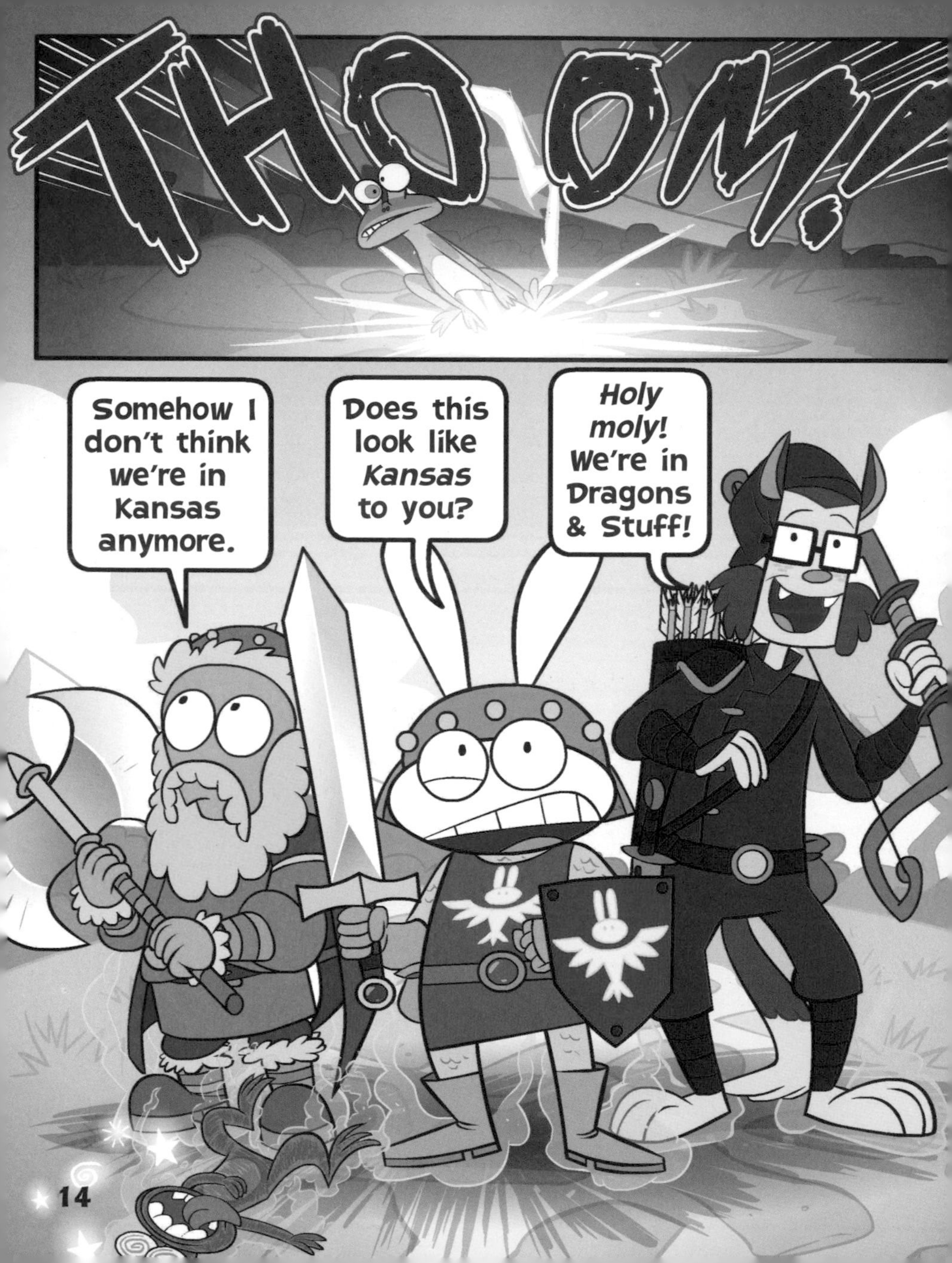
THOOM!
Somehow I don't think we're in Kansas anymore.
Does this look like *Kansas* to you?
Holy moly! We're in Dragons & Stuff!

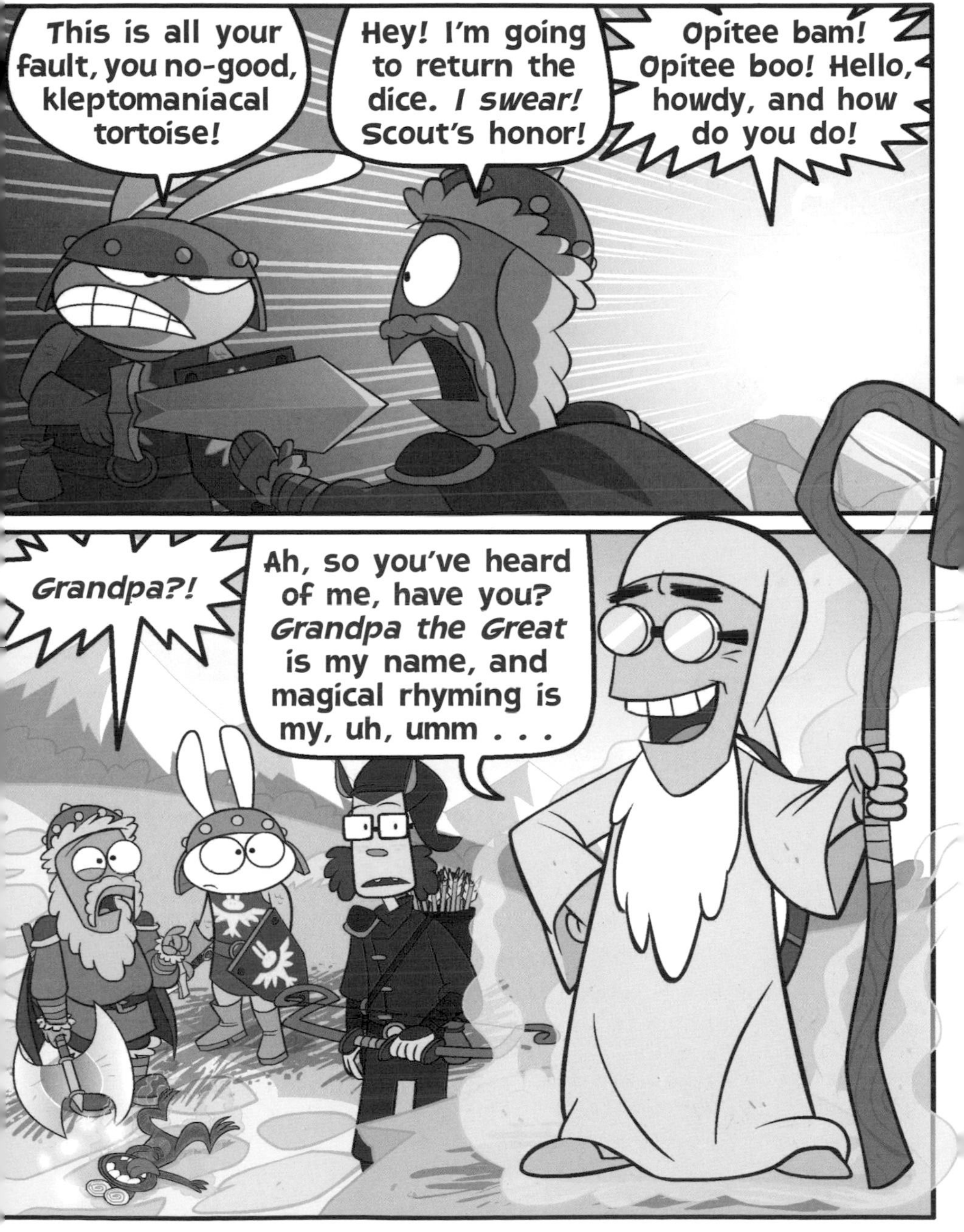
This is all your fault, you no-good, kleptomaniacal tortoise!
Hey! I'm going to return the dice. *I swear!* Scout's honor!
Opitee bam! Opitee boo! Hello, howdy, and how do you do!
Grandpa?!
Ah, so you've heard of me, have you? *Grandpa the Great* is my name, and magical rhyming is my, uh, umm . . .

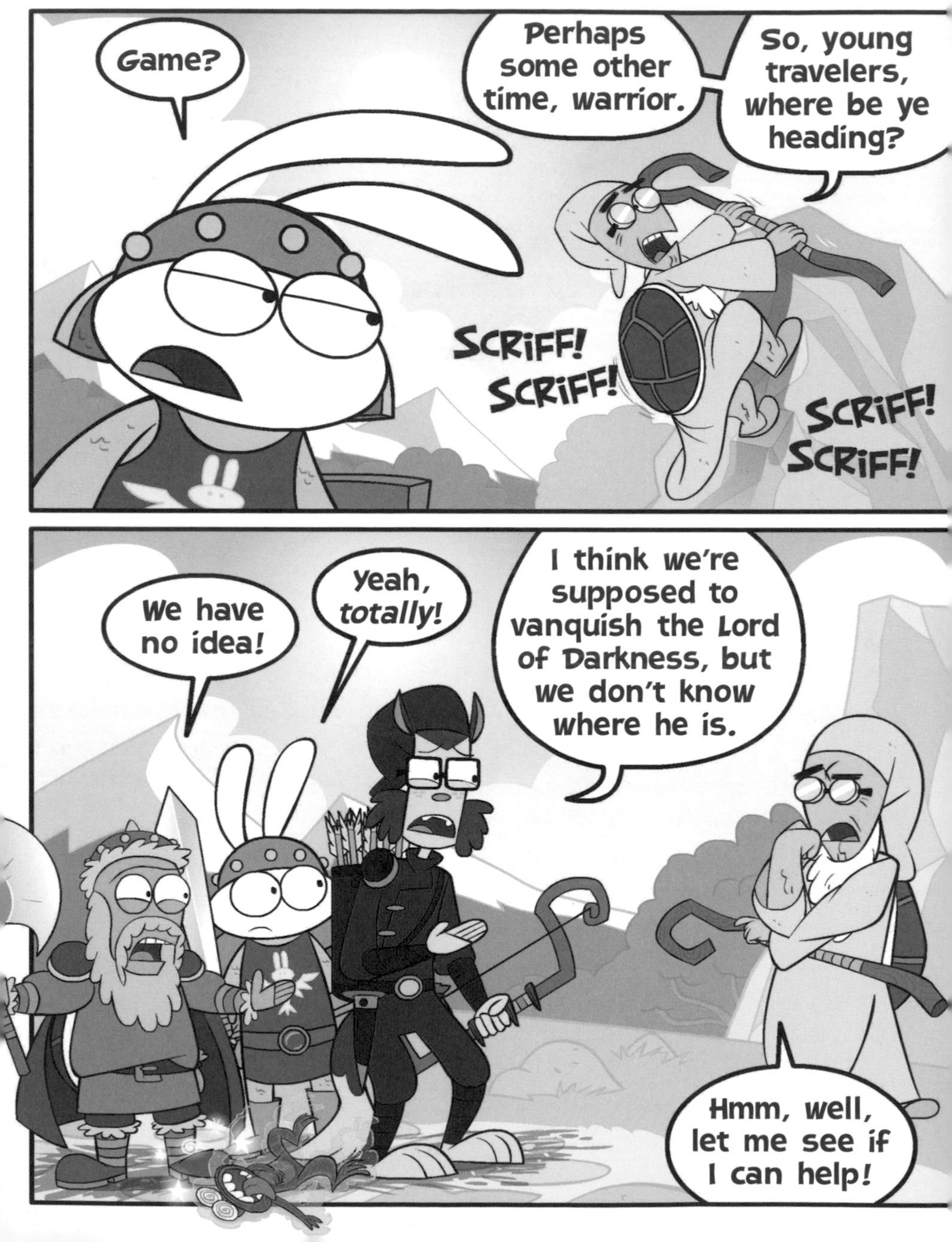
Game?
Perhaps some other time, warrior.
So, young travelers, where be ye heading?
SCRIFF! SCRIFF!
SCRIFF! SCRIFF!
We have no idea!
Yeah, *totally*!
I think *we're* supposed to vanquish the Lord of Darkness, but we don't know where he is.
Hmm, well, let me see if I can help!

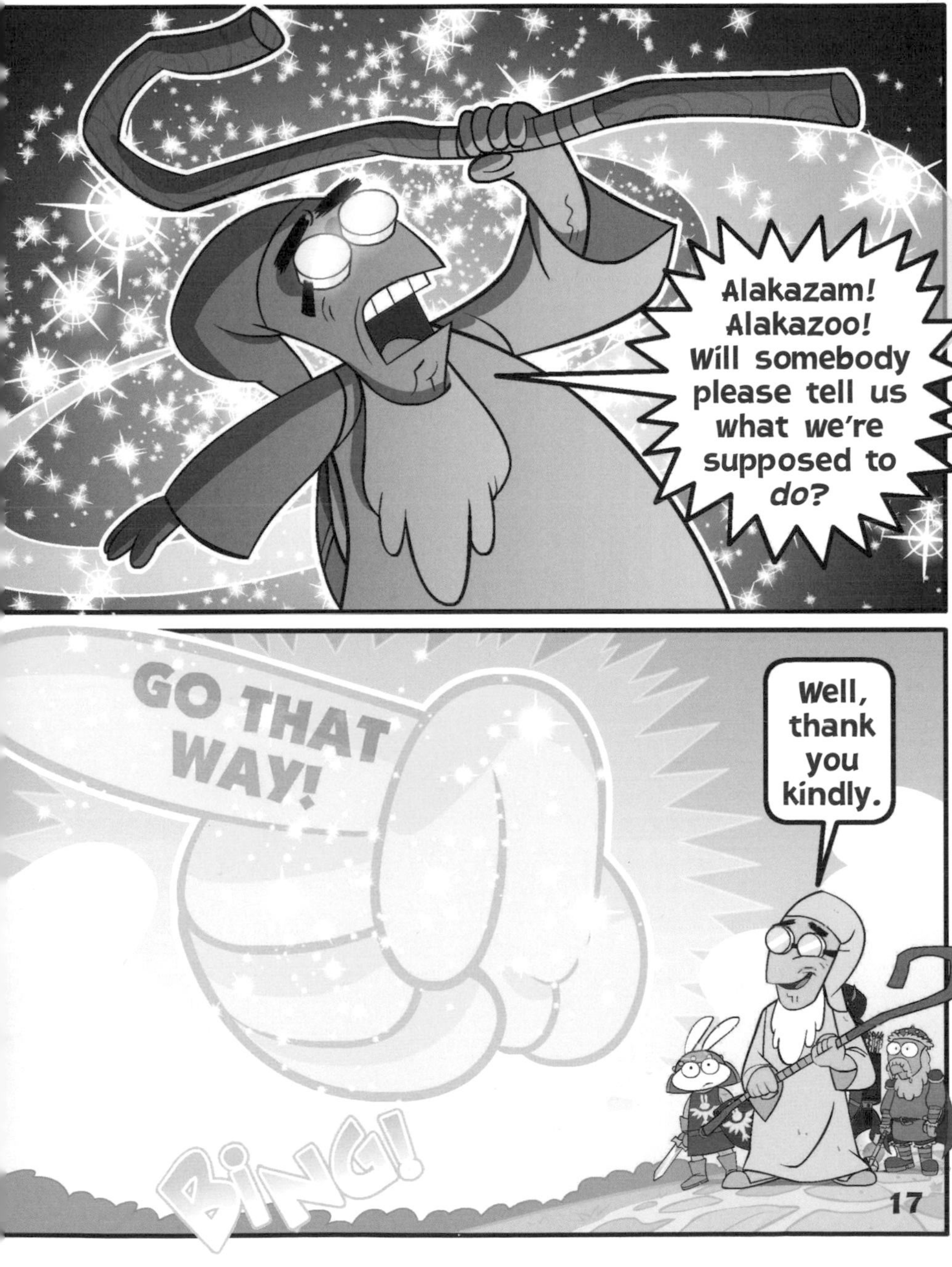
Alakazam! Alakazoo! Will somebody please tell us what we're supposed to *do?*
GO THAT WAY!
Well, thank you kindly.
BING!

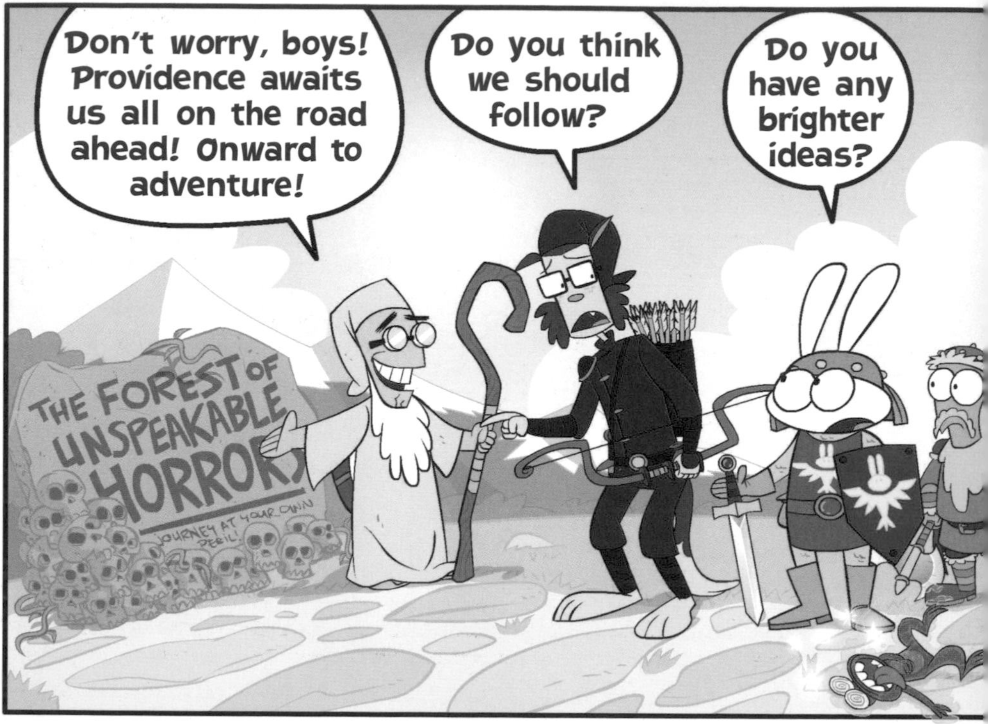
Don't worry, boys! Providence awaits us all on the road ahead! Onward to adventure!
Do you think we should follow?
Do you have any brighter ideas?
THE FOREST OF UNSPEAKABLE HORROR
JOURNEY AT YOUR OWN PERIL!

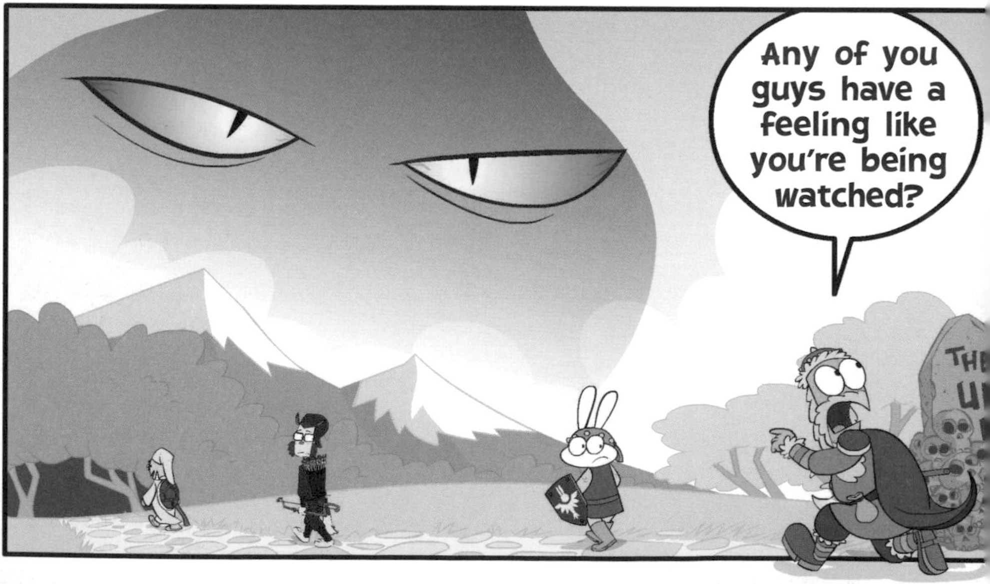
Any of you guys have a feeling like you're being watched?

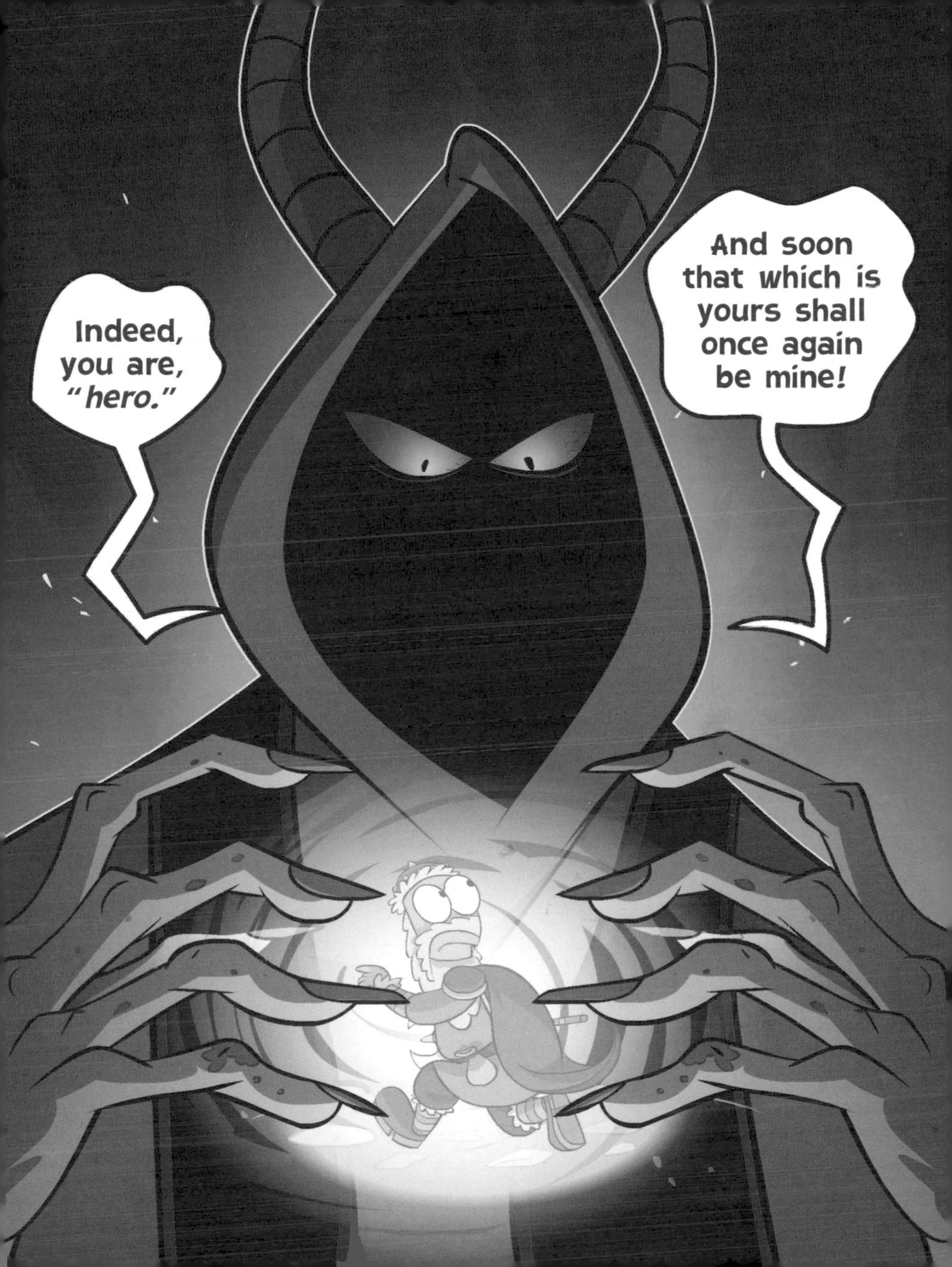
Indeed, you are, "*hero.*"
And soon that which is yours shall once again be mine!

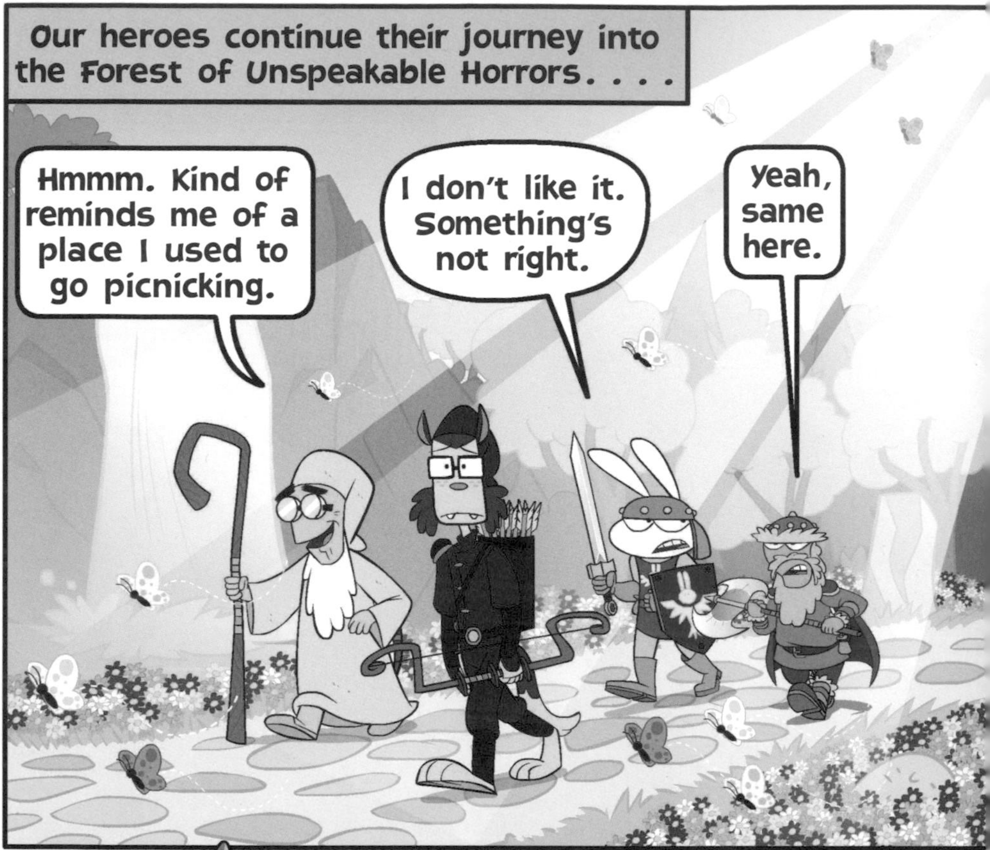
Our heroes continue their journey into the Forest of Unspeakable Horrors. . . .
Hmmm. Kind of reminds me of a place I used to go picnicking.
I don't like it. Something's not right.
Yeah, same here.

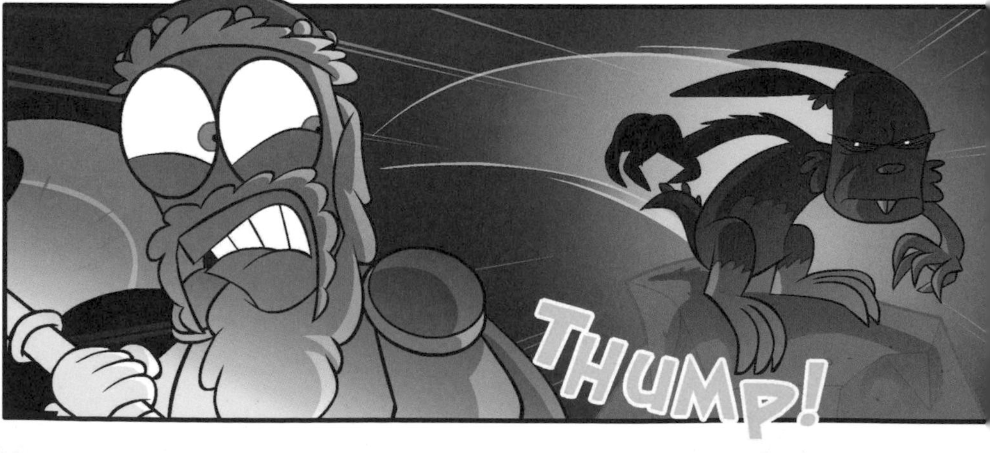
THUMP!

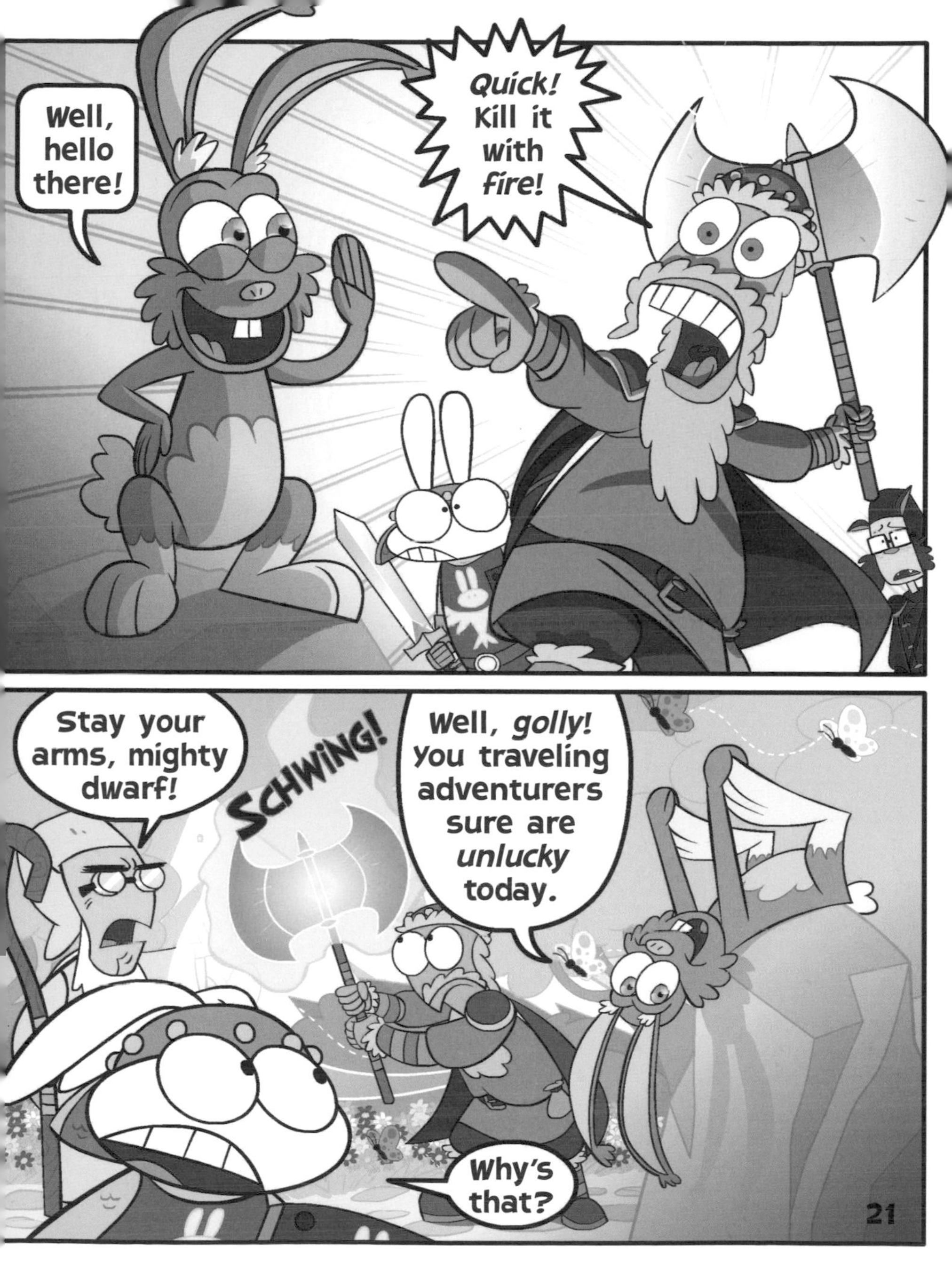
Well, hello there!
Quick! Kill it with *fire!*
Stay your arms, mighty dwarf!
SCHWING!
Well, *golly!* You traveling adventurers sure are *unlucky* today.
Why's that?

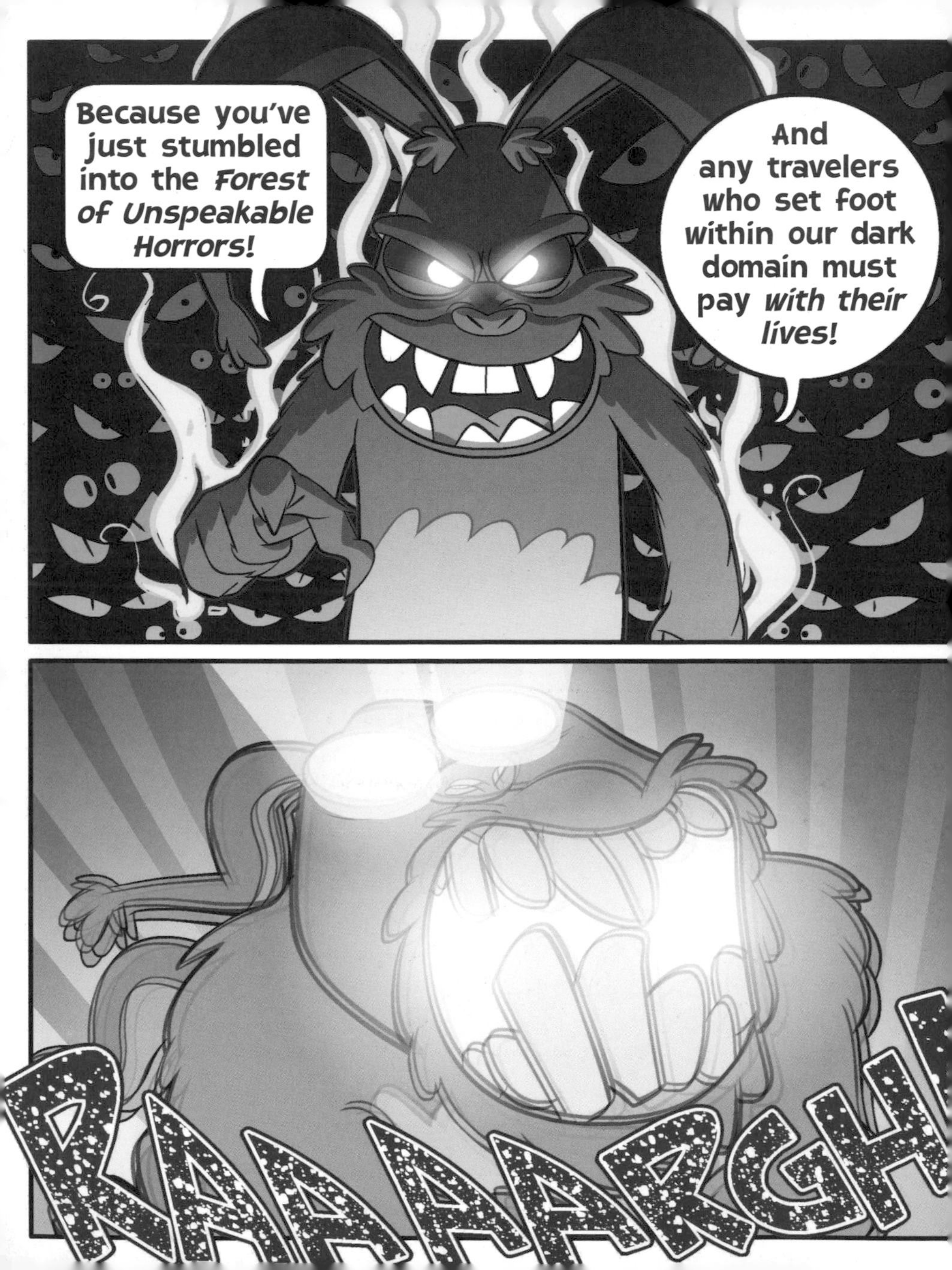
Because you've just stumbled into the *Forest of Unspeakable Horrors!*
And any travelers who set foot within our dark domain must pay *with their lives!*
RAAARGH!

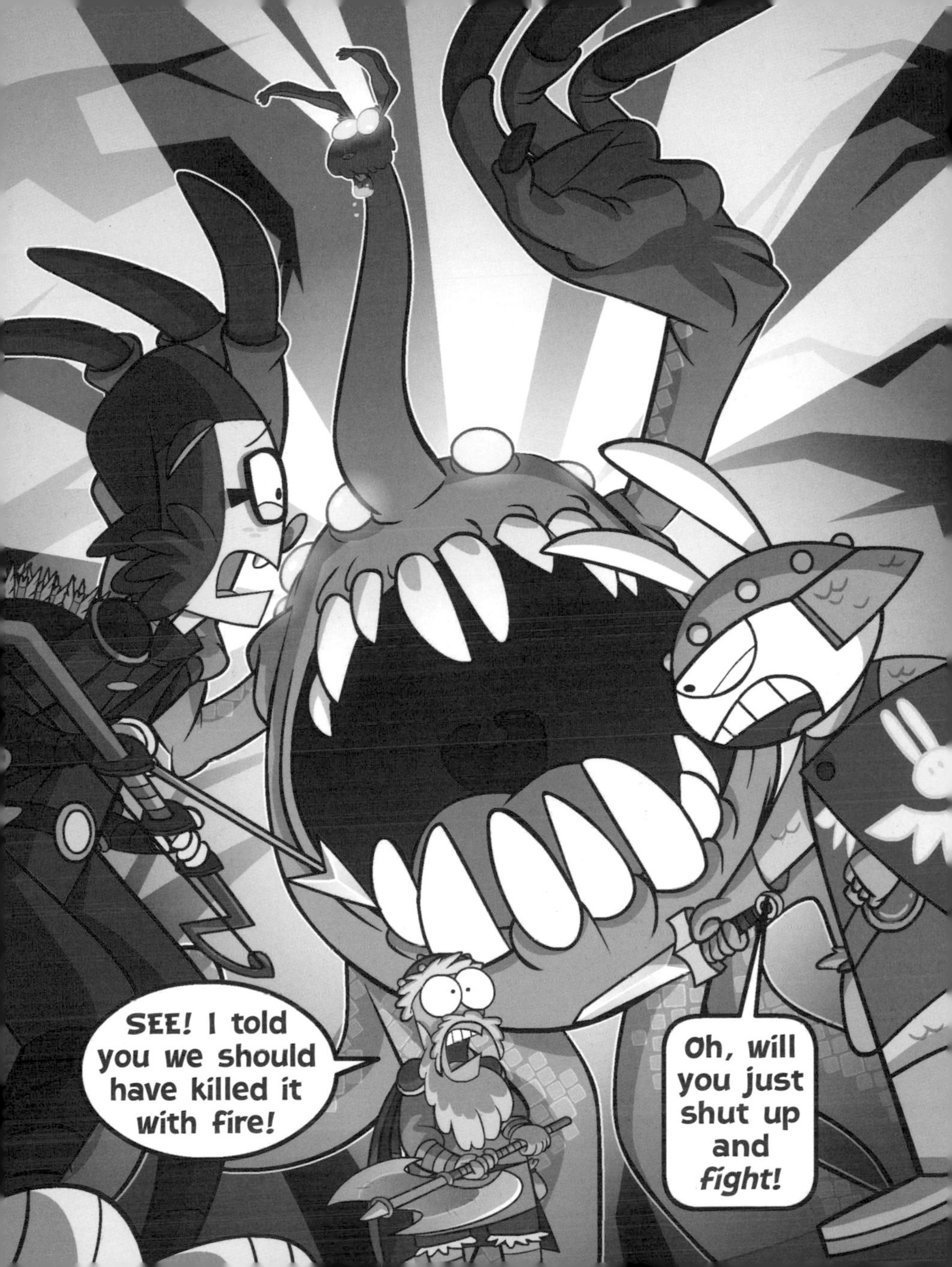
SEE! I told you we should have killed it with fire!
Oh, will you just shut up and *fight*!

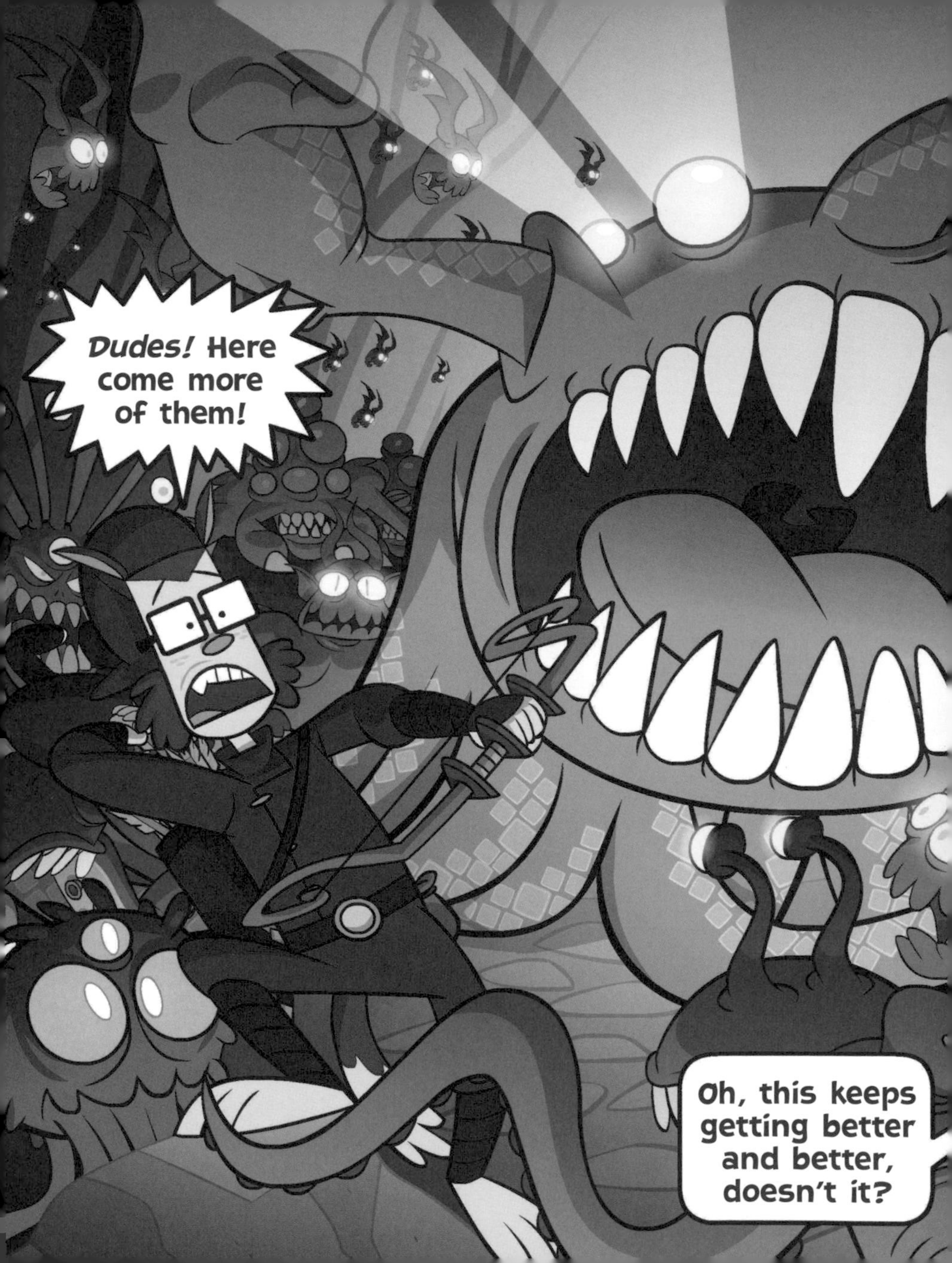
Dudes! Here come more of them!
Oh, this keeps getting better and better, doesn't it?

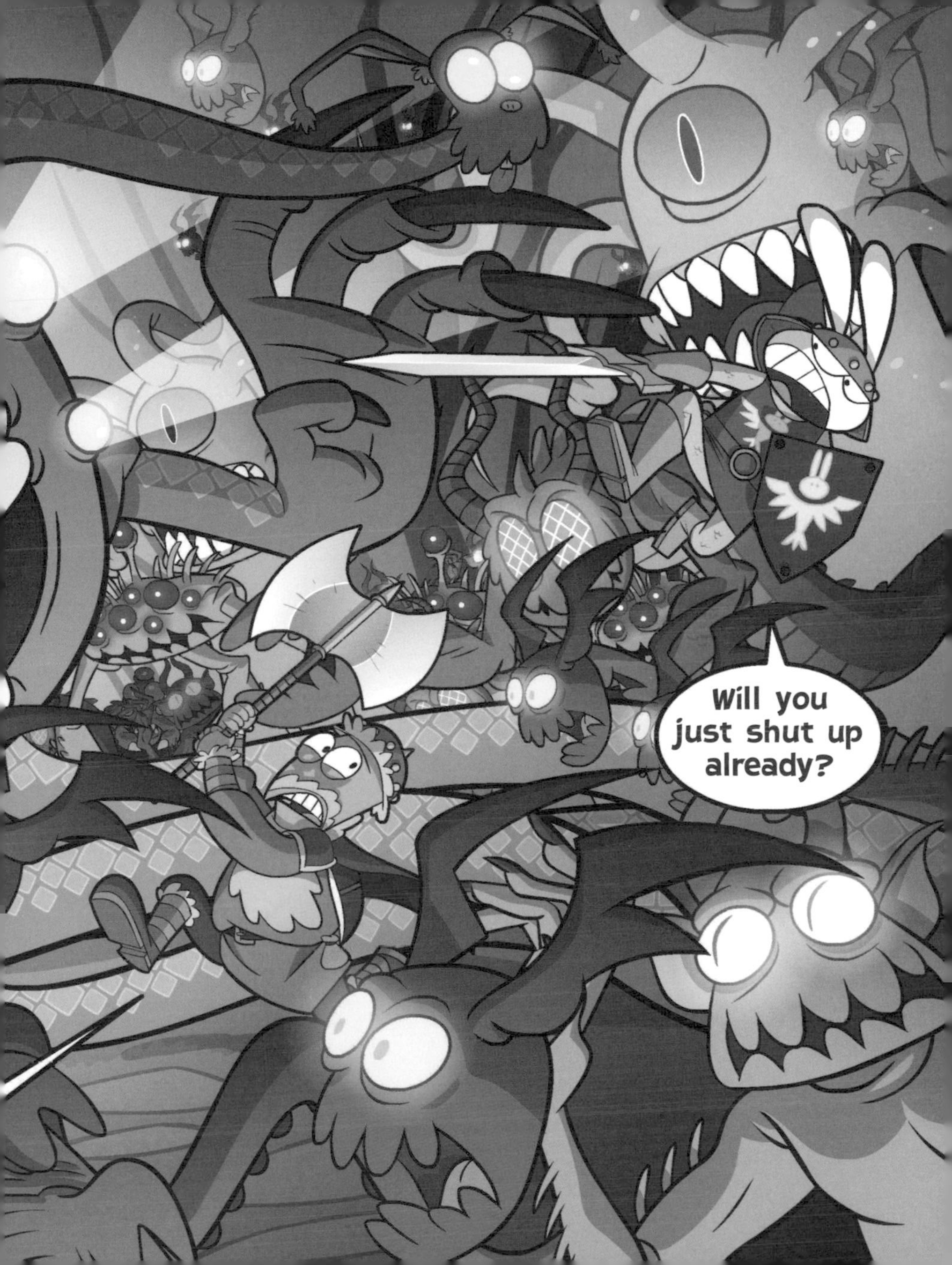
Will you just shut up already?

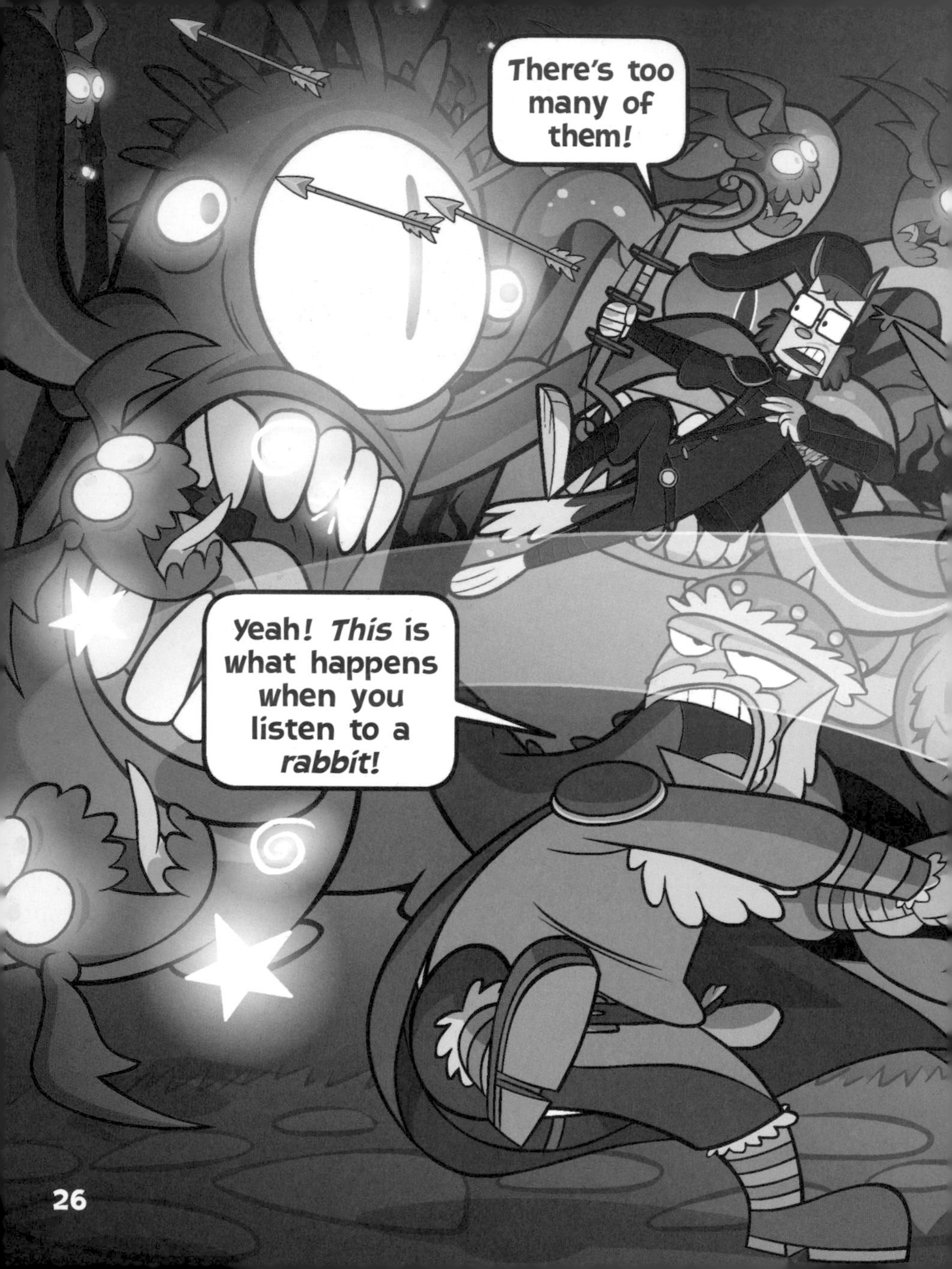
There's too many of them!
Yeah! *This* is what happens when you listen to a *rabbit*!

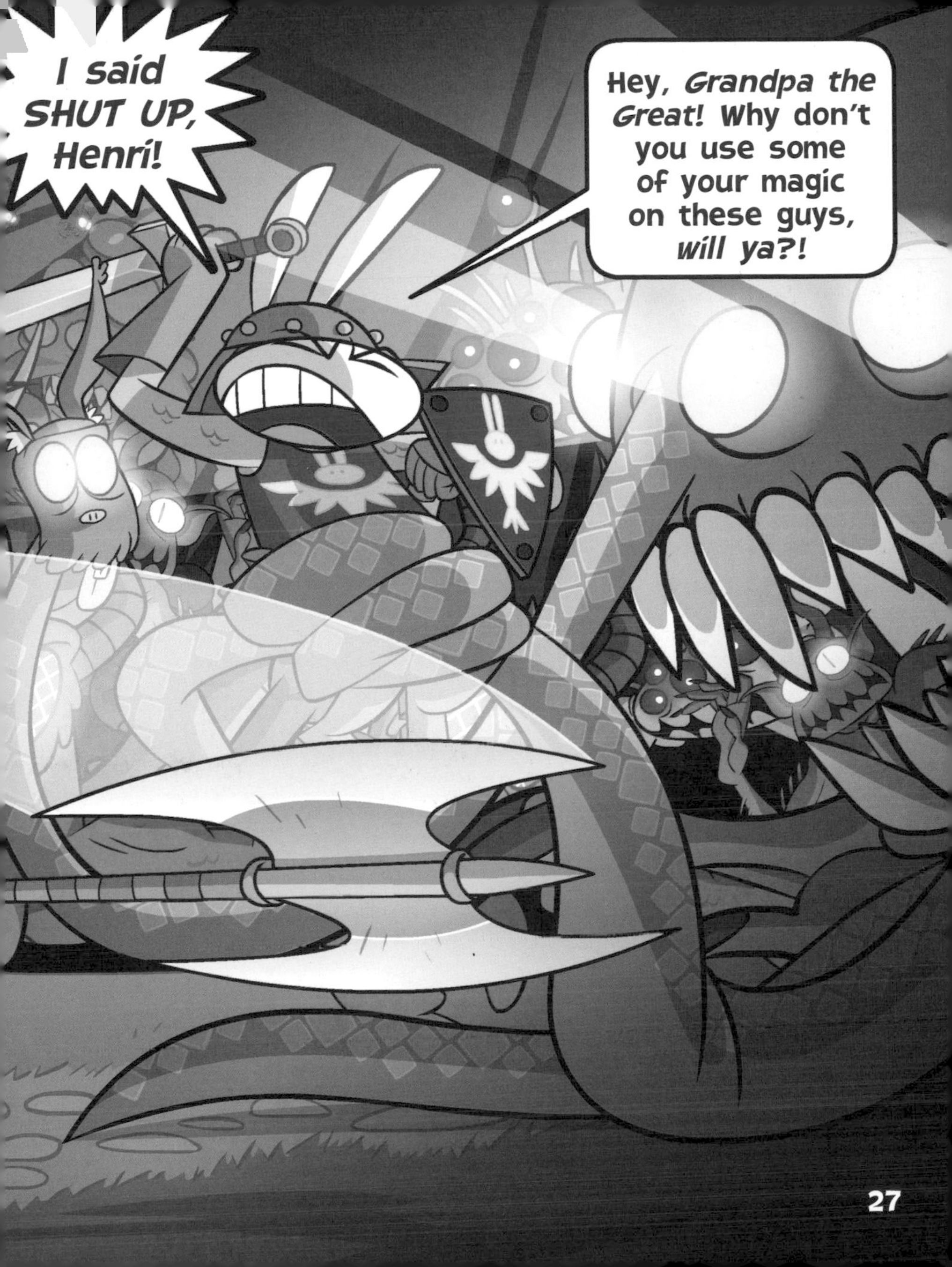
I said SHUT UP, Henri!
Hey, Grandpa the Great! Why don't you use some of your magic on these guys, will ya?!

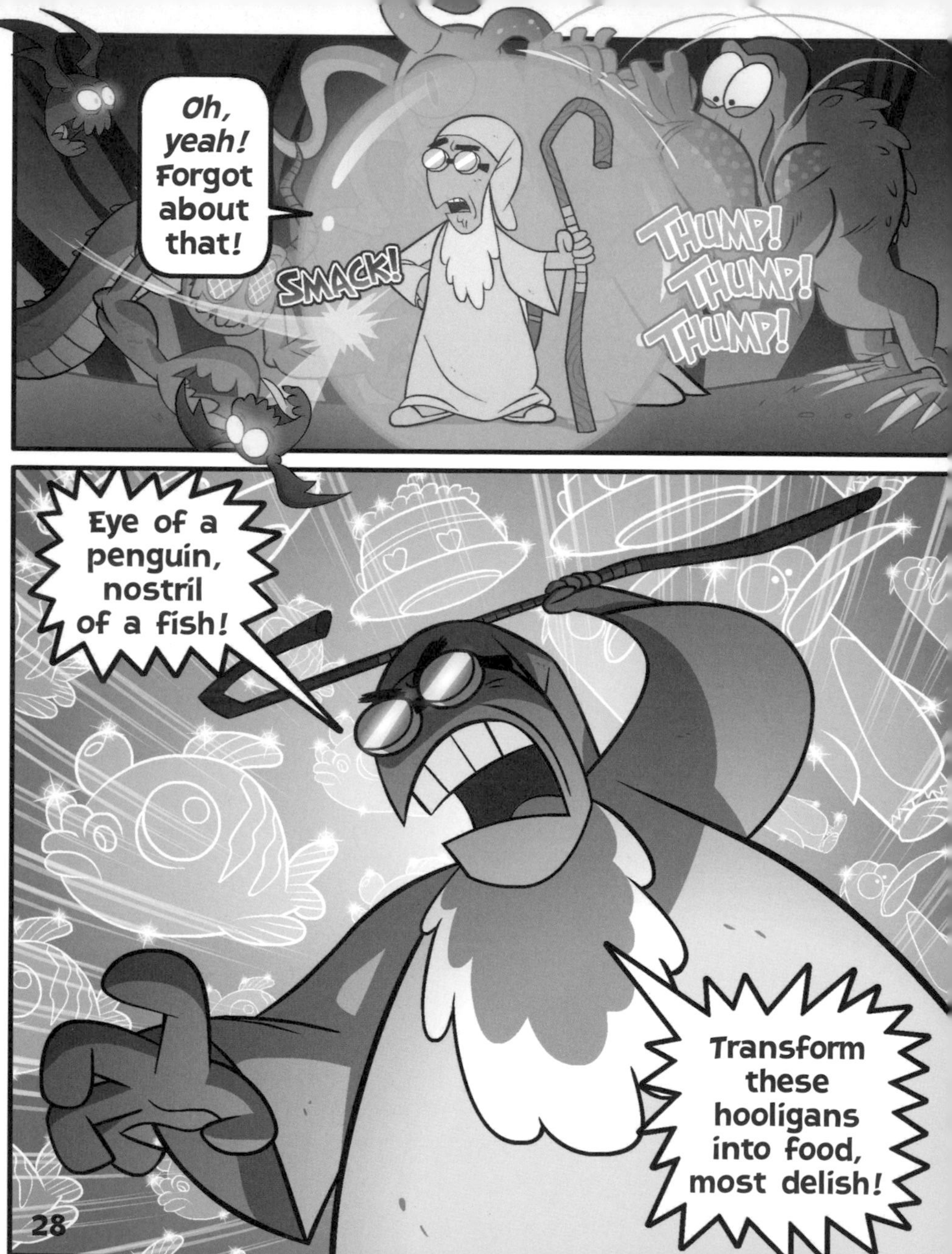

Oh, yeah! Forgot about that!
SMACK!
THUMP! THUMP! THUMP!
Eye of a penguin, nostril of a fish!
Transform these hooligans into food, most delish!

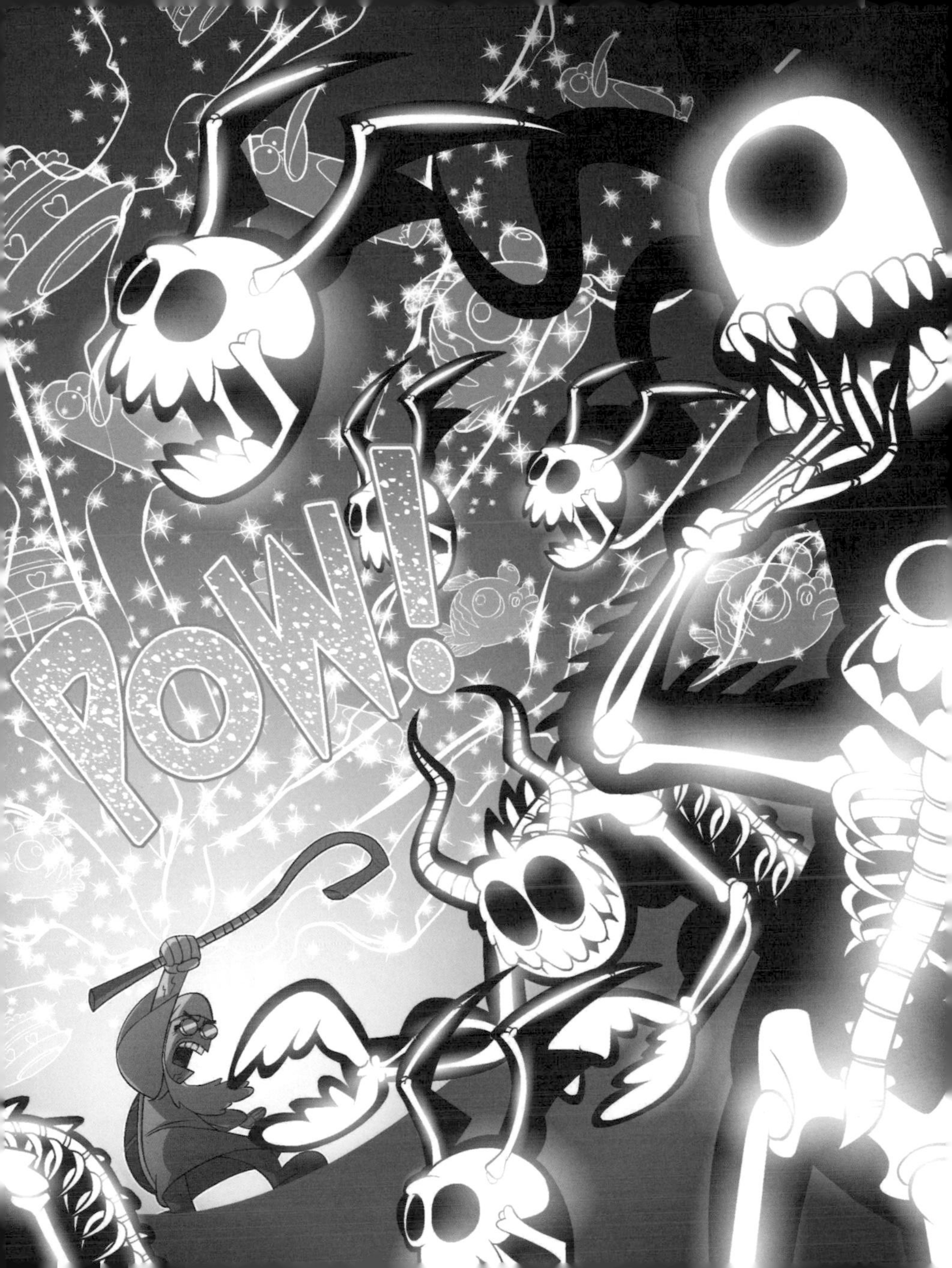
POW!

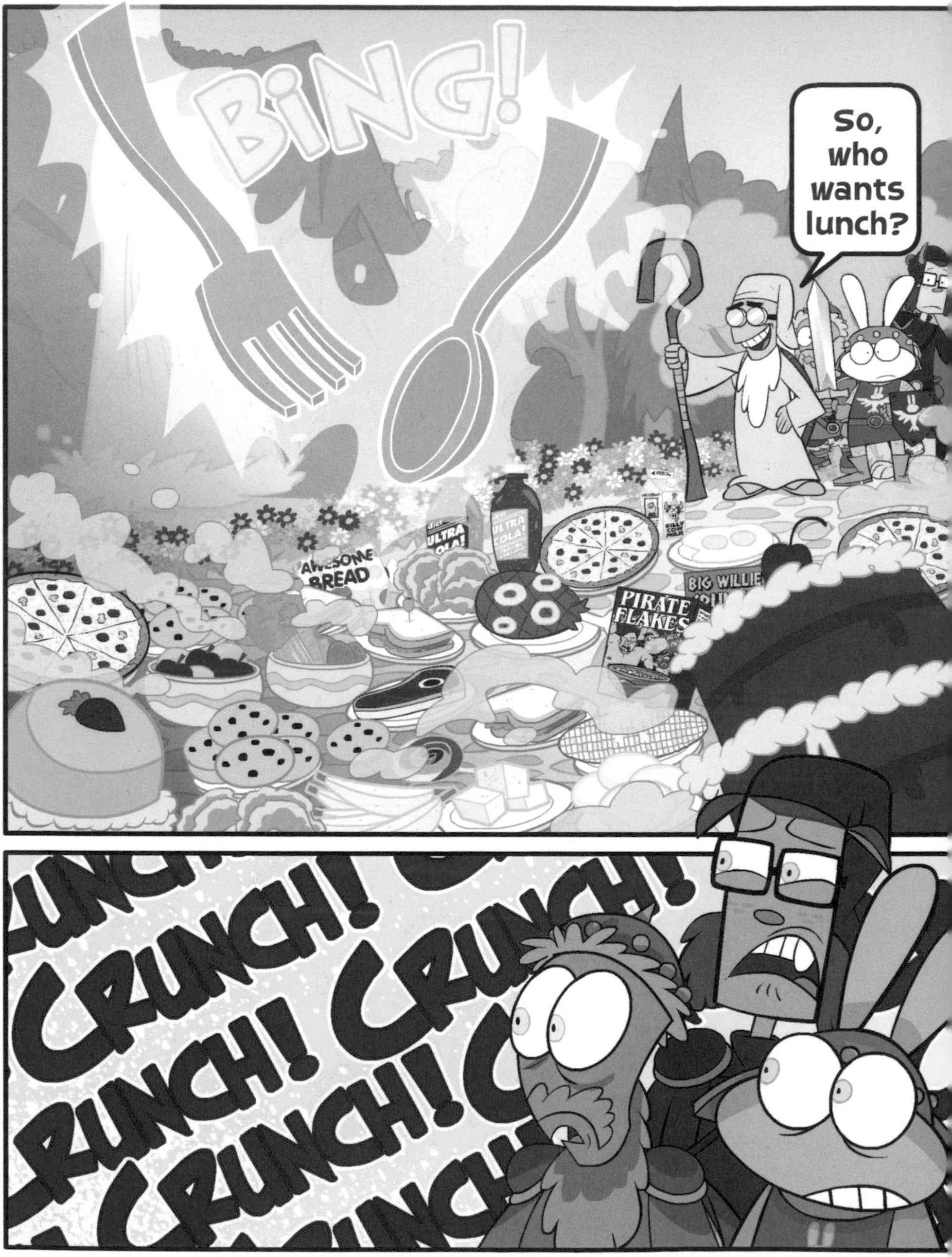
BiNG!
So, who wants lunch?
AWESOME BREAD
diet ULTRA COLA!
ULTRA COLA!
PIRATE FLAKES
CRUNCH! CRUNCH!
CRUNCH! CRUNCH!
CRUNCH!
CRUNCH!

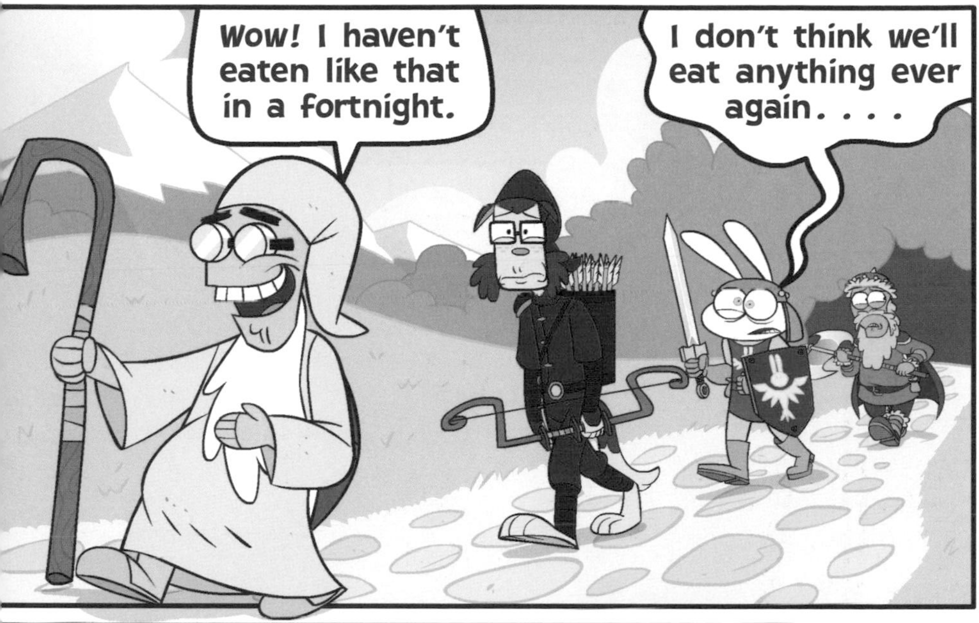
Wow! I haven't eaten like that in a fortnight.
I don't think we'll eat anything ever again. . . .

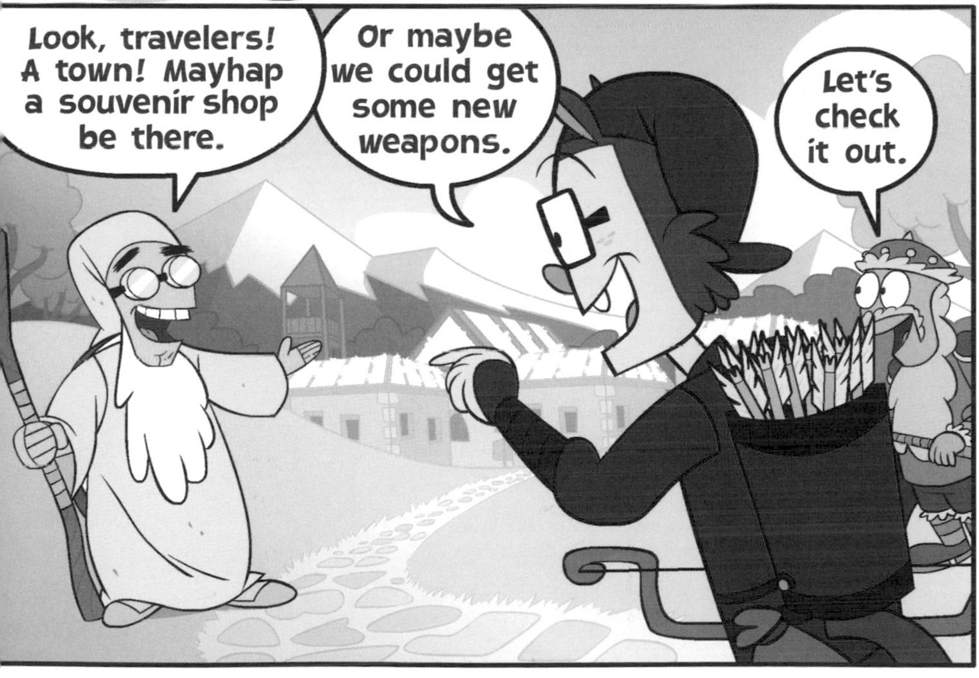
Look, travelers! A town! Mayhap a souvenir shop be there.
Or maybe we could get some new weapons.
Let's check it out.

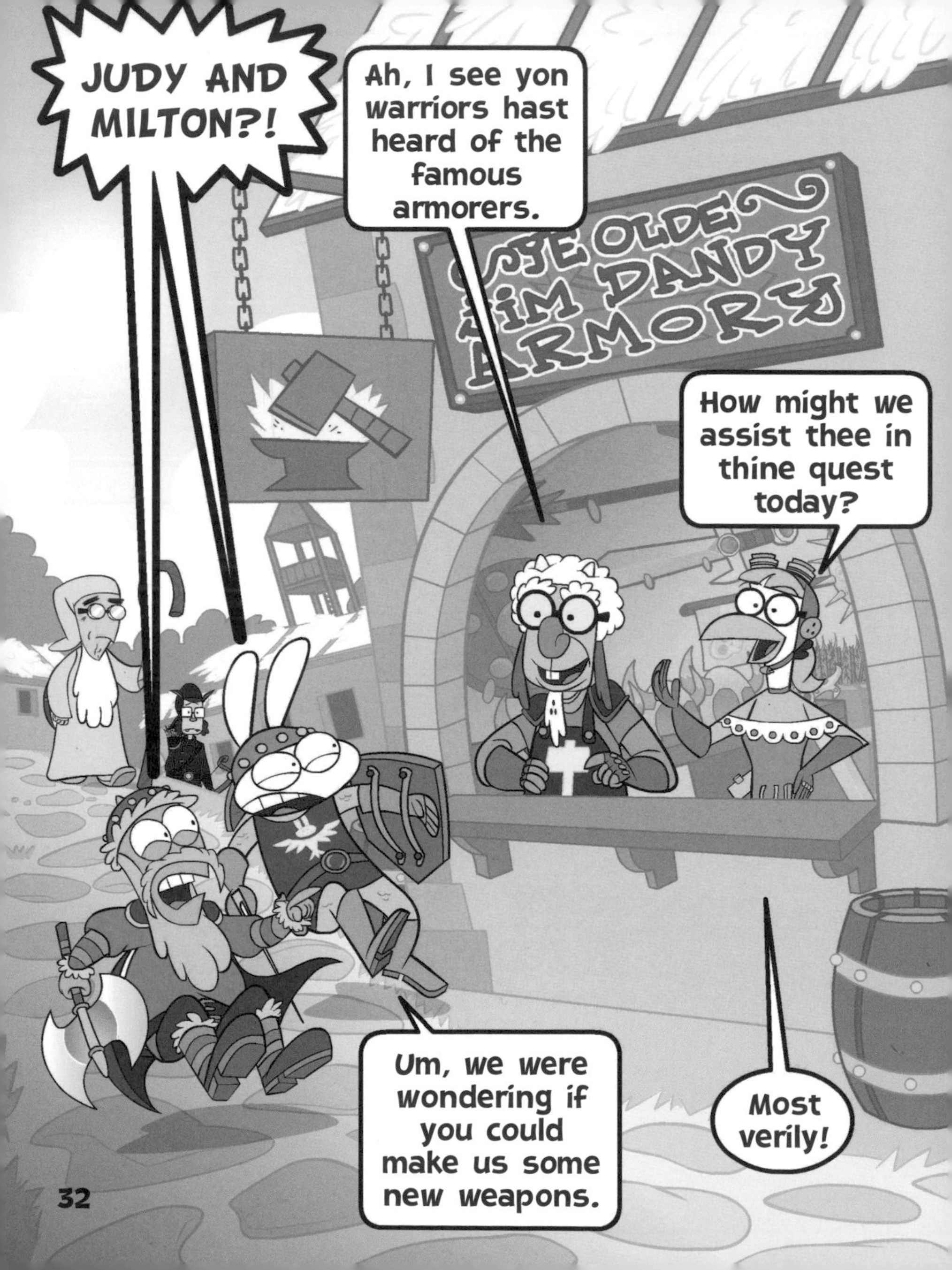
JUDY AND MILTON?!
Ah, I see yon warriors hast heard of the famous armorers.
YE OLDE JIM DANDY ARMORY
How might we assist thee in thine quest today?
Um, we were wondering if you could make us some new weapons.
Most verily!

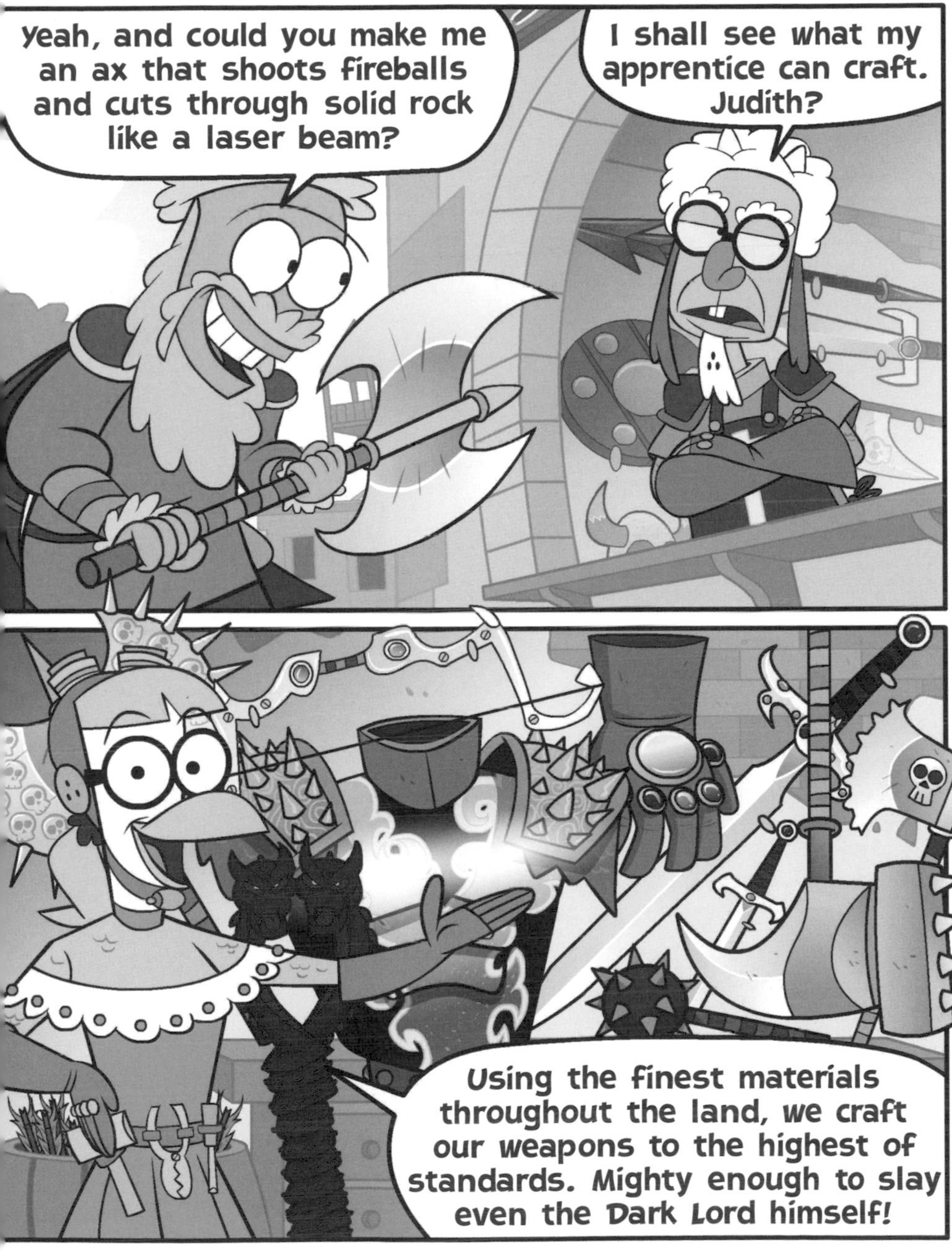
Yeah, and could you make me an ax that shoots fireballs and cuts through solid rock like a laser beam?
I shall see what my apprentice can craft. Judith?
Using the finest materials throughout the land, we craft our weapons to the highest of standards. Mighty enough to slay even the Dark Lord himself!

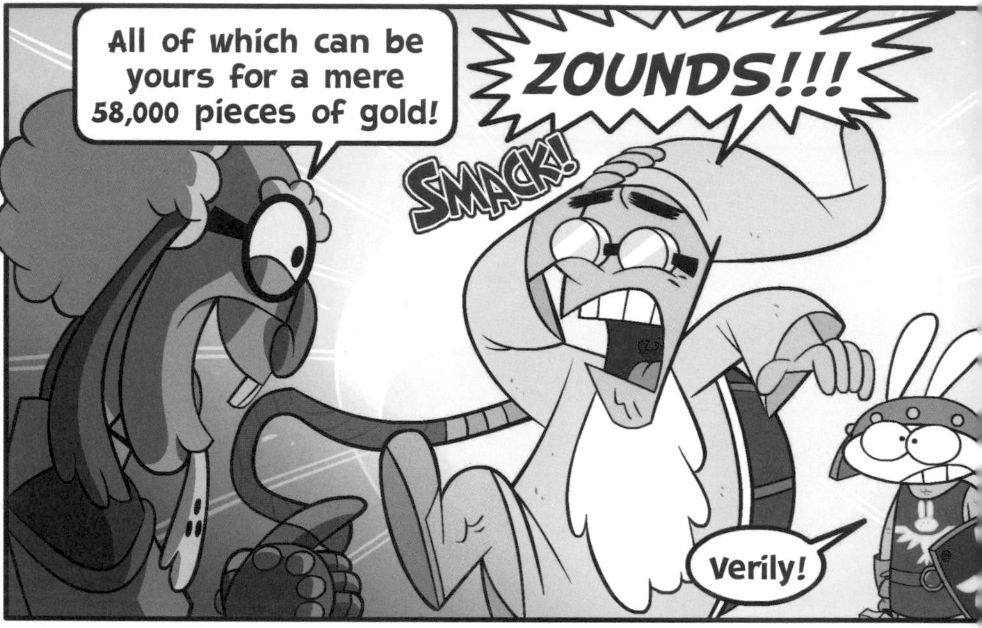
All of which can be yours for a mere 58,000 pieces of gold!
ZOUNDS!!!
SMACK!
Verily!

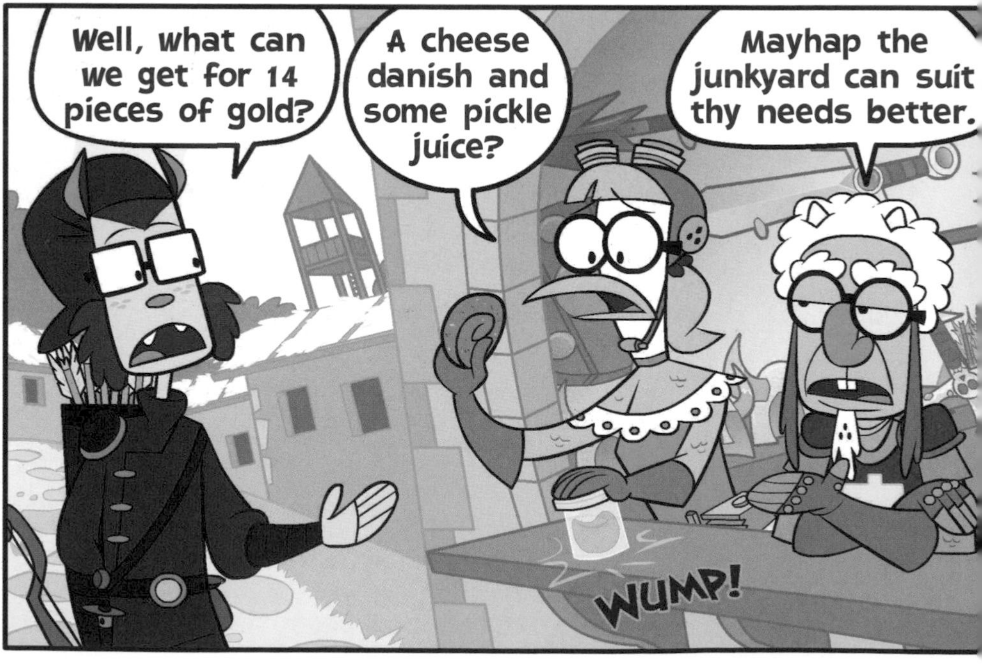
Well, what can we get for 14 pieces of gold?
A cheese danish and some pickle juice?
Mayhap the junkyard can suit thy needs better.
WUMP!

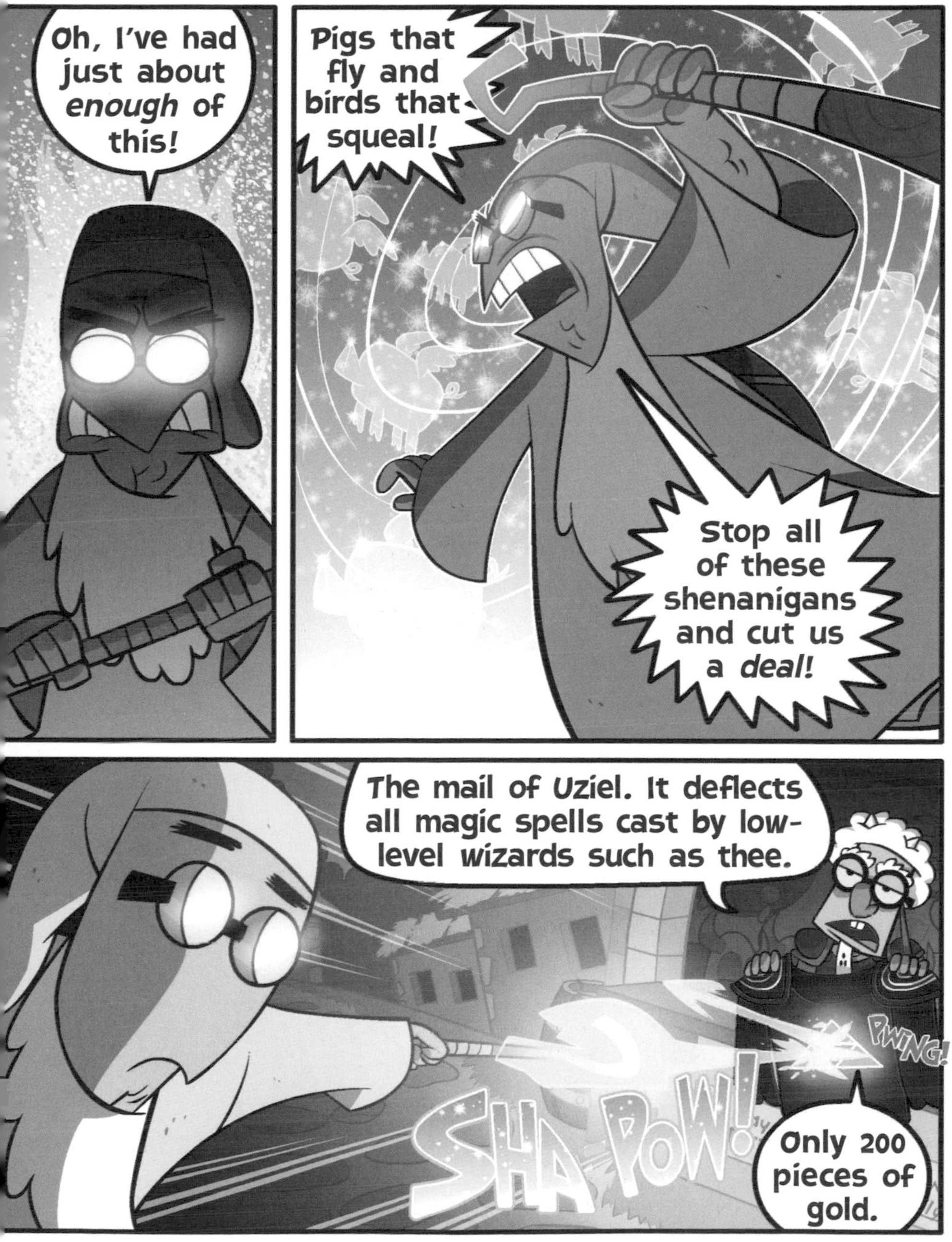
Oh, I've had just about *enough* of this!
Pigs that fly and birds that squeal!
Stop all of these shenanigans and cut us a *deal!*
The mail of Uziel. It deflects all magic spells cast by low-level wizards such as thee.
PWING!
SHA-POW!
Only 200 pieces of gold.

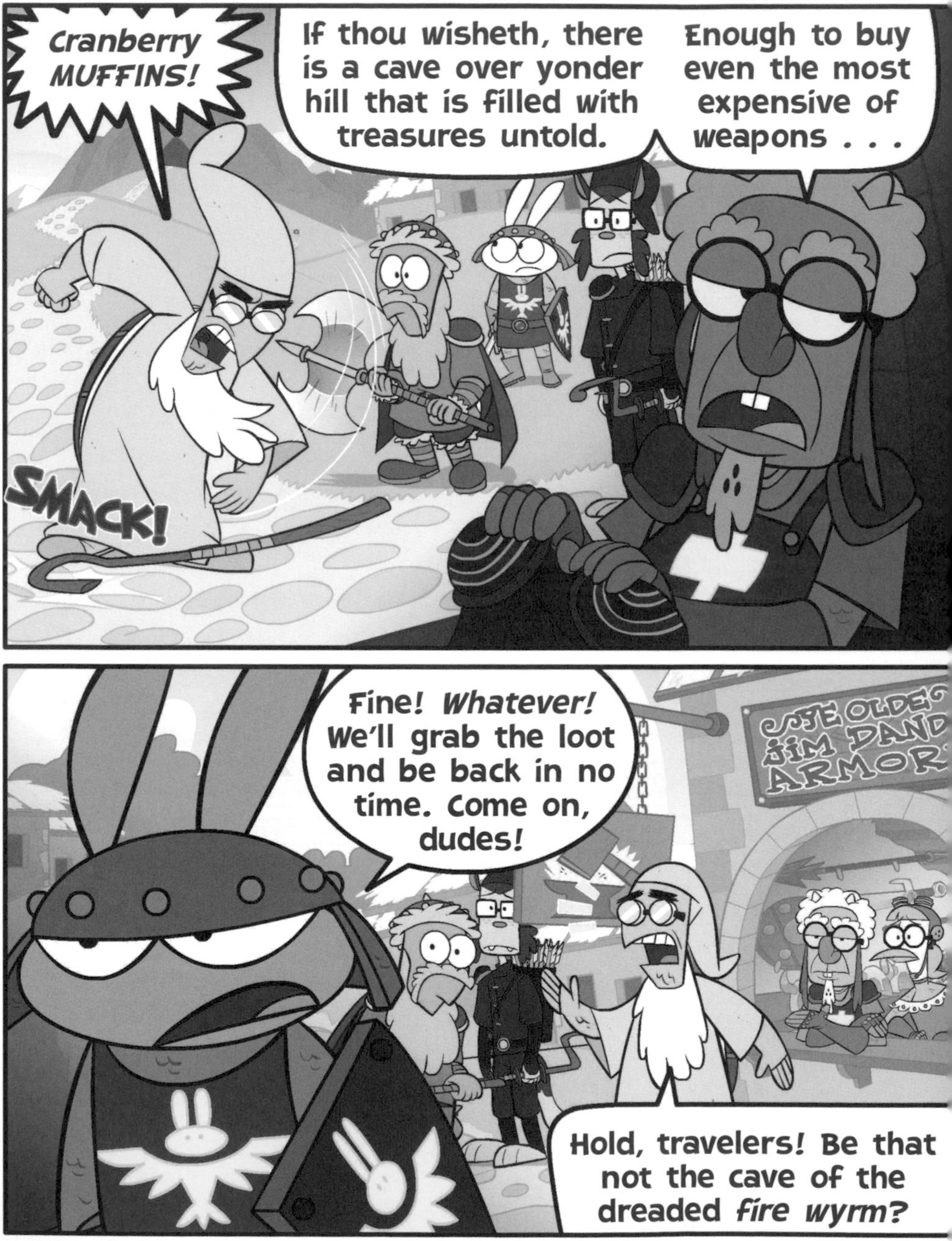
Cranberry MUFFINS!
If thou wisheth, there is a cave over yonder hill that is filled with treasures untold.
Enough to buy even the most expensive of weapons . . .
SMACK!
Fine! Whatever! We'll grab the loot and be back in no time. Come on, dudes!
Hold, travelers! Be that not the cave of the dreaded fire wyrm?

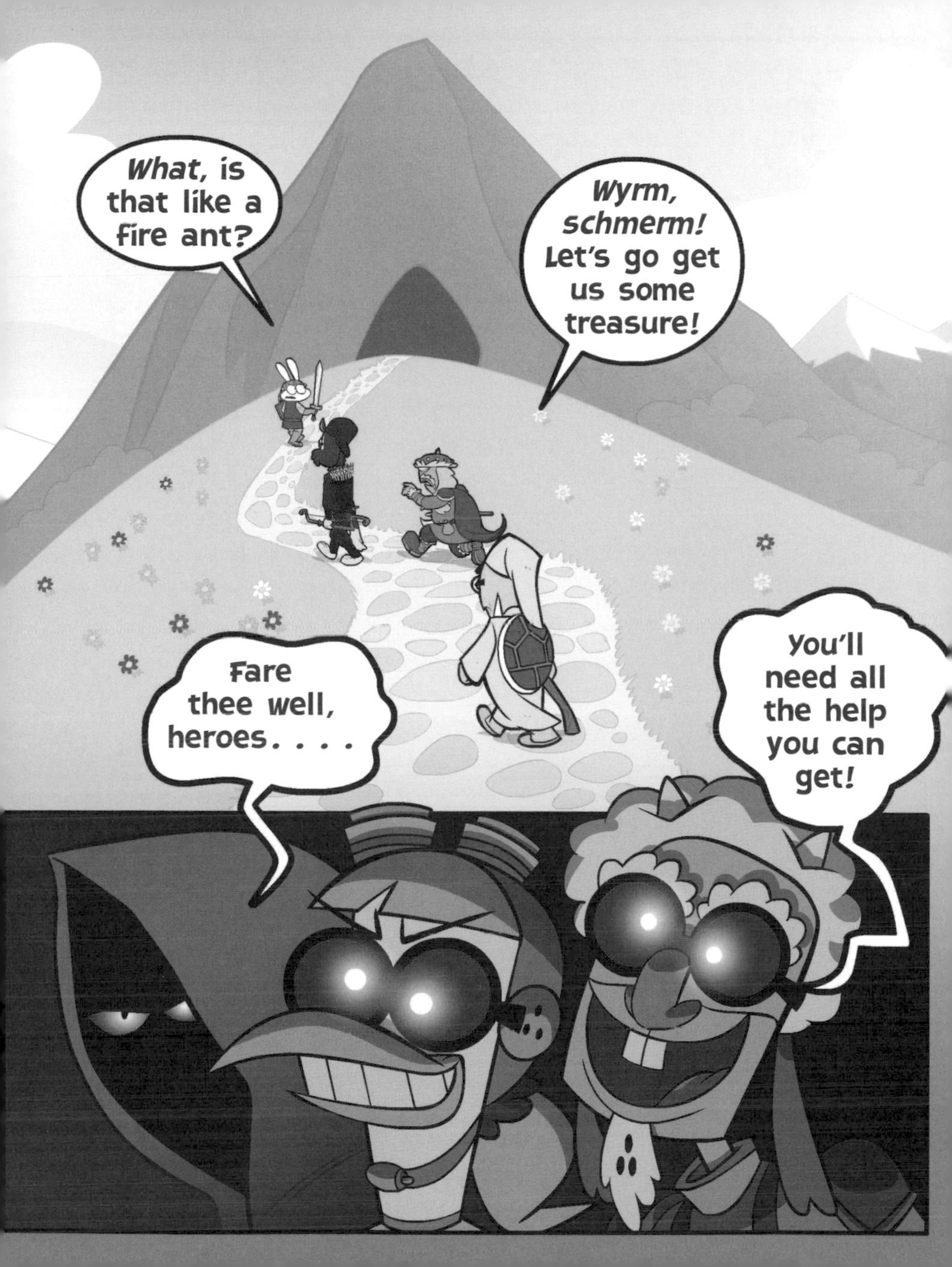

What, is that like a fire ant?
Wyrm, schmerm! Let's go get us some treasure!
Fare thee well, heroes. . . .
You'll need all the help you can get!

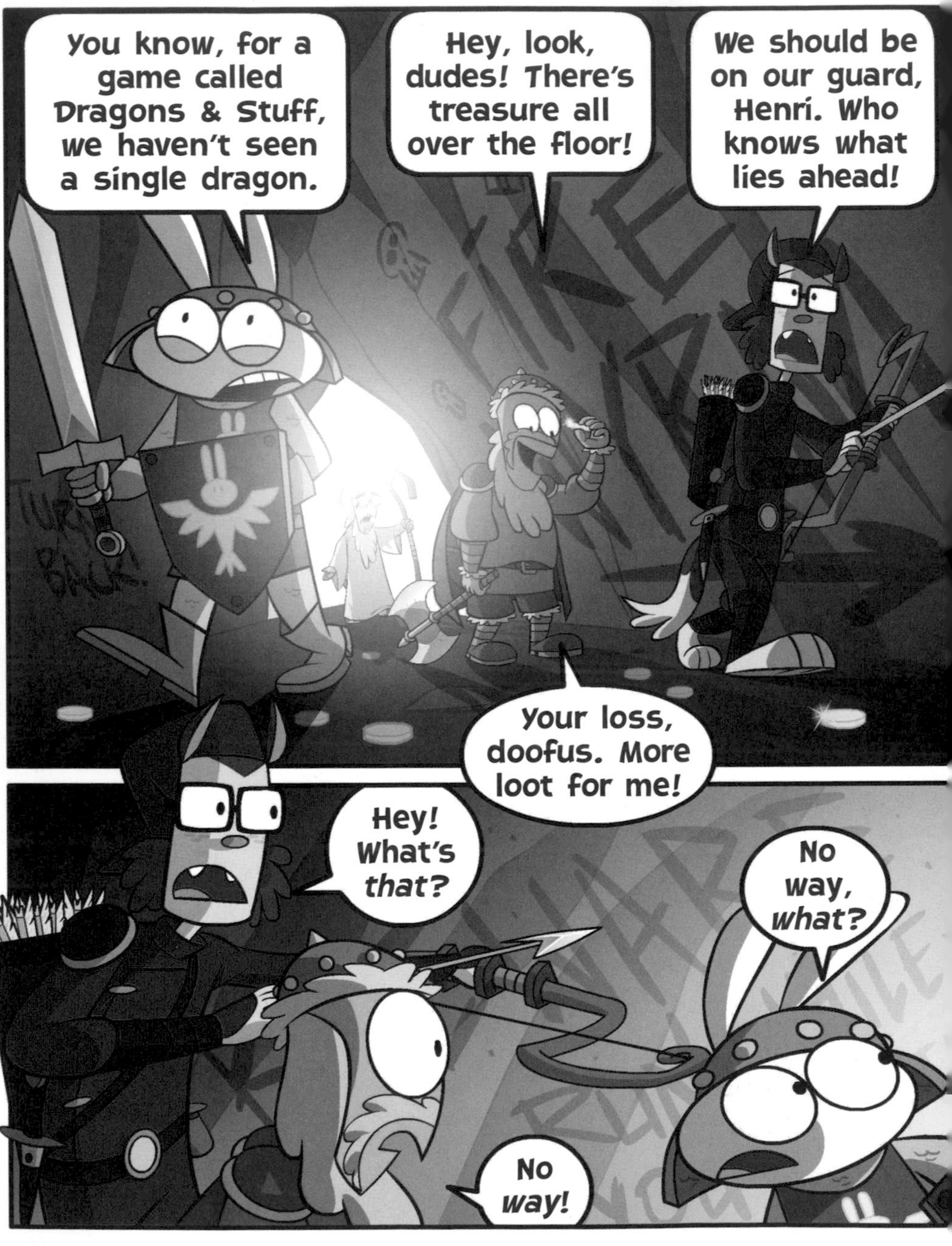
You know, for a game called Dragons & Stuff, we haven't seen a single dragon.
Hey, look, dudes! There's treasure all over the floor!
We should be on our guard, Henri. Who knows what lies ahead!
Your loss, doofus. More loot for me!
Hey! What's *that*?
No way, *what*?
No *way*!

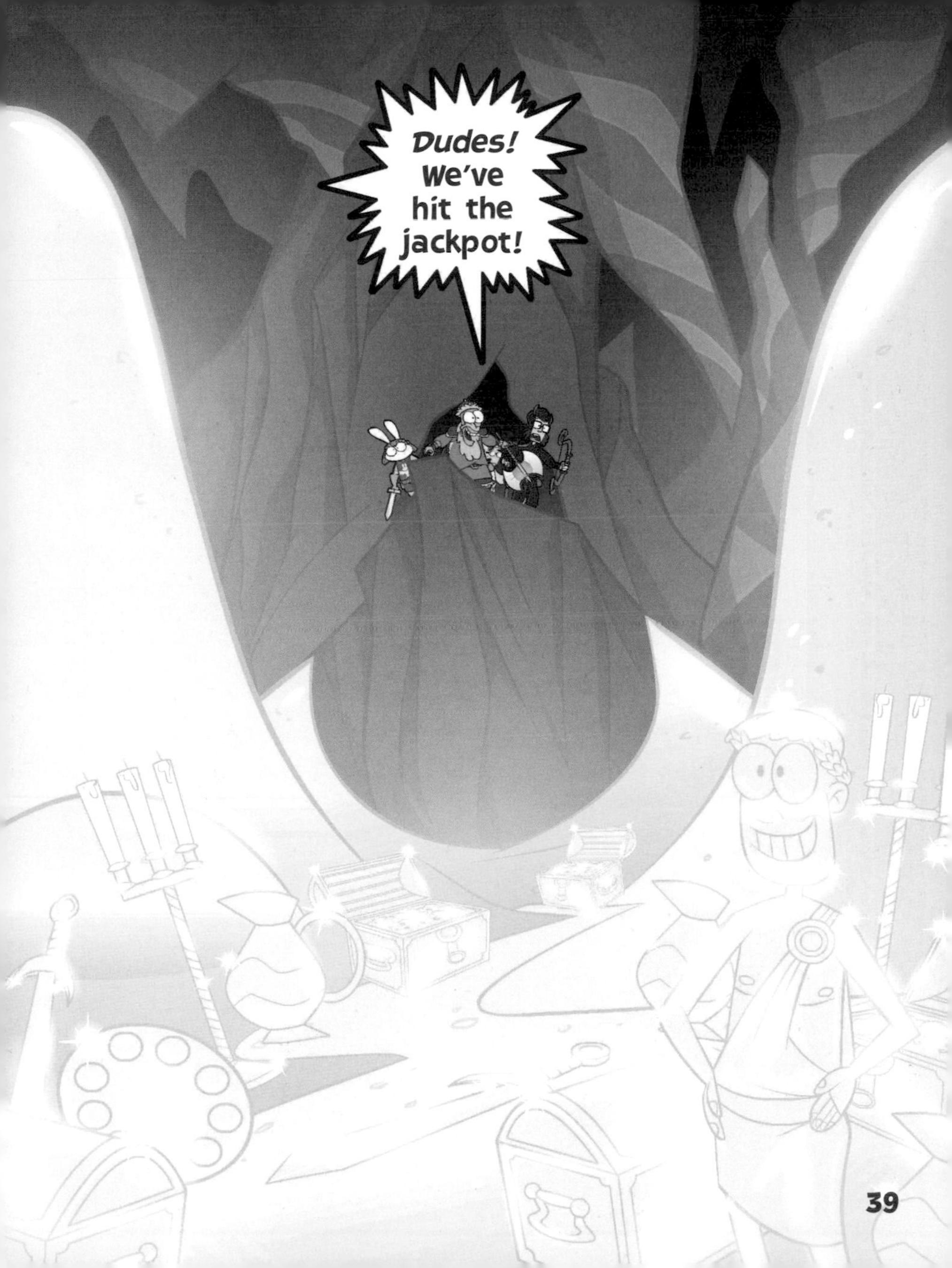
Dudes! We've hit the jackpot!

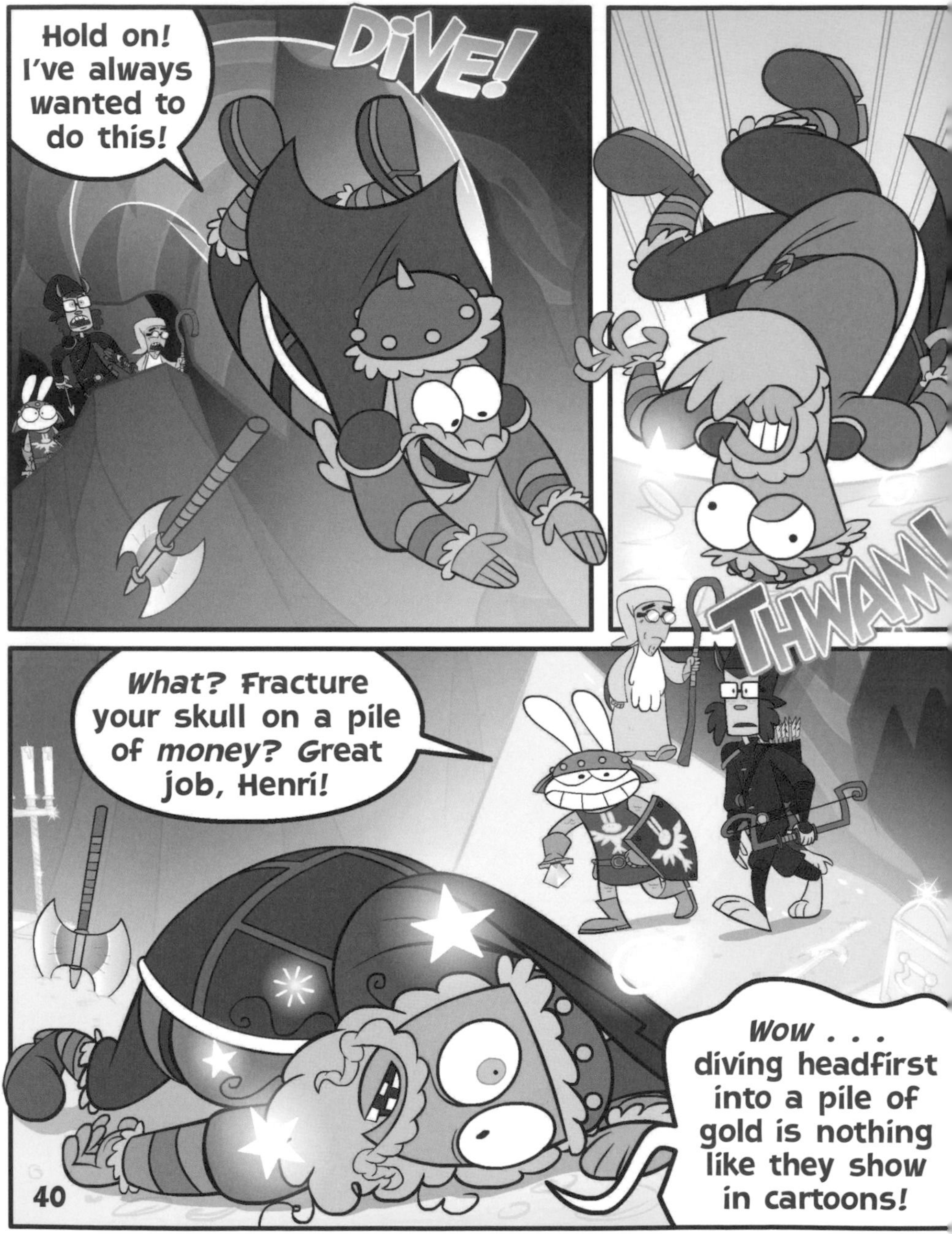
Hold on! I've always wanted to do this!
DIVE!
THWAM!
What? Fracture your skull on a pile of money? Great job, Henri!
Wow . . . diving headfirst into a pile of gold is nothing like they show in cartoons!

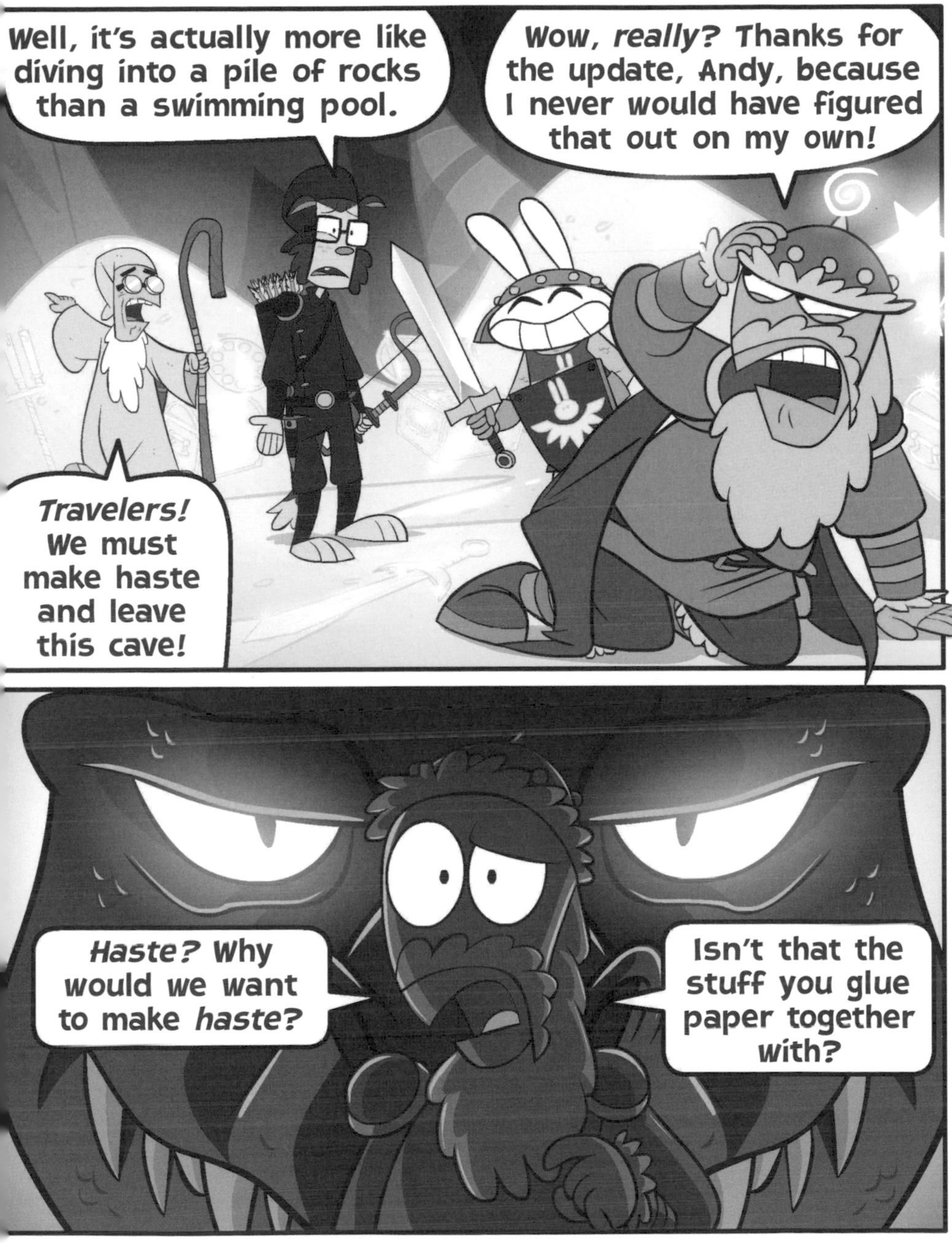
Well, it's actually more like diving into a pile of rocks than a swimming pool.
Wow, really? Thanks for the update, Andy, because I never would have figured that out on my own!
Travelers! We must make haste and leave this cave!
Haste? Why would we want to make *haste?*
Isn't that the stuff you glue paper together with?

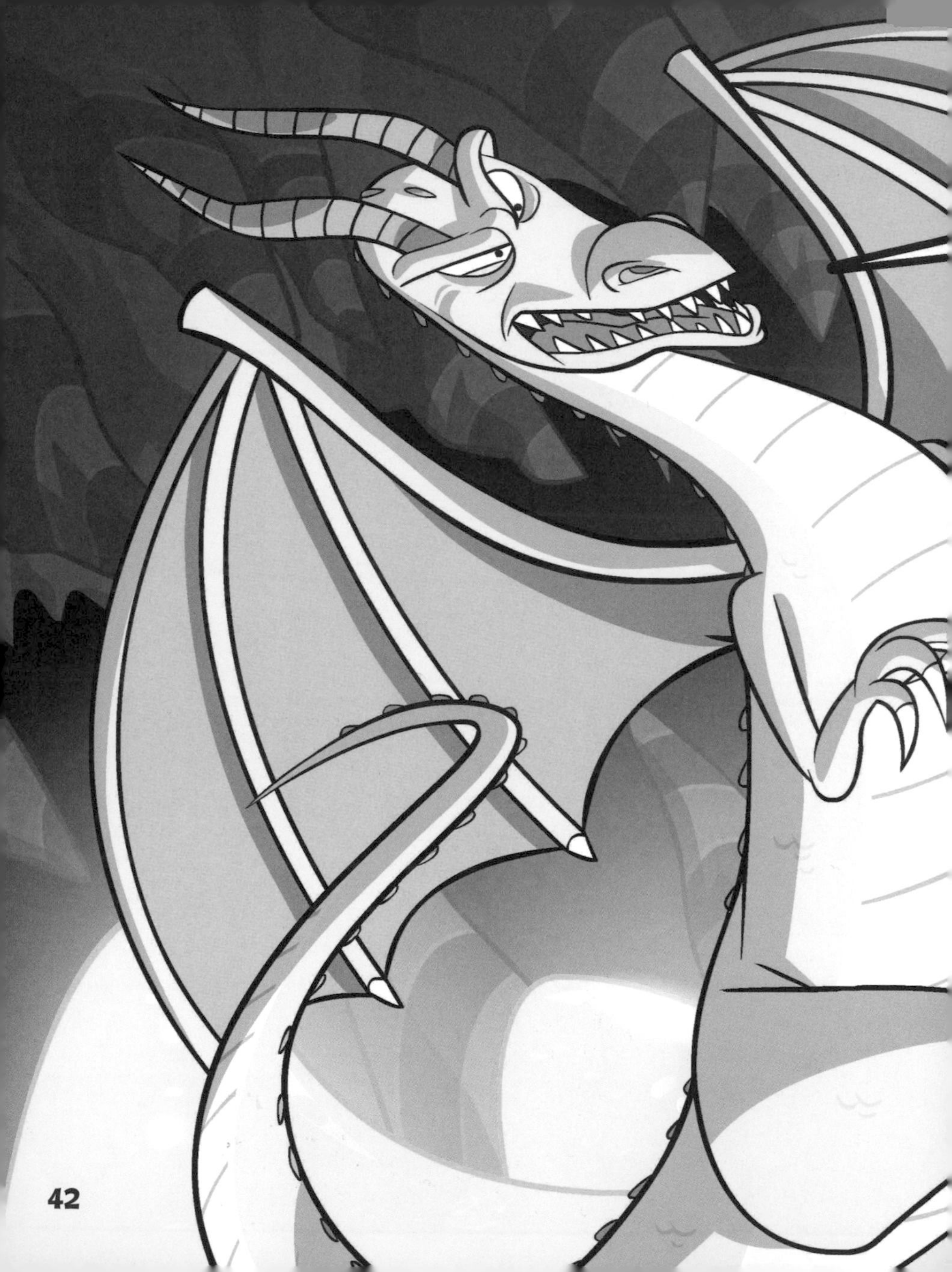

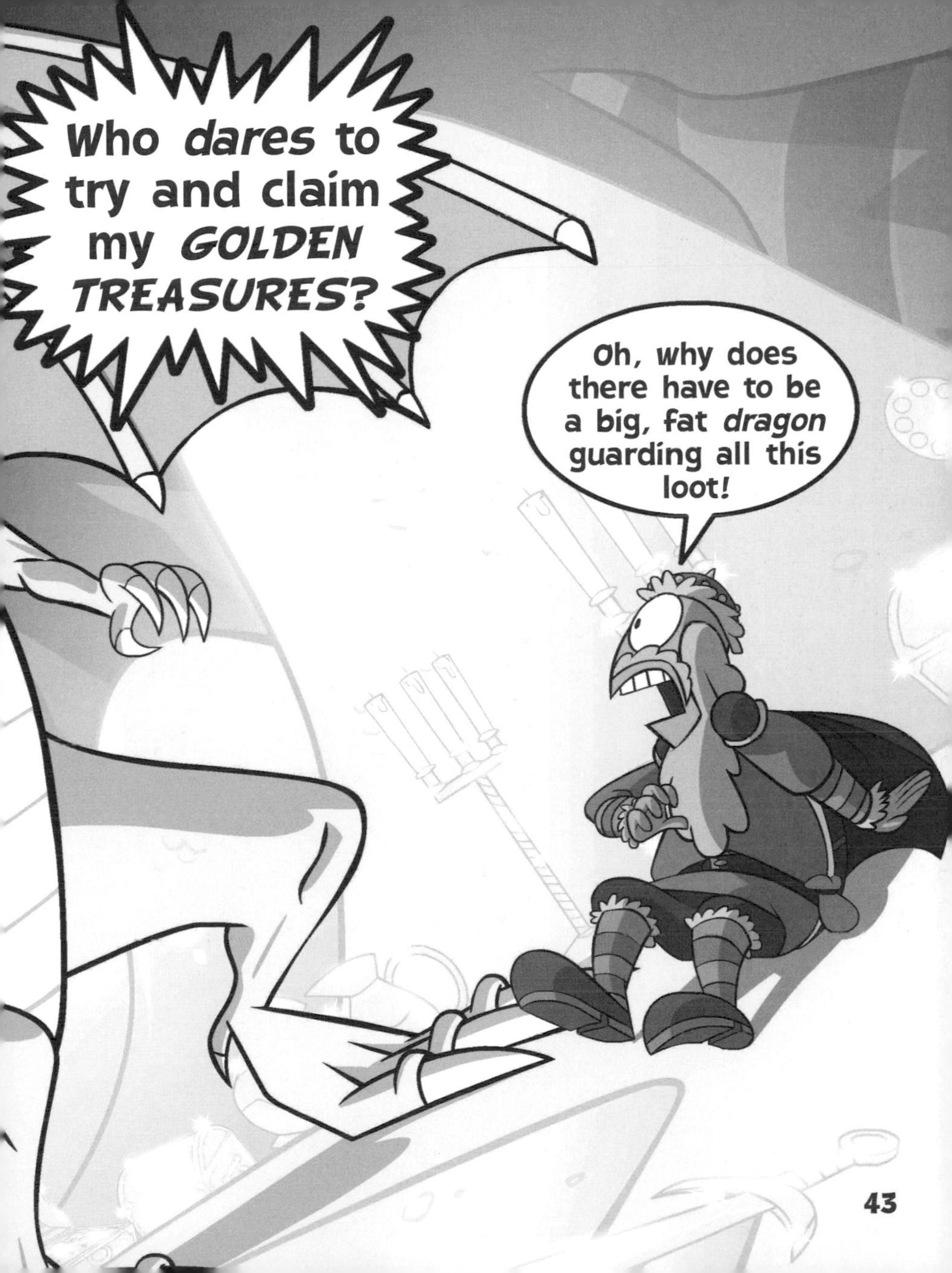
Who *dares* to try and claim my *GOLDEN TREASURES?*
Oh, why does there have to be a big, fat *dragon* guarding all this loot!

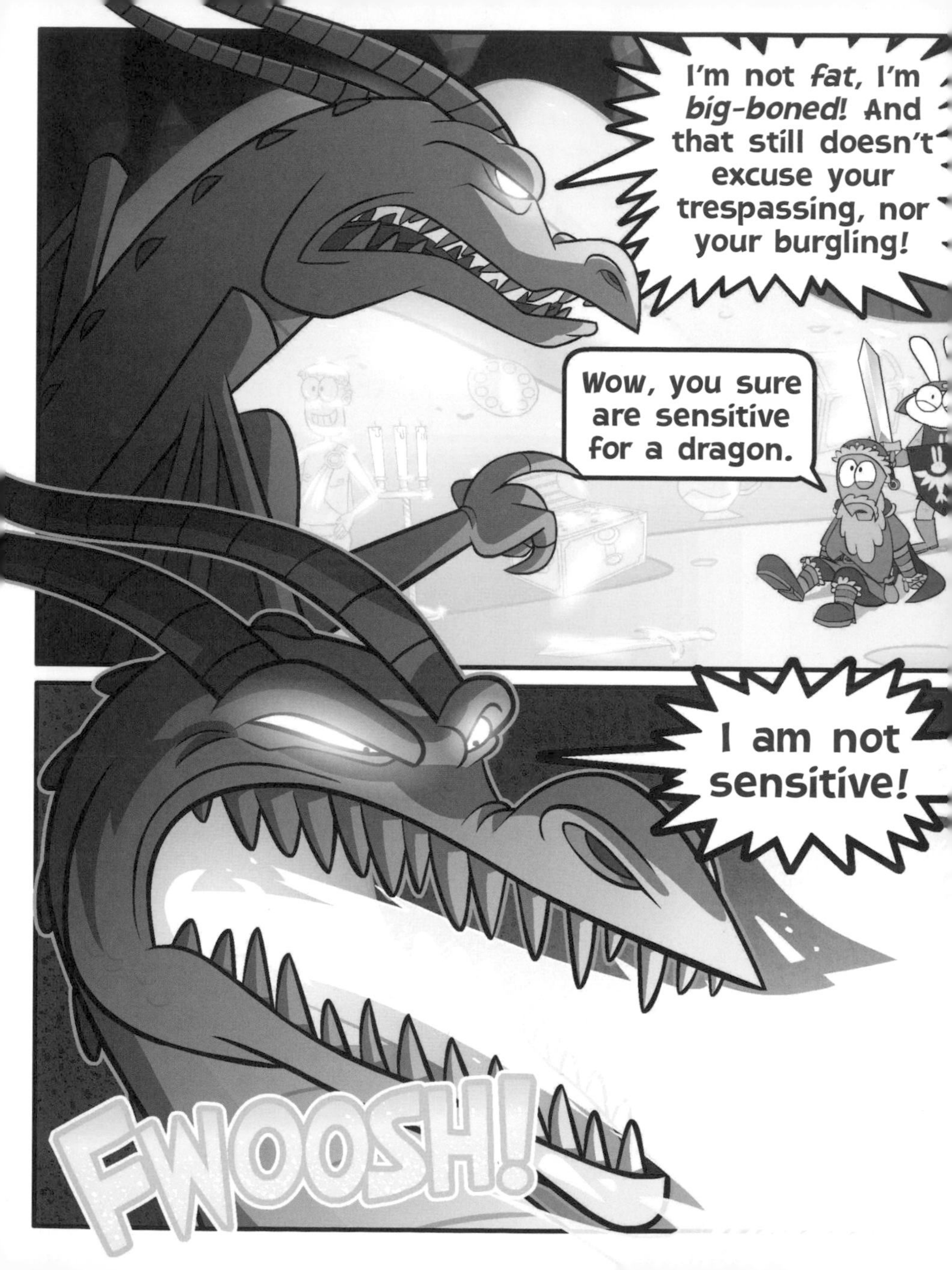
I'm not *fat*, I'm *big-boned*! And that still doesn't excuse your trespassing, nor your burgling!
Wow, you sure are sensitive for a dragon.
I am not sensitive!
FWOOSH!

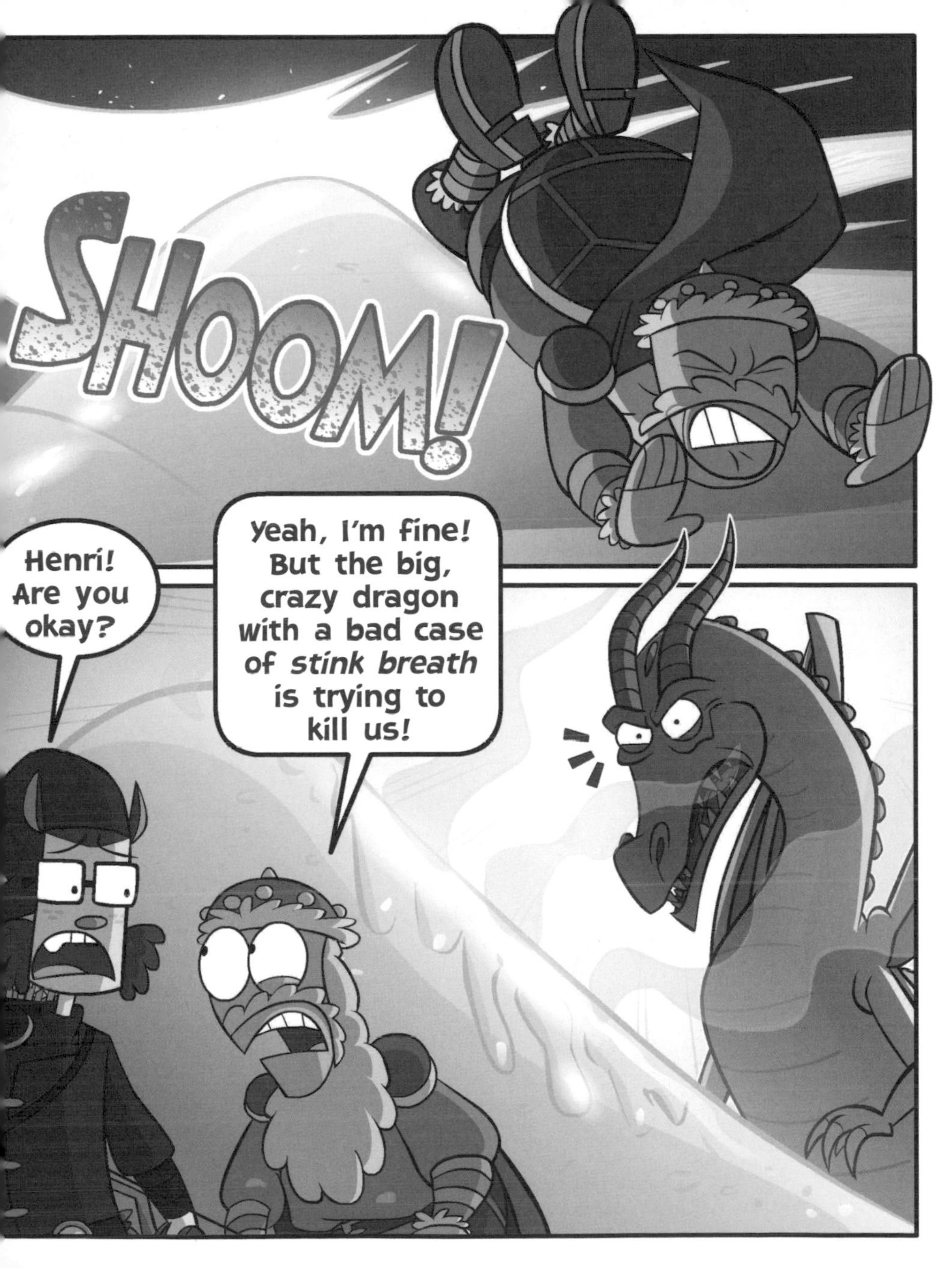
SHOOM!
Henri! Are you okay?
Yeah, I'm fine! But the big, crazy dragon with a bad case of *stink breath* is trying to kill us!

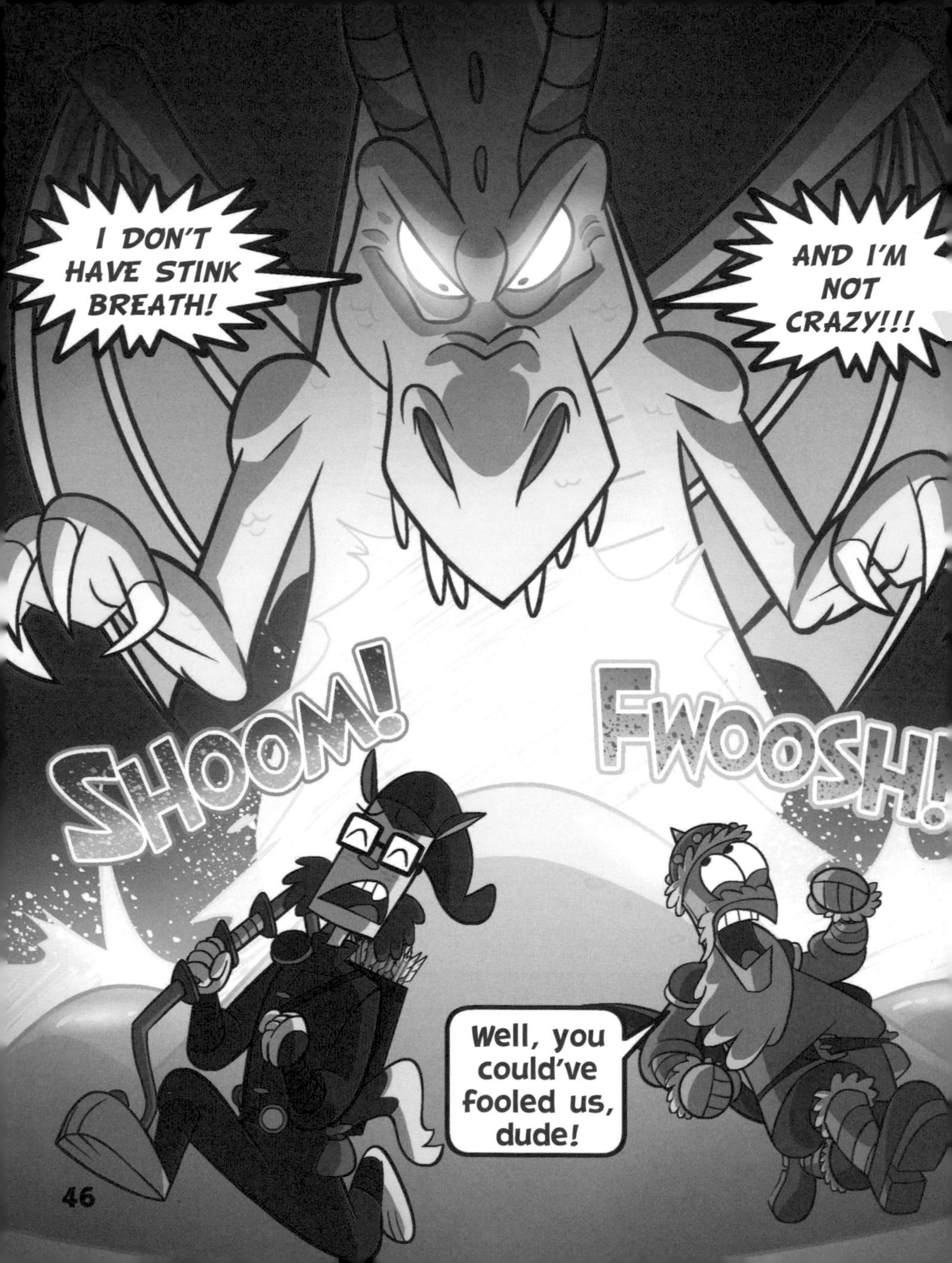
I DON'T HAVE STINK BREATH!
AND I'M NOT CRAZY!!!
SHOOM!
FWOOSH!
Well, you could've fooled us, dude!

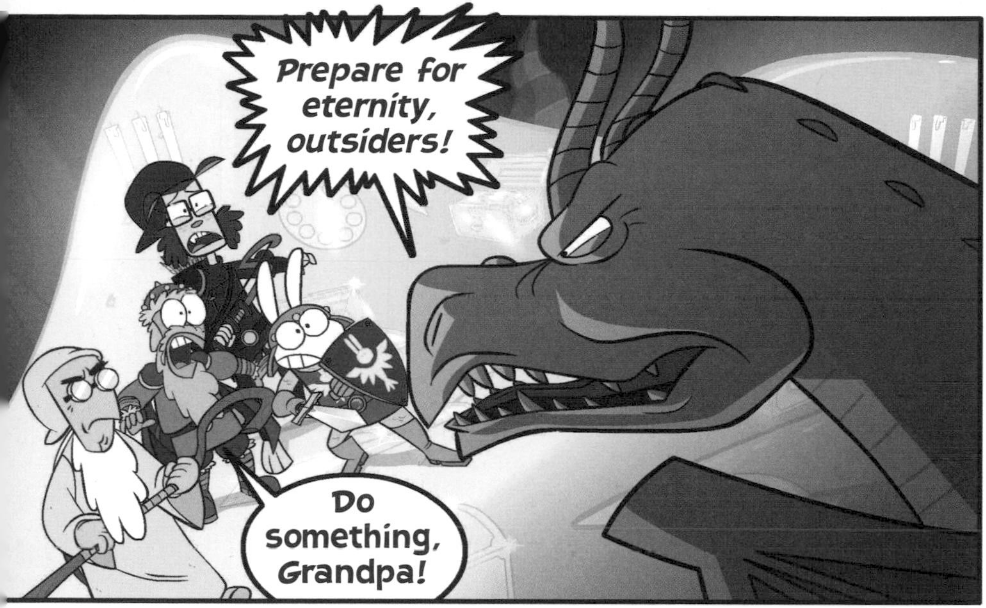
Prepare for eternity, outsiders!
Do something, Grandpa!

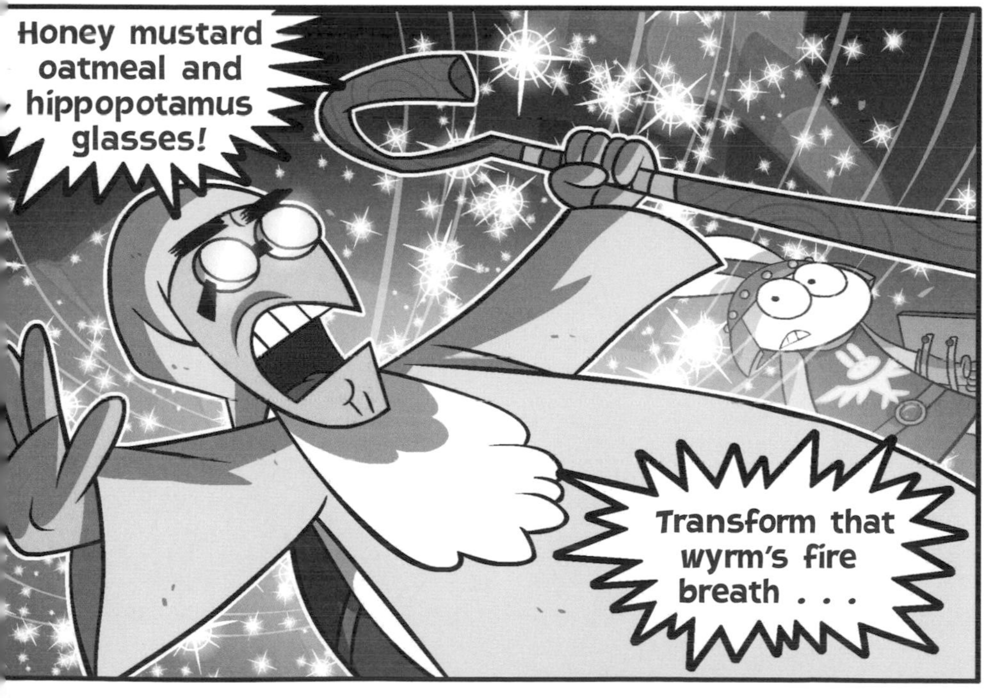
Honey mustard oatmeal and hippopotamus glasses!
Transform that wyrm's fire breath . . .

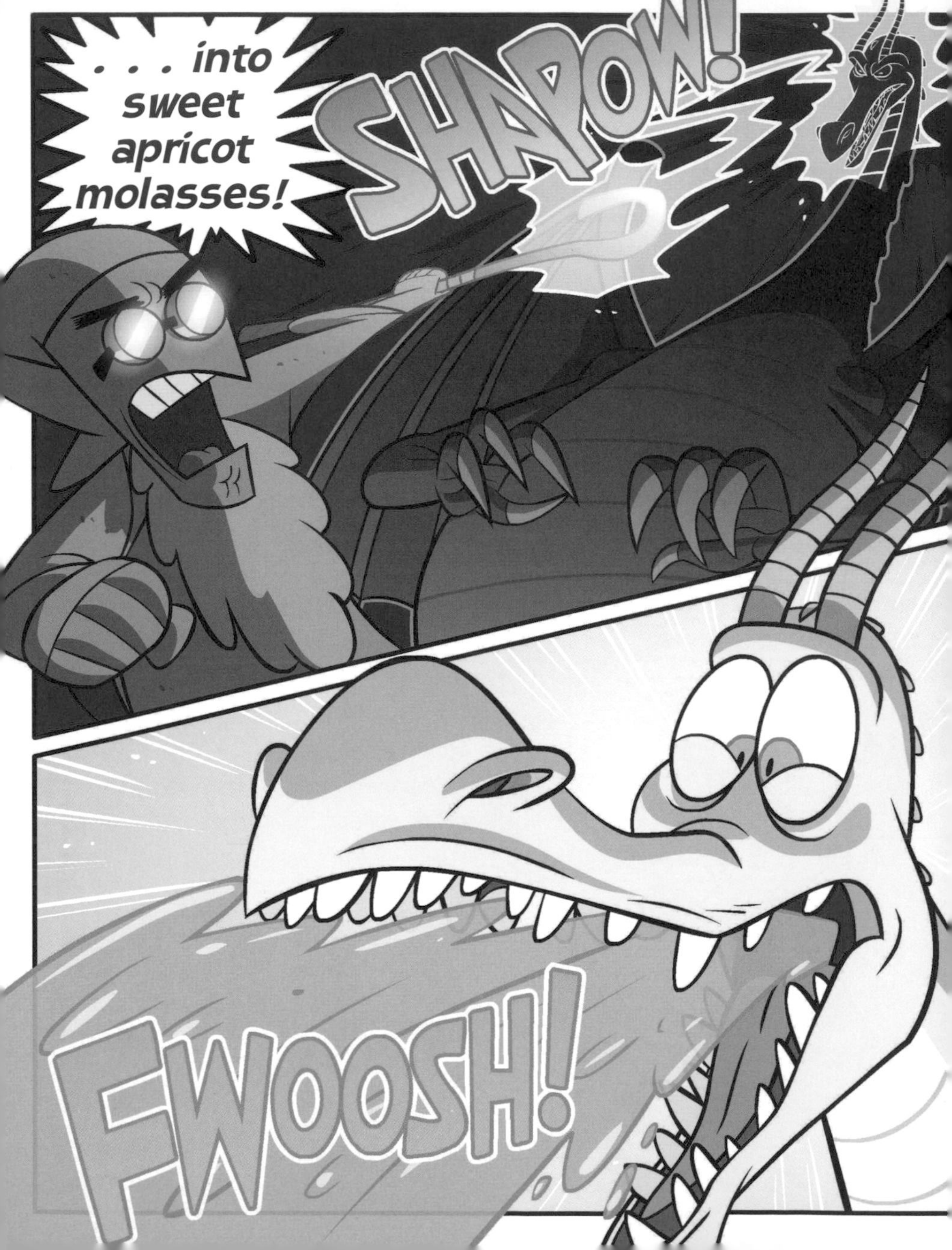
. . . into sweet apricot molasses!
SHAPOW!
FWOOSH!

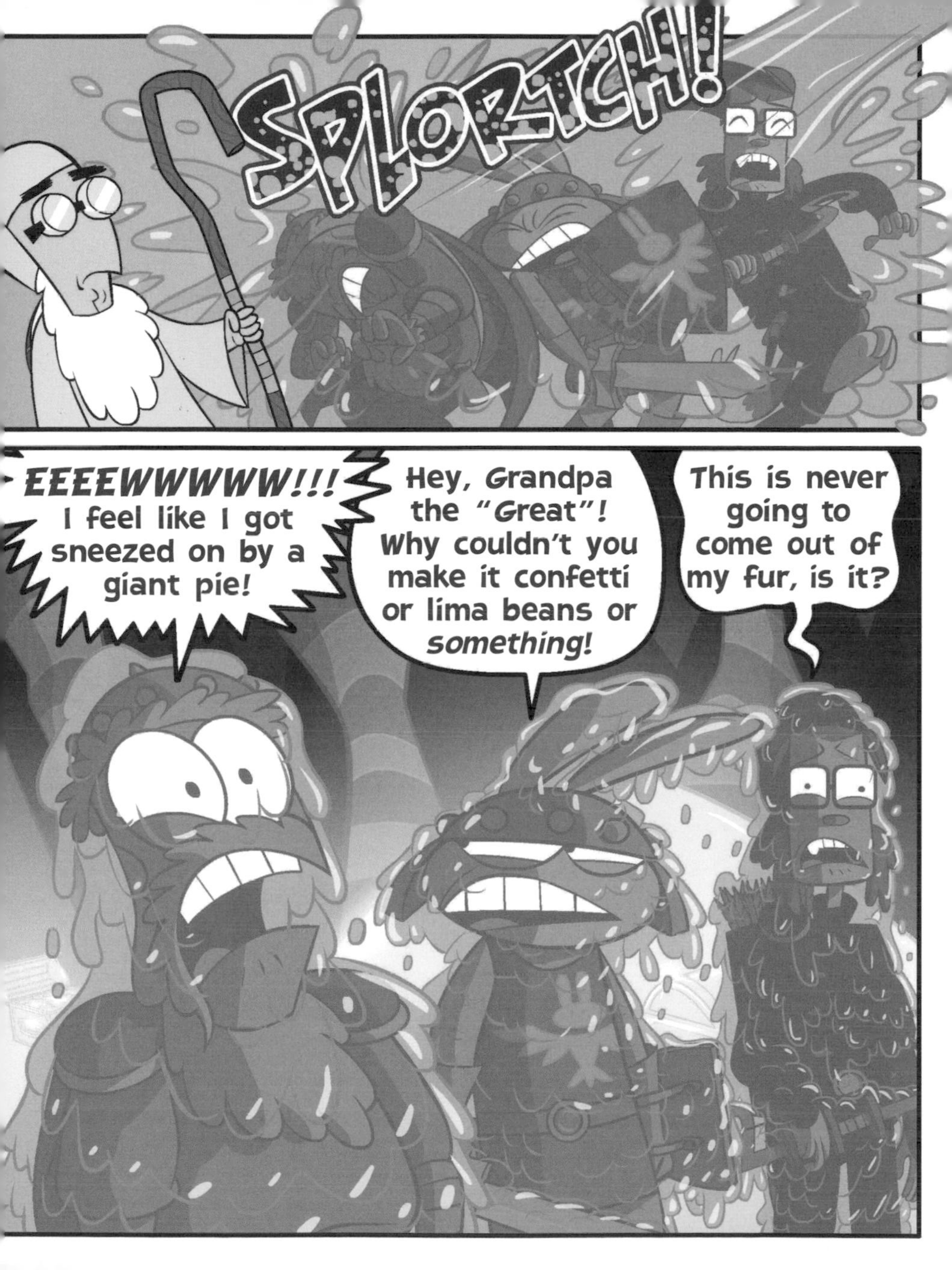
SPLORTCH!!
EEEEWWWWW!!! I feel like I got sneezed on by a giant pie!
Hey, Grandpa the "Great"! Why couldn't you make it confetti or lima beans or *something*!
This is never going to come out of my fur, is it?

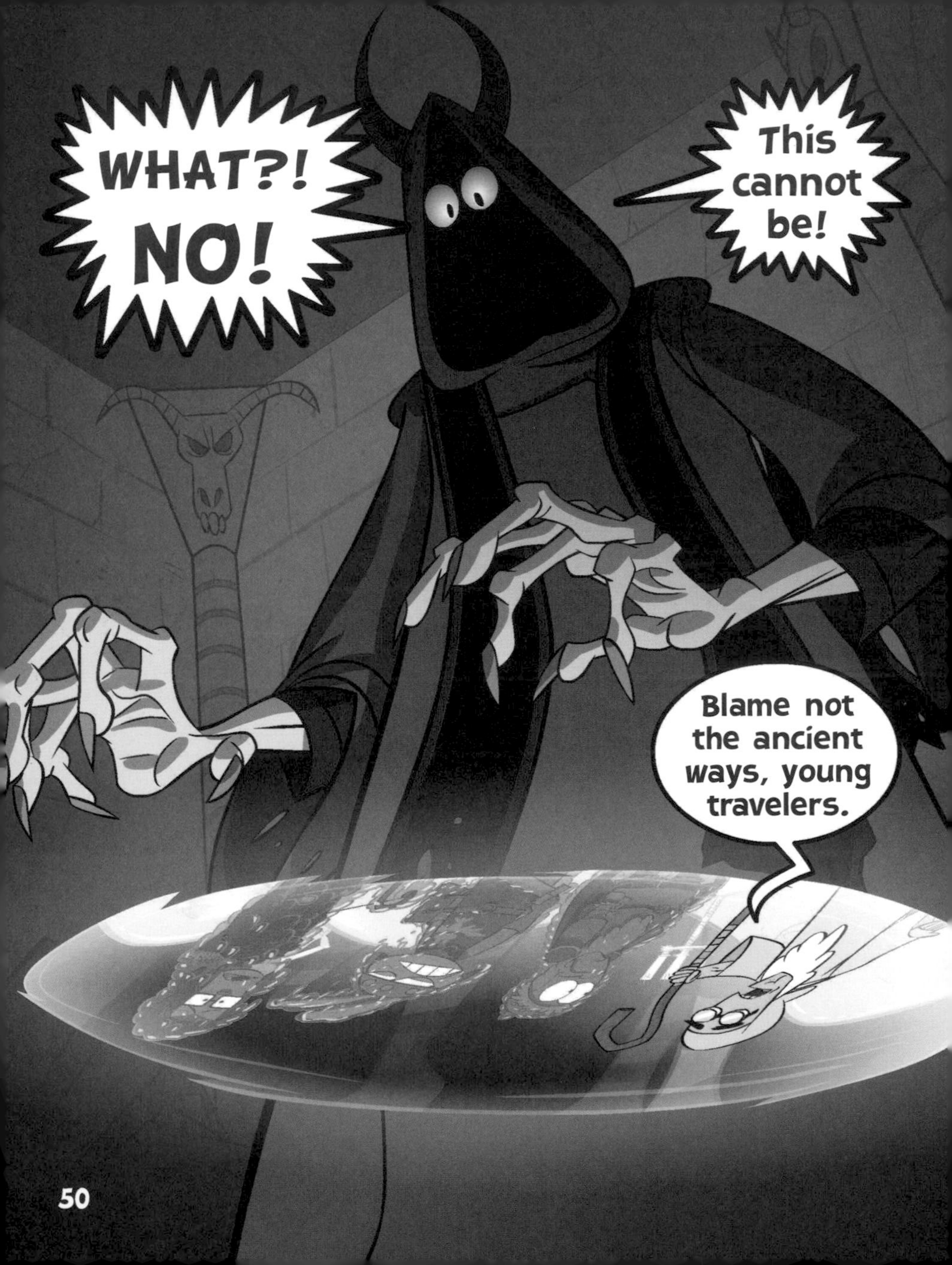
WHAT?! NO!
This cannot be!
Blame not the ancient ways, young travelers.

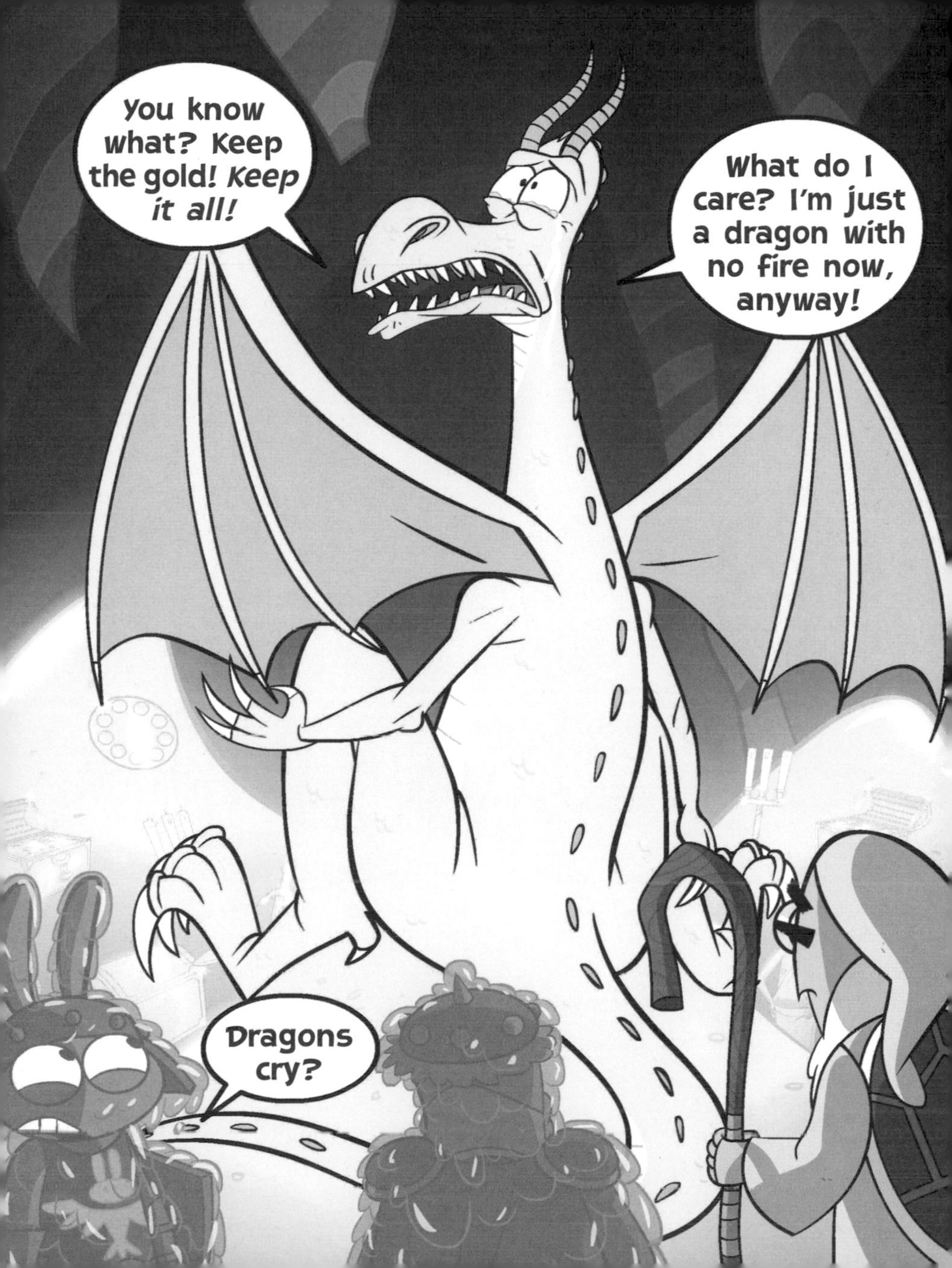
You know what? Keep the gold! *Keep it all!*
What do I care? I'm just a dragon with no fire now, anyway!
Dragons cry?

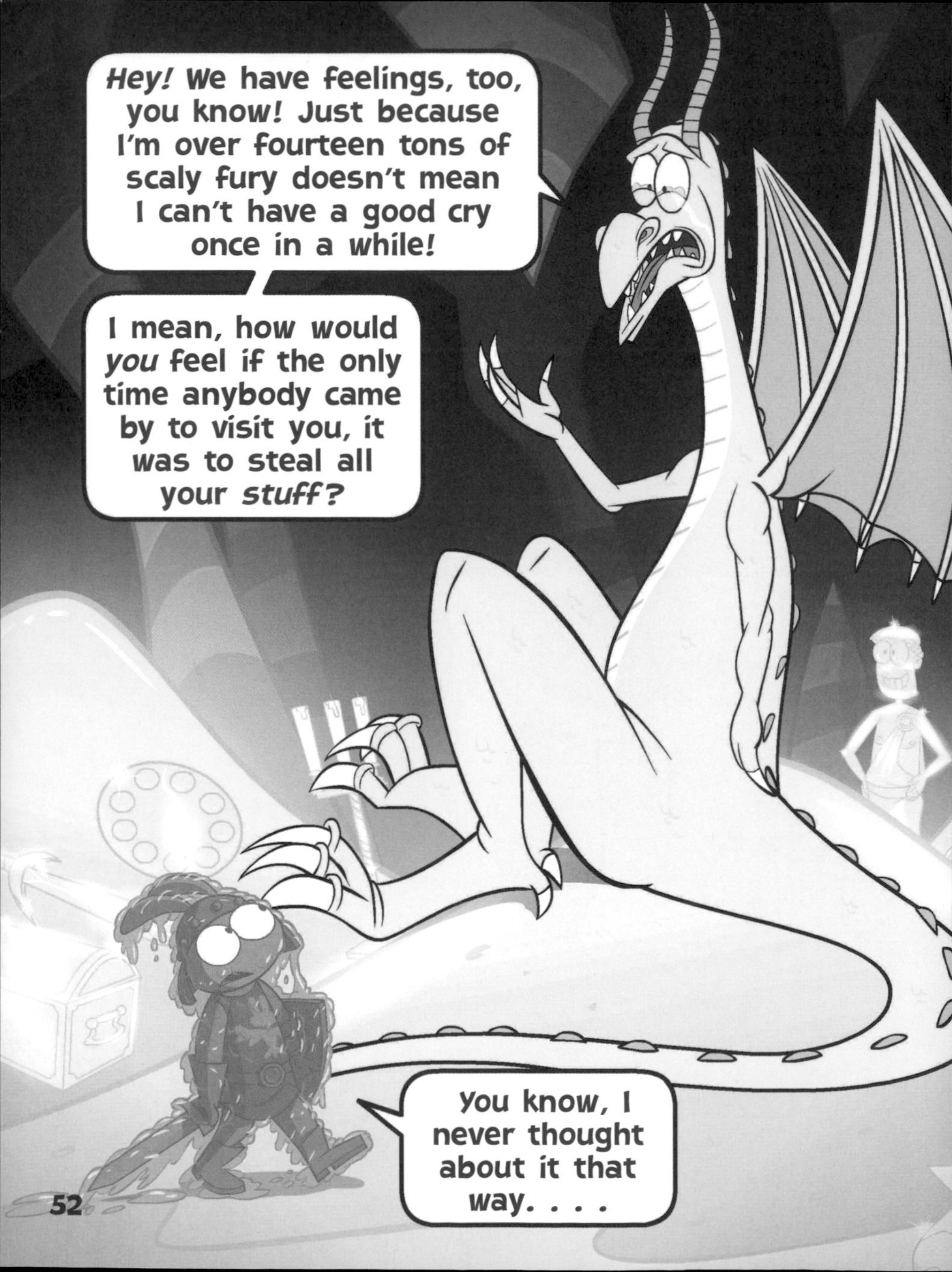
Hey! We have feelings, too, you know! Just because I'm over fourteen tons of scaly fury doesn't mean I can't have a good cry once in a *while!*
I mean, how would *you* feel if the only time anybody came by to visit you, it was to steal all your *stuff?*
You know, I never thought about it that way. . . .

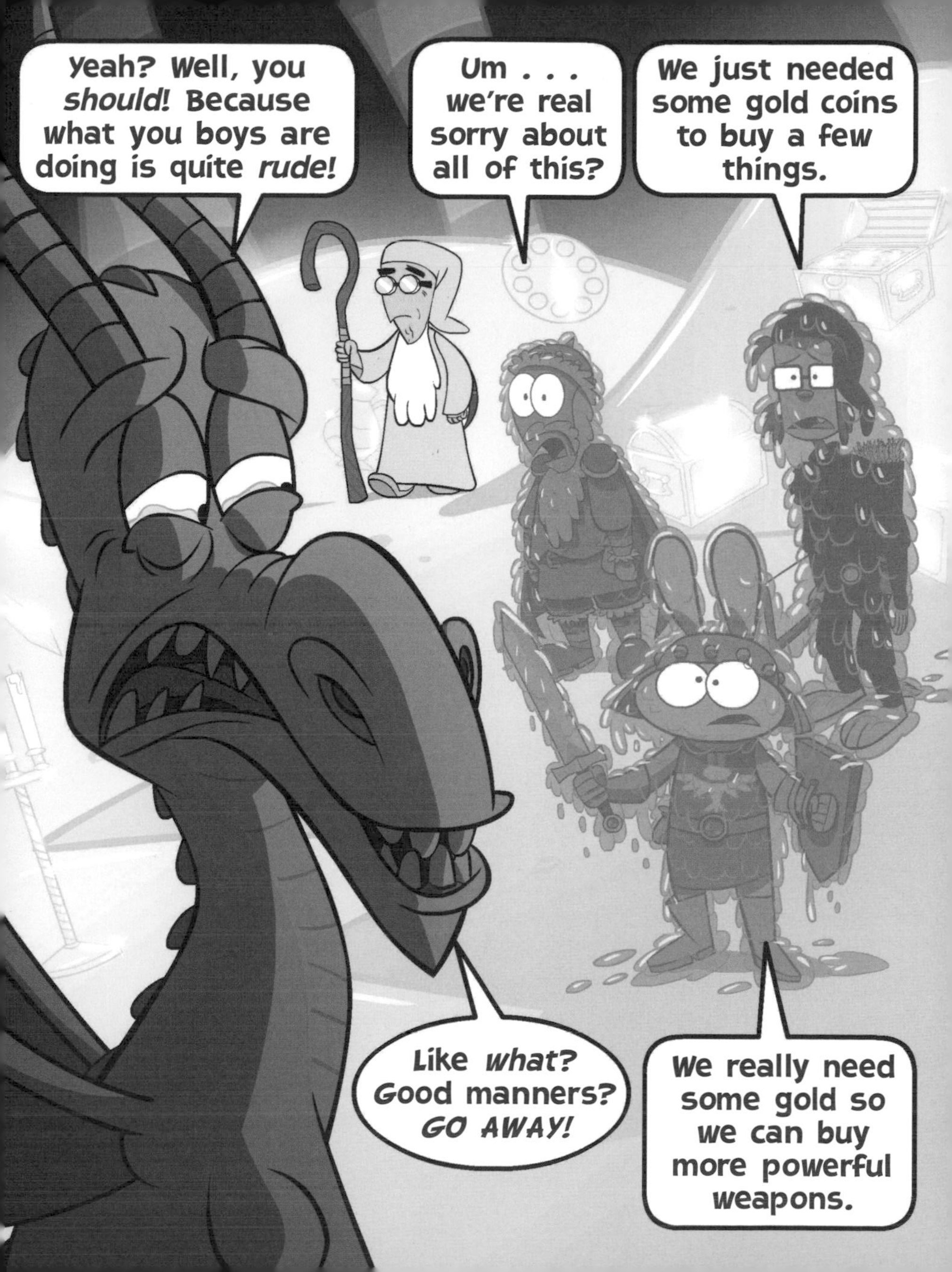
Yeah? Well, you *should*! Because what you boys are doing is quite *rude*!
Um . . . we're real sorry about all of this?
We just needed some gold coins to buy a few things.
Like *what*? Good manners? *GO AWAY!*
We really need some gold so we can buy more powerful weapons.

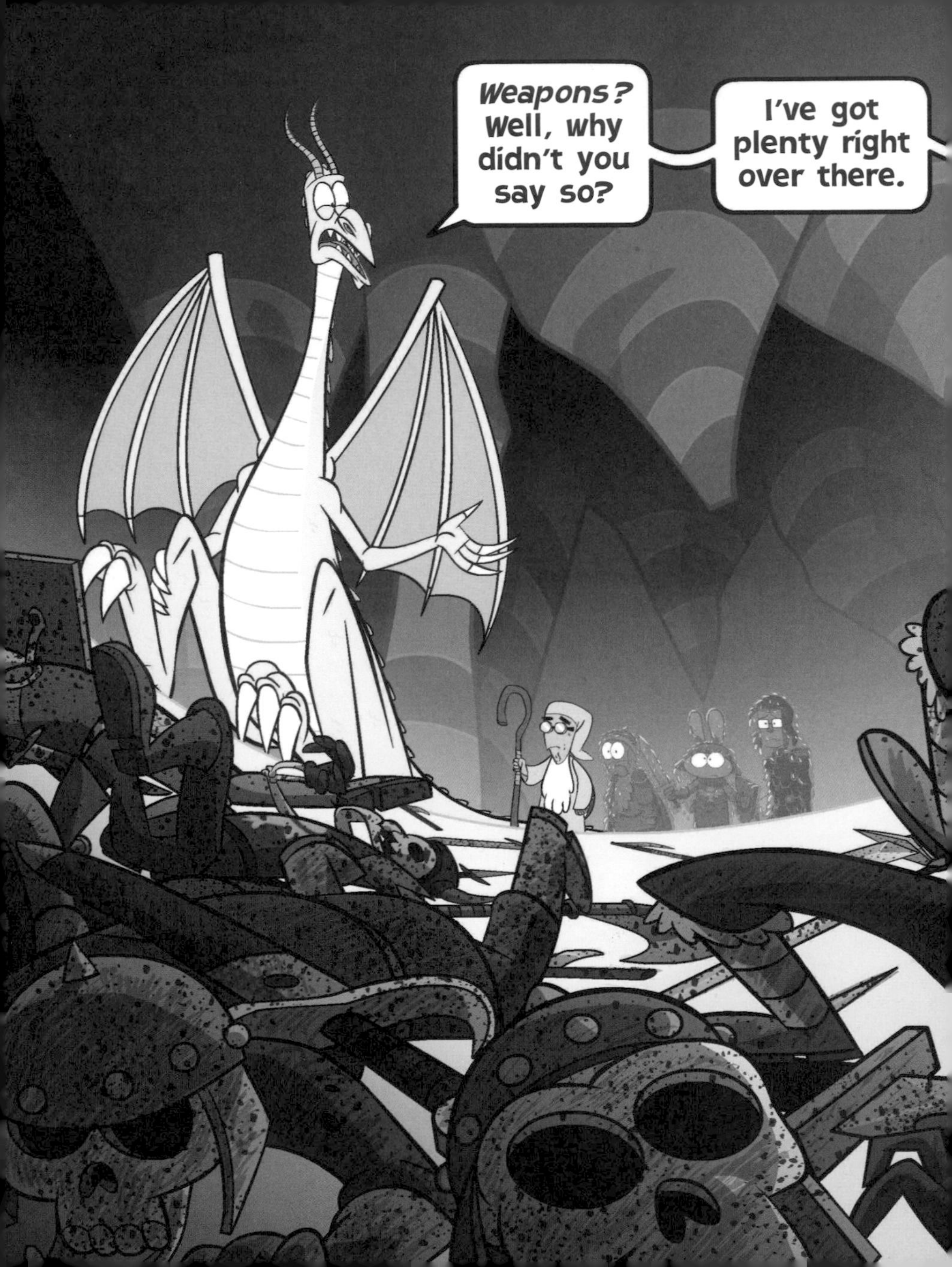
Weapons? Well, why didn't you say so?
I've got plenty right over there.

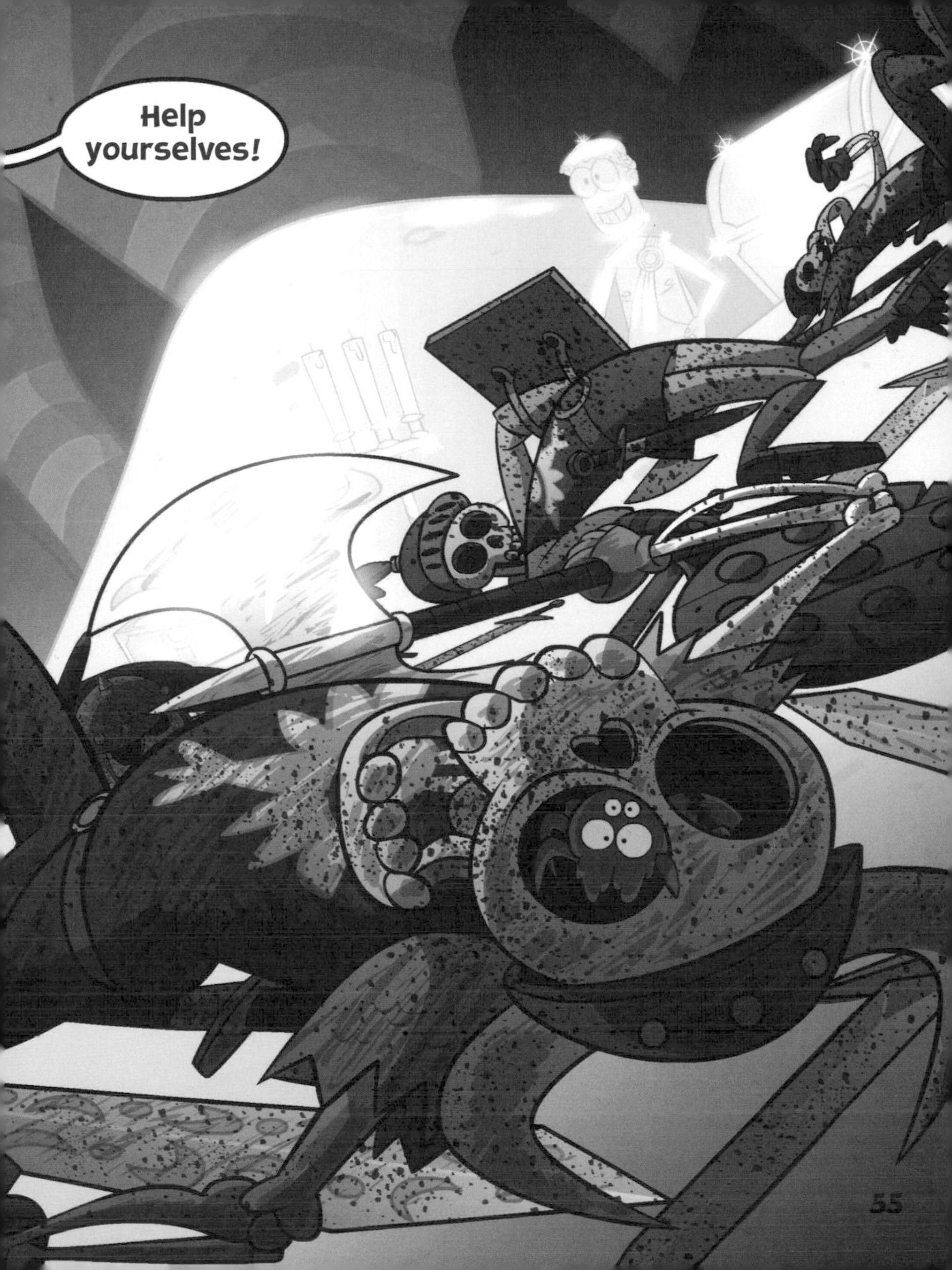
Help yourselves!

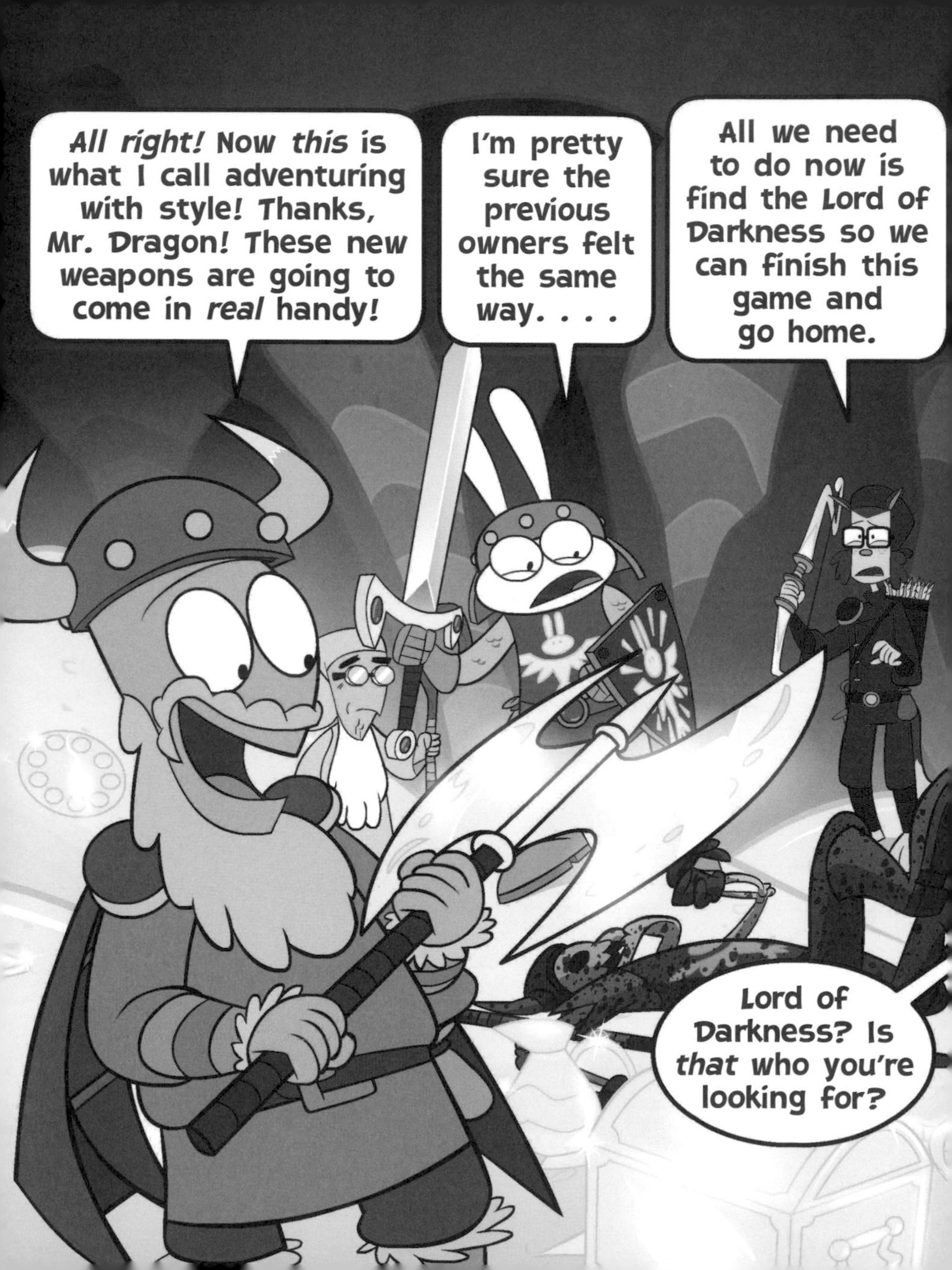
All right! Now *this* is what I call adventuring with style! Thanks, Mr. Dragon! These new weapons are going to come in *real* handy!
I'm pretty sure the previous owners felt the same way. . . .
All we need to do now is find the Lord of Darkness so we can finish this game and go home.
Lord of Darkness? Is *that* who you're looking for?

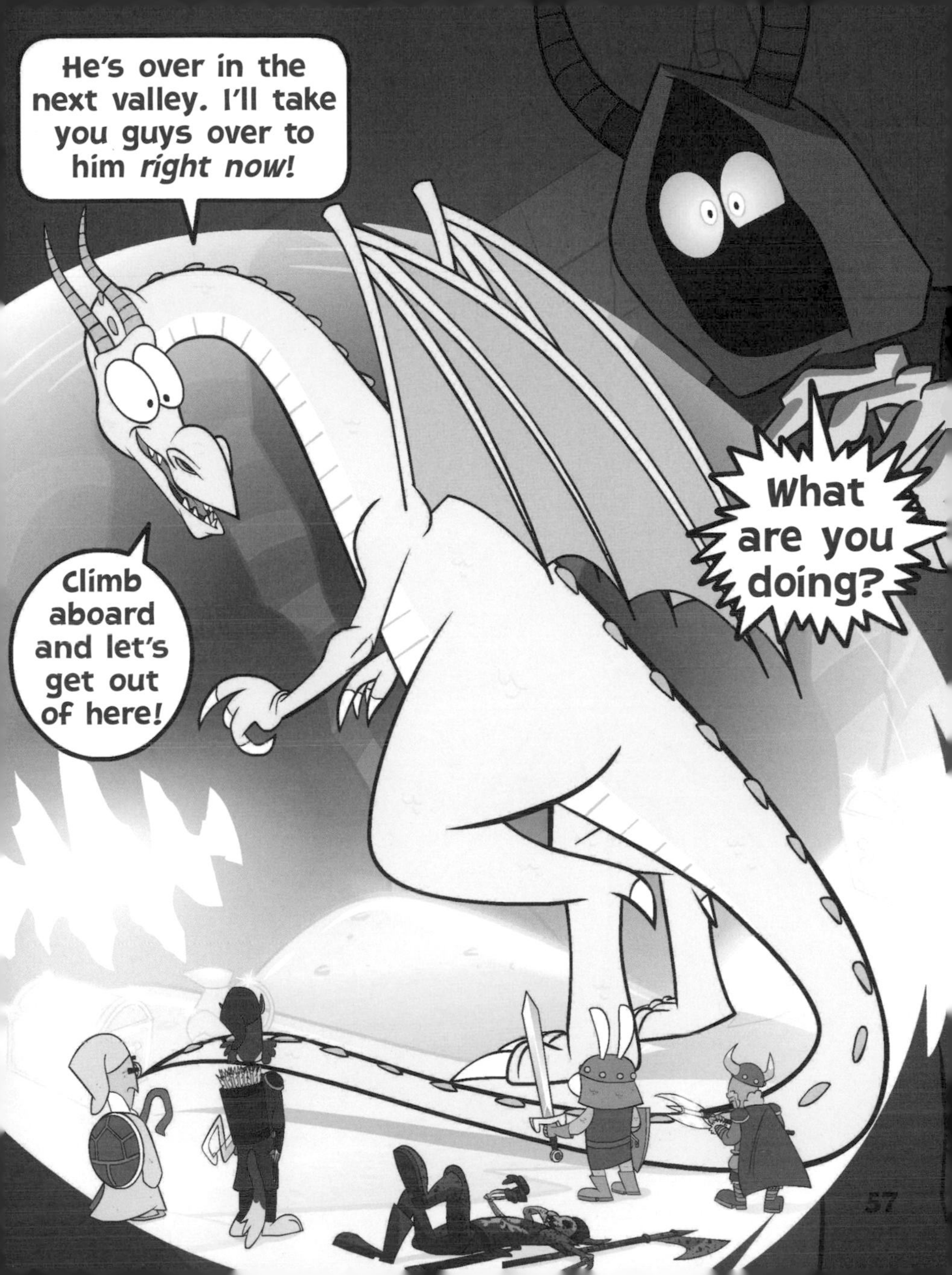
He's over in the next valley. I'll take you guys over to him *right now*!
Climb aboard and let's get out of here!
What are you doing?

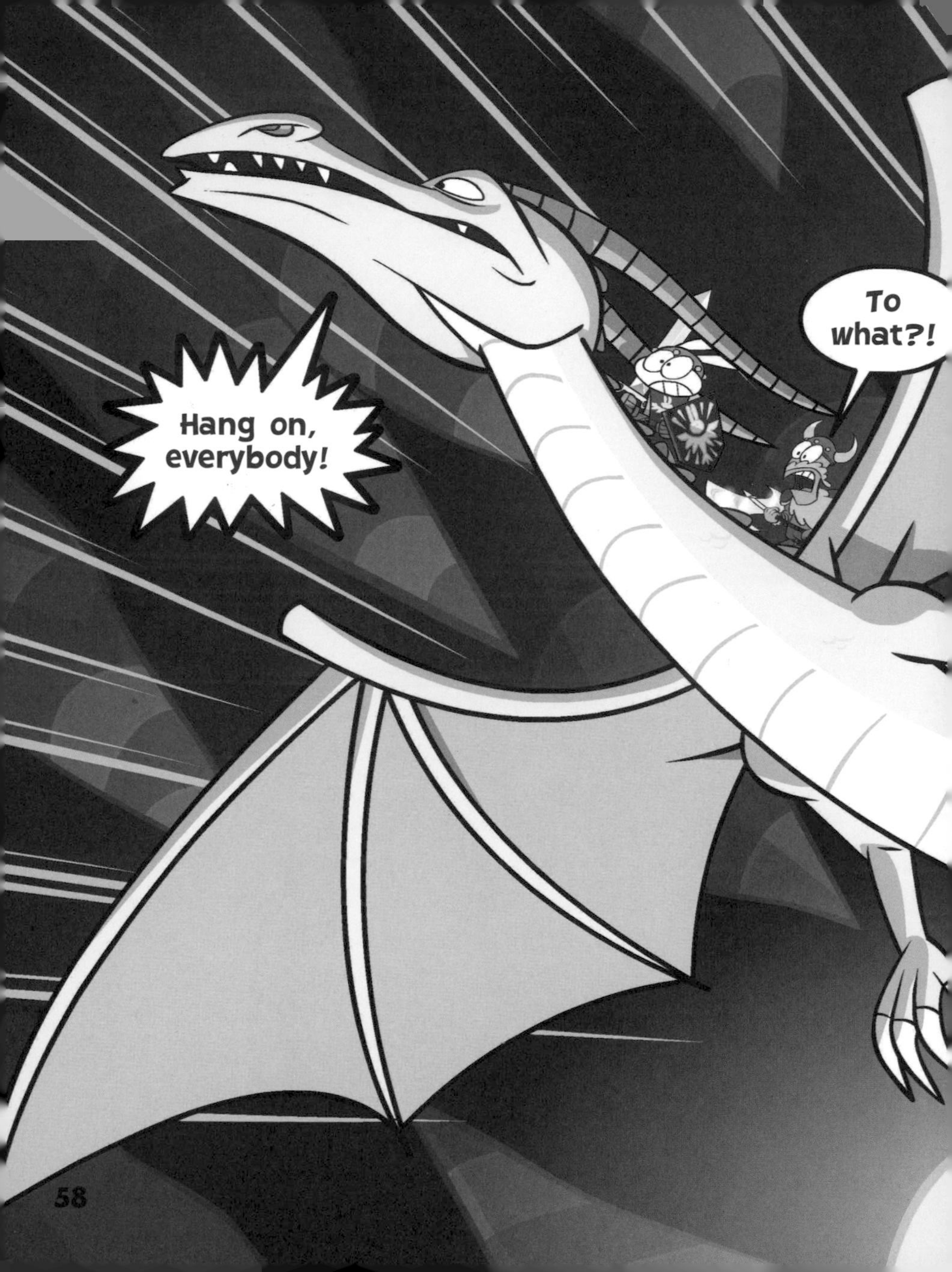
Hang on, everybody!
To what?!

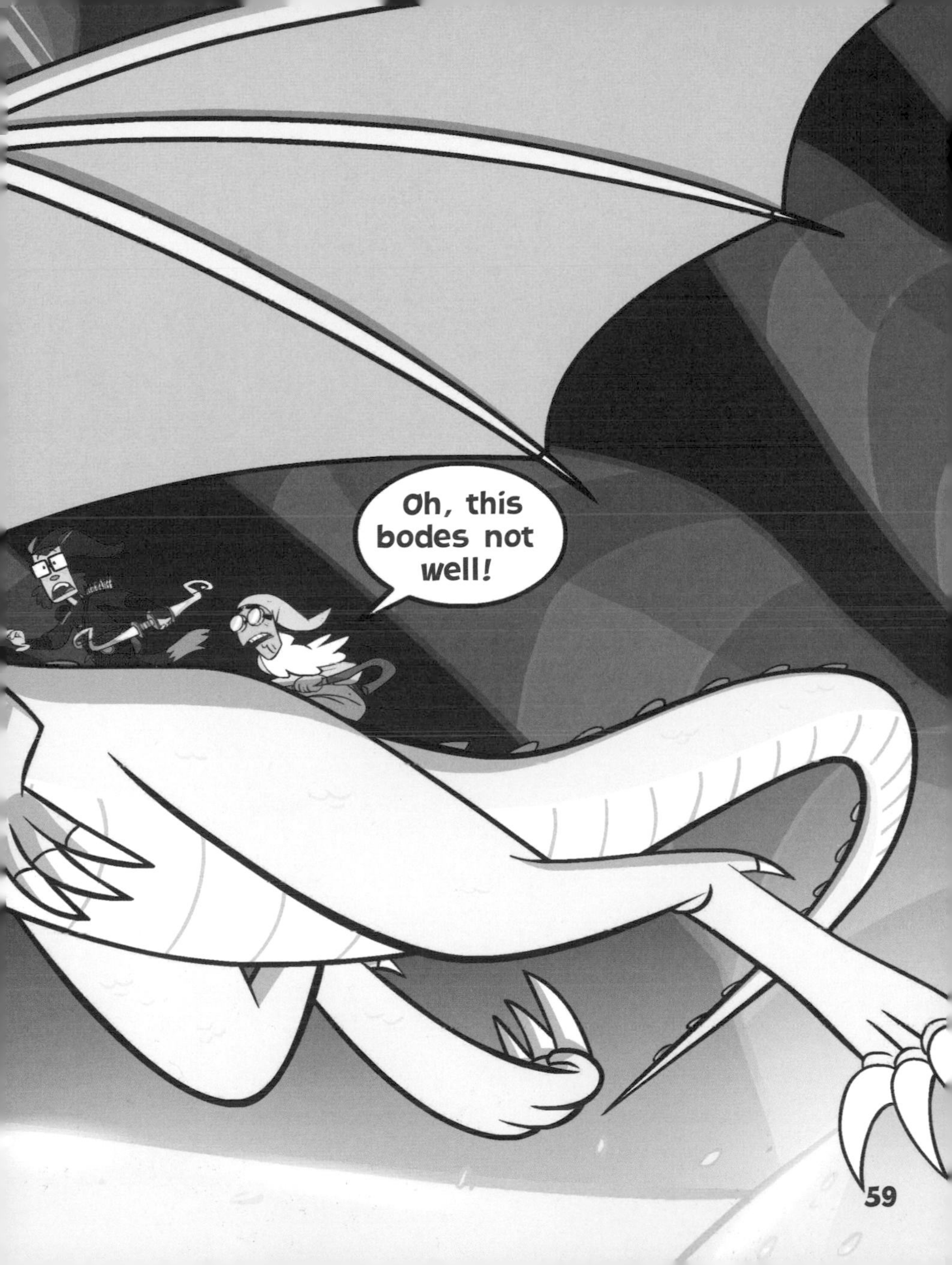
Oh, this bodes not well!

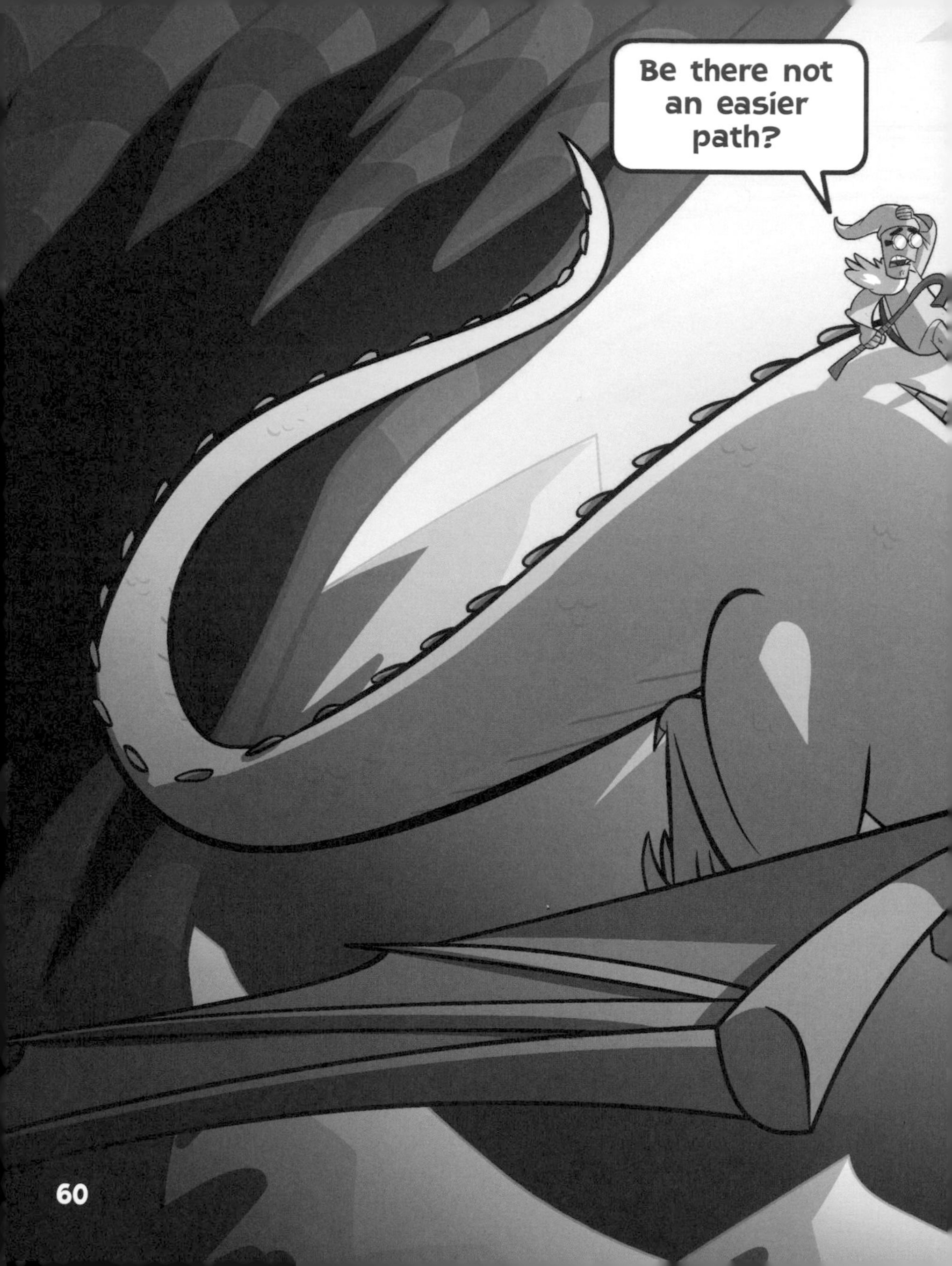
Be there not an easier path?

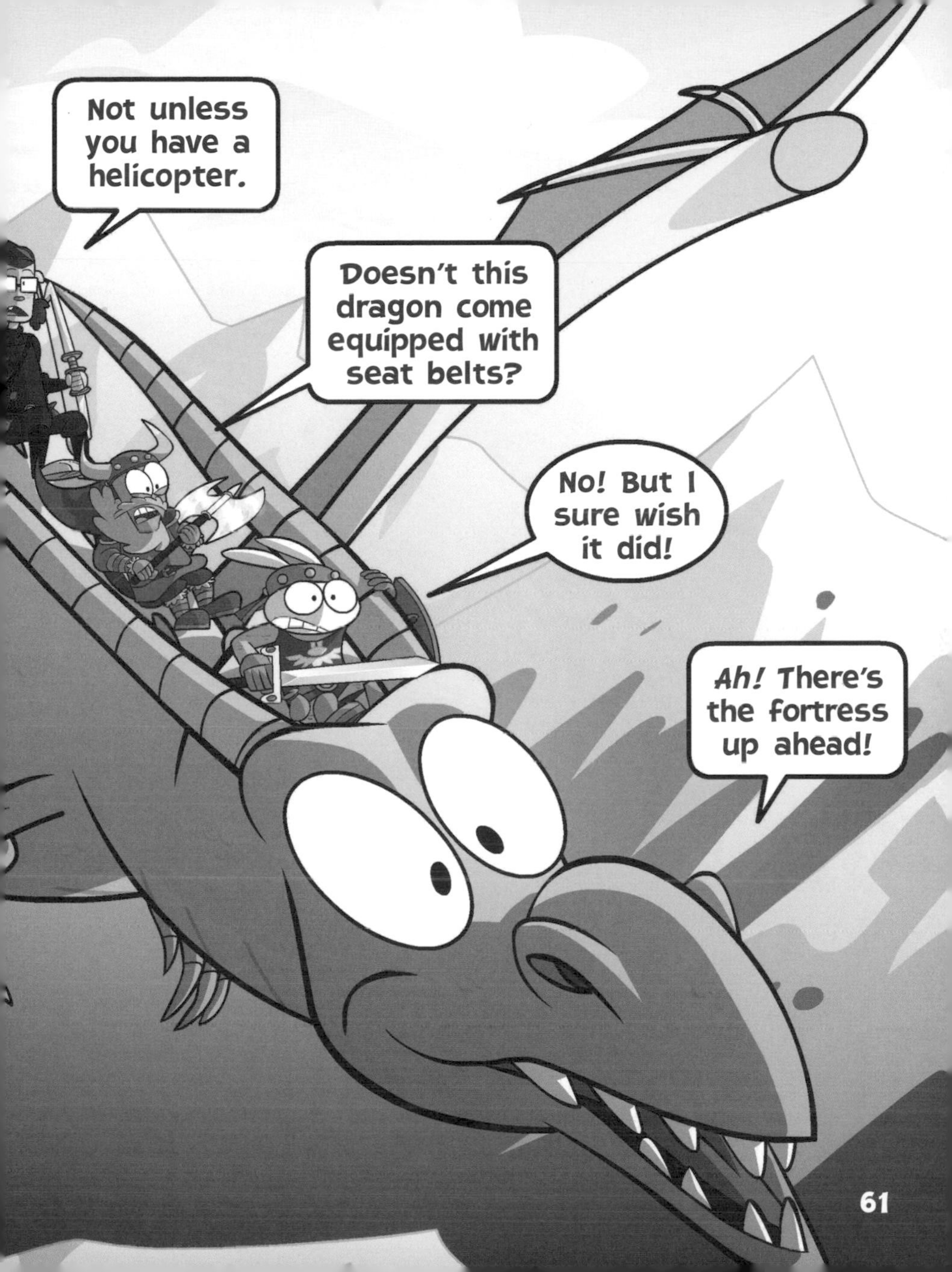
Not unless you have a helicopter.
Doesn't this dragon come equipped with seat belts?
No! But I sure wish it did!
Ah! There's the fortress up ahead!

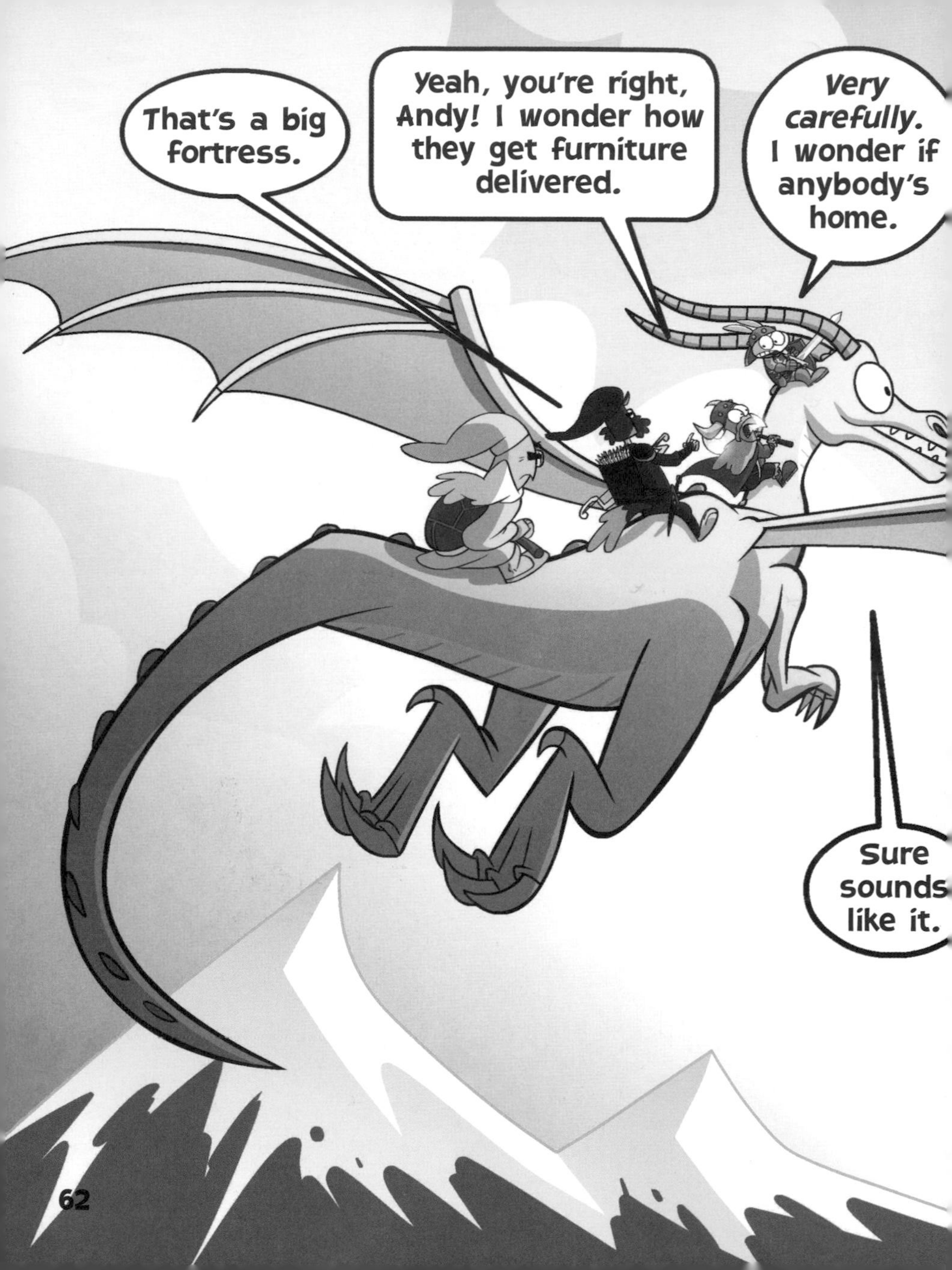
That's a big fortress.
Yeah, you're right, Andy! I wonder how they get furniture delivered.
Very carefully. I wonder if anybody's home.
Sure sounds like it.

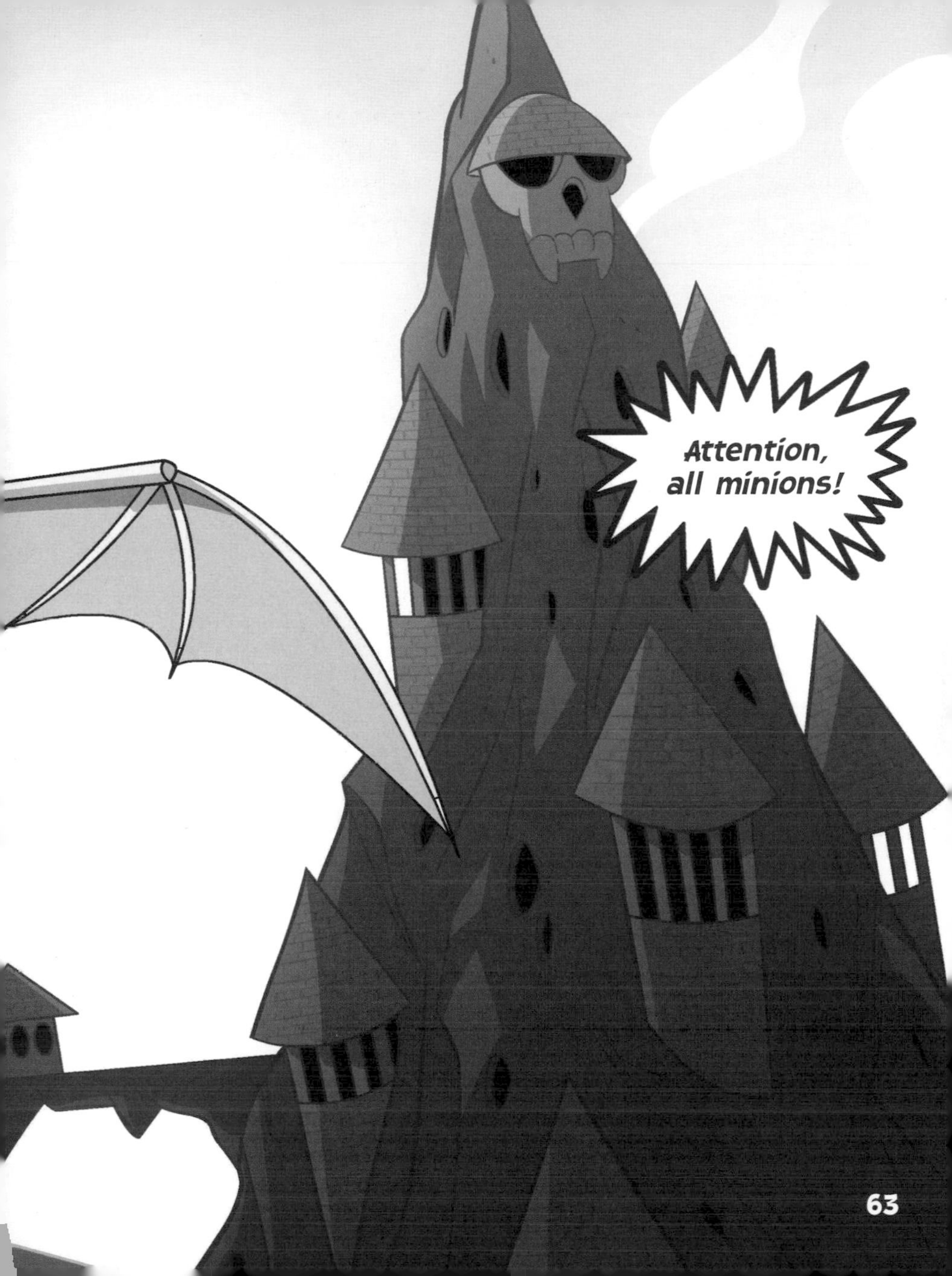
Attention, all minions!

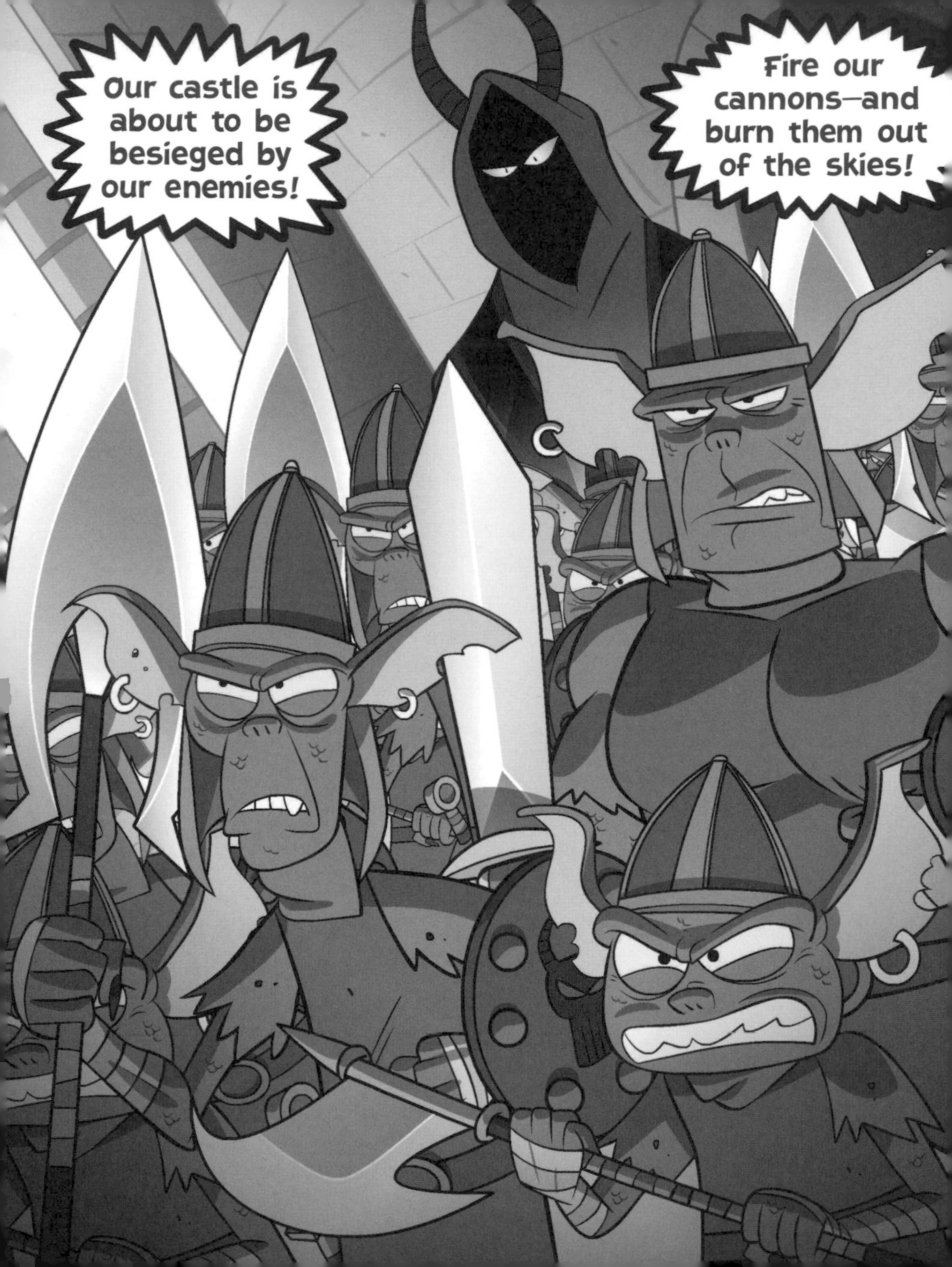

Our castle is about to be besieged by our enemies!
Fire our cannons—and burn them out of the skies!

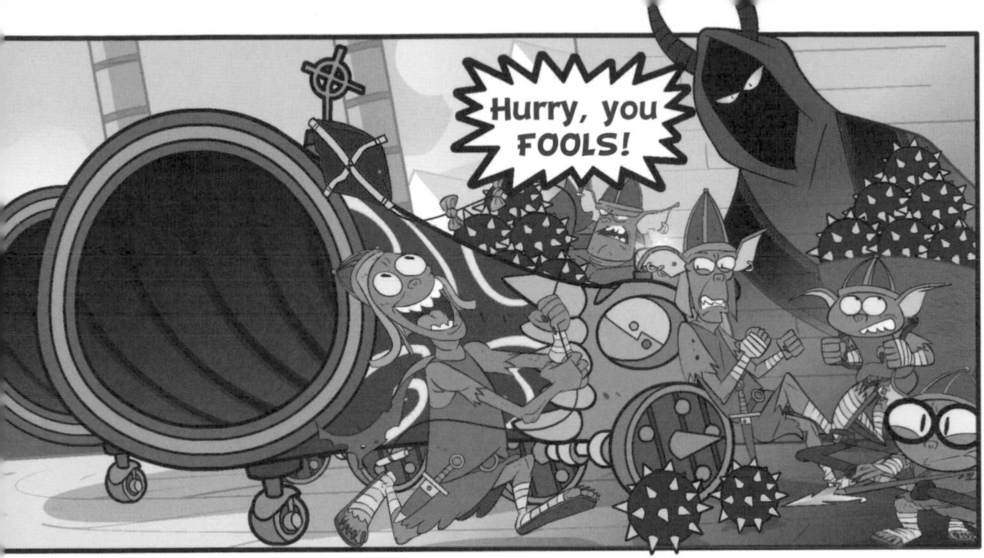
Hurry, you FOOLS!

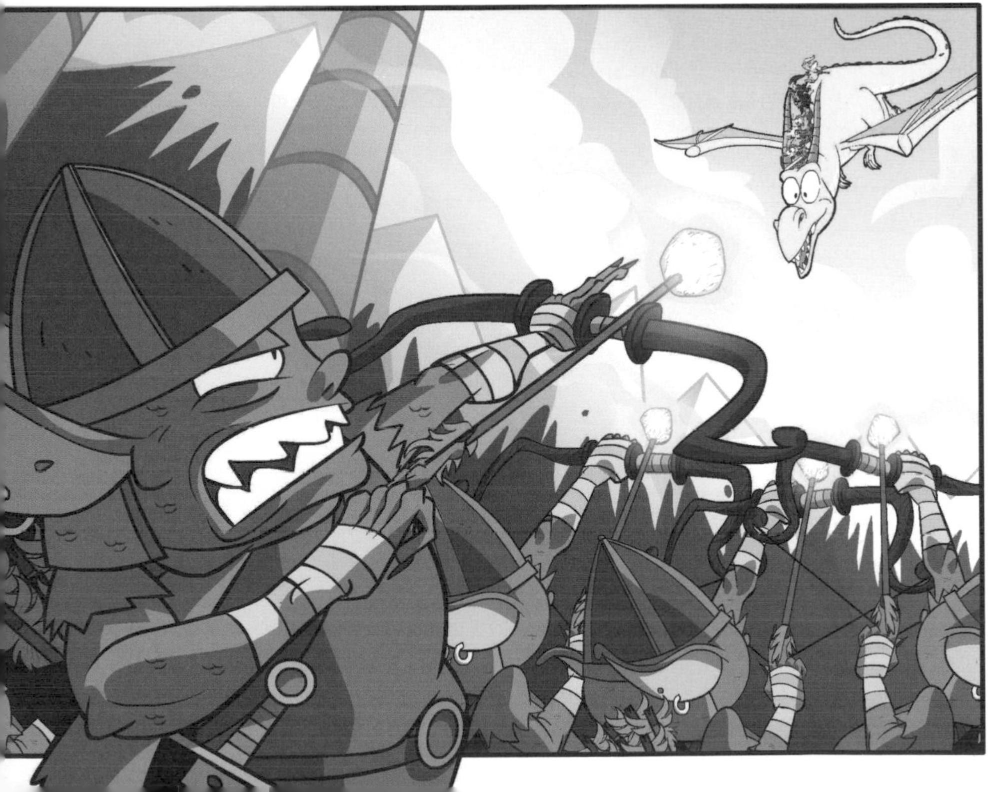

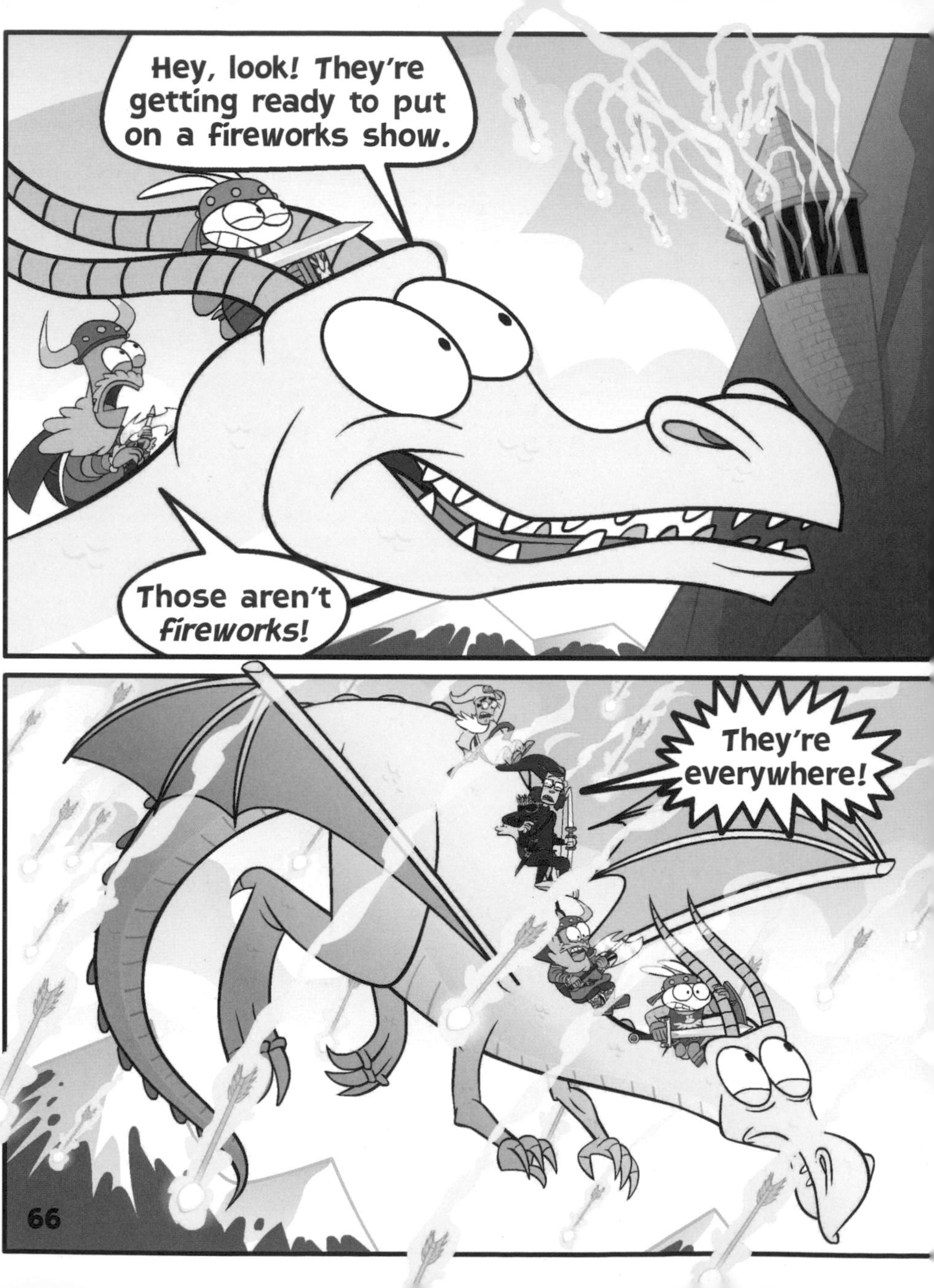
Hey, look! They're getting ready to put on a fireworks show.
Those aren't *fireworks*!
They're everywhere!

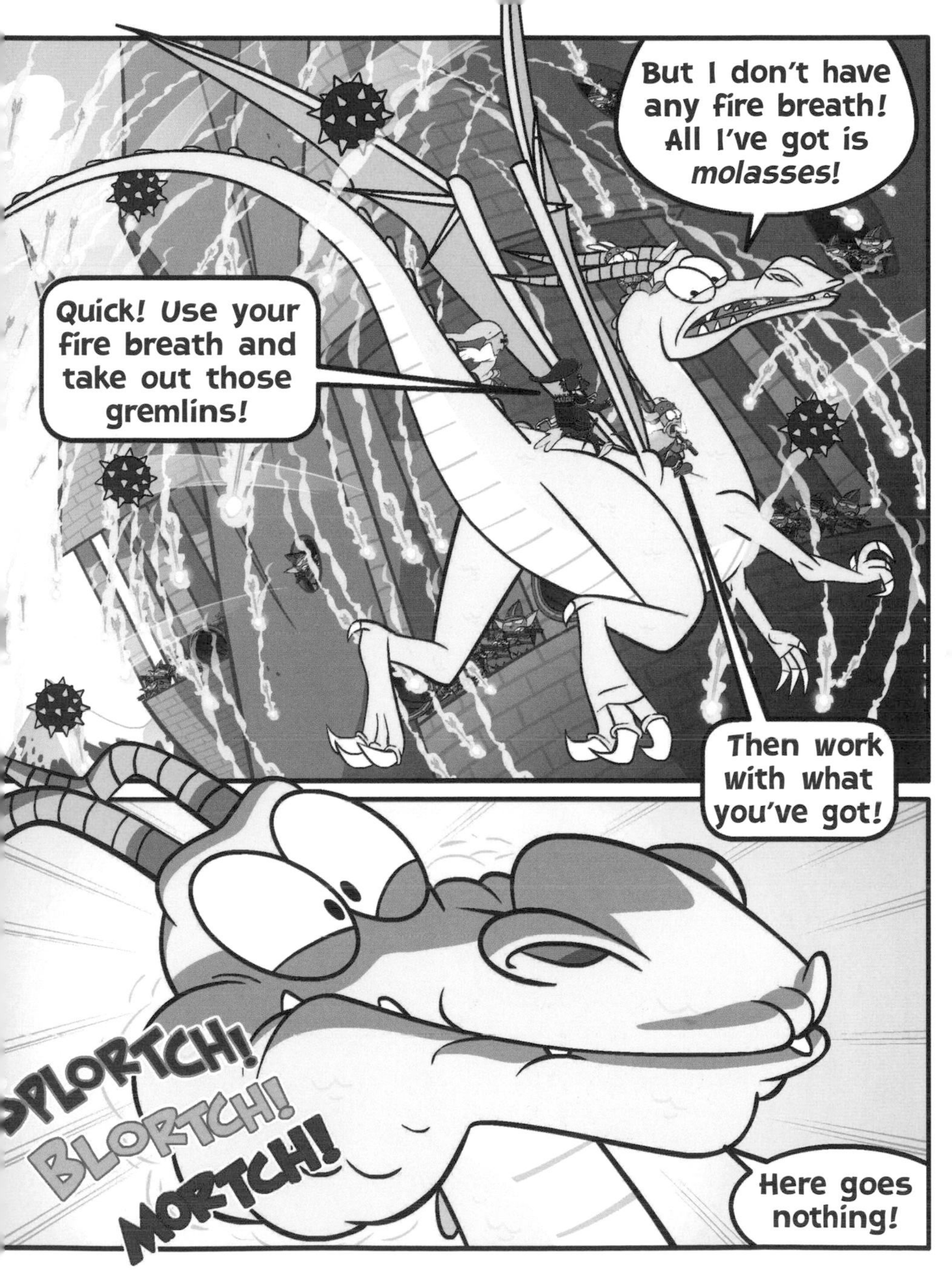
But I don't have any fire breath! All I've got is *molasses!*
Quick! Use your fire breath and take out those gremlins!
Then work with what you've got!
Here goes nothing!
SPLORTCH! BLORTCH! MORTCH!

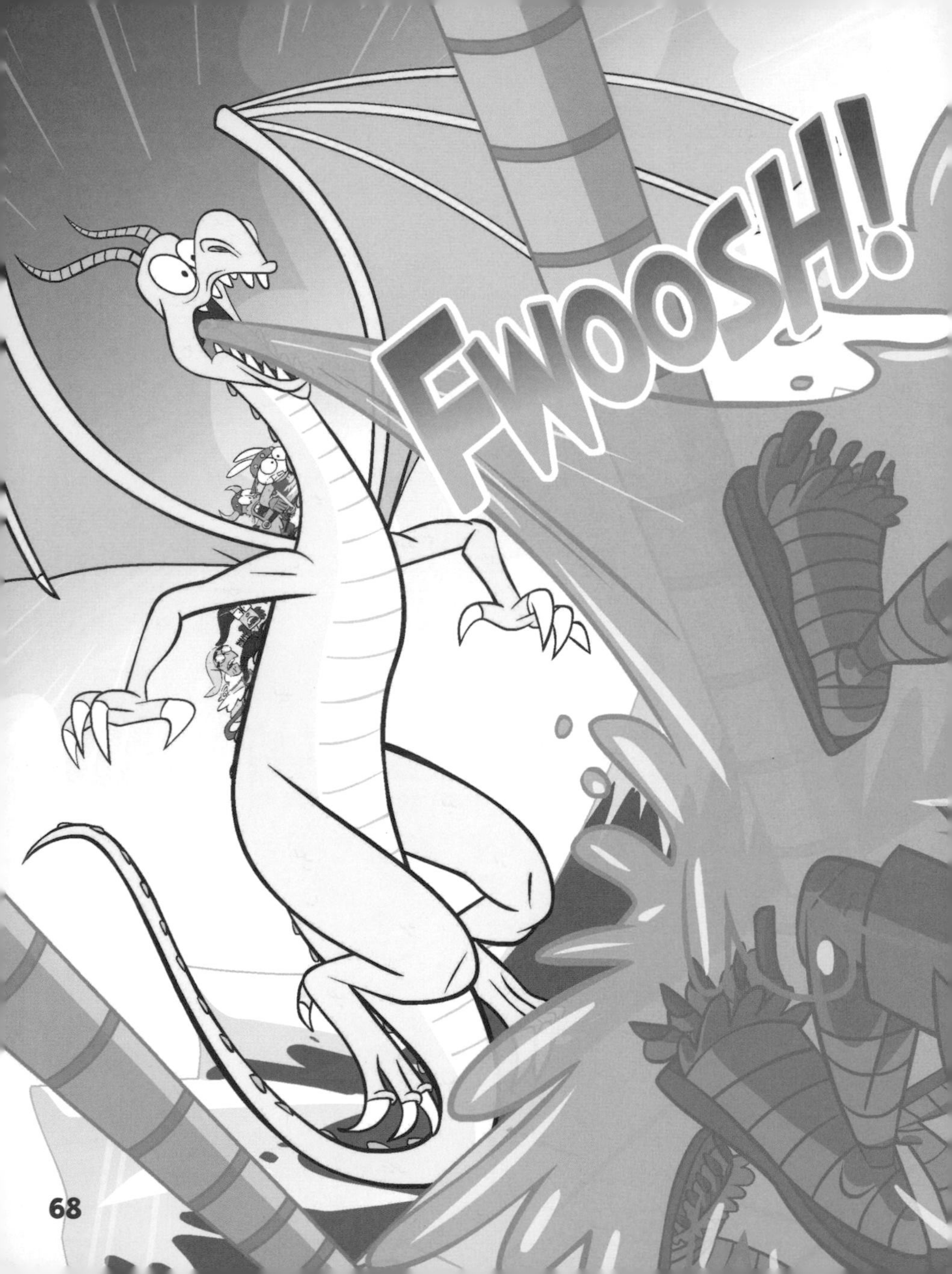
FWOOSH!

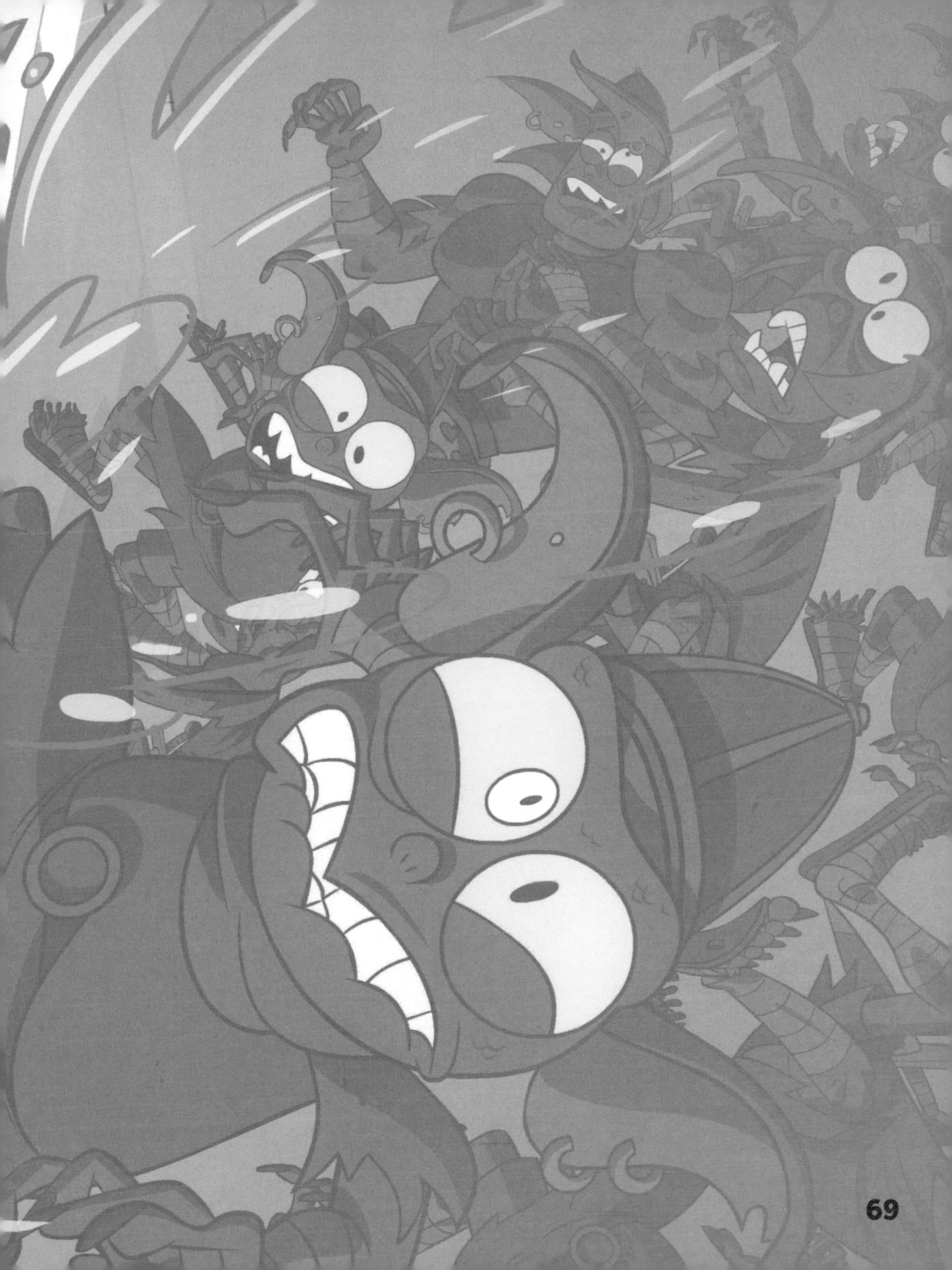

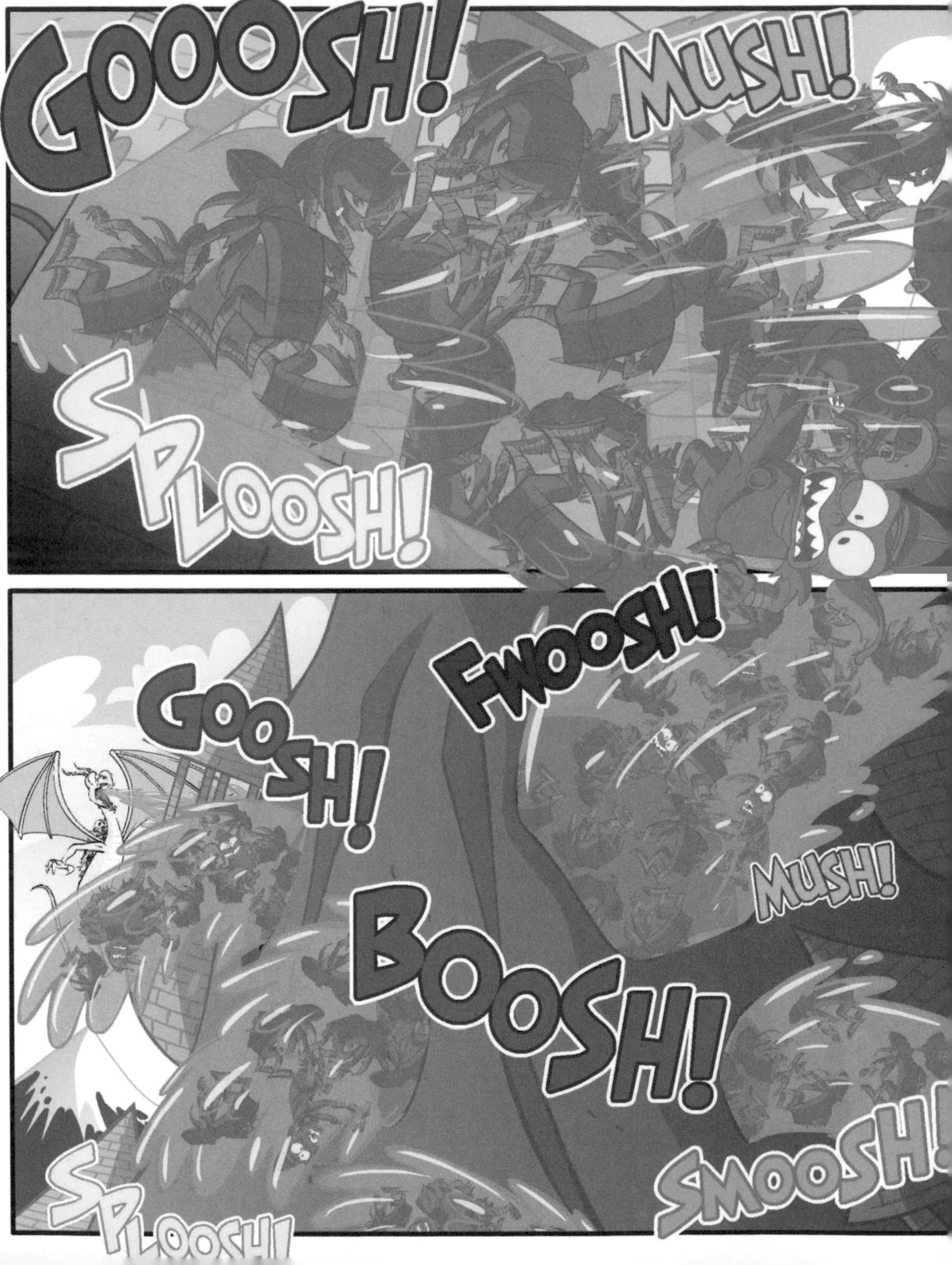
GOOOSH!
MUSH!
SPLOOSH!
FWOOSH!
GOOSH!
MUSH!
BOOSH!
SPLOOSH!
SMOOSH!

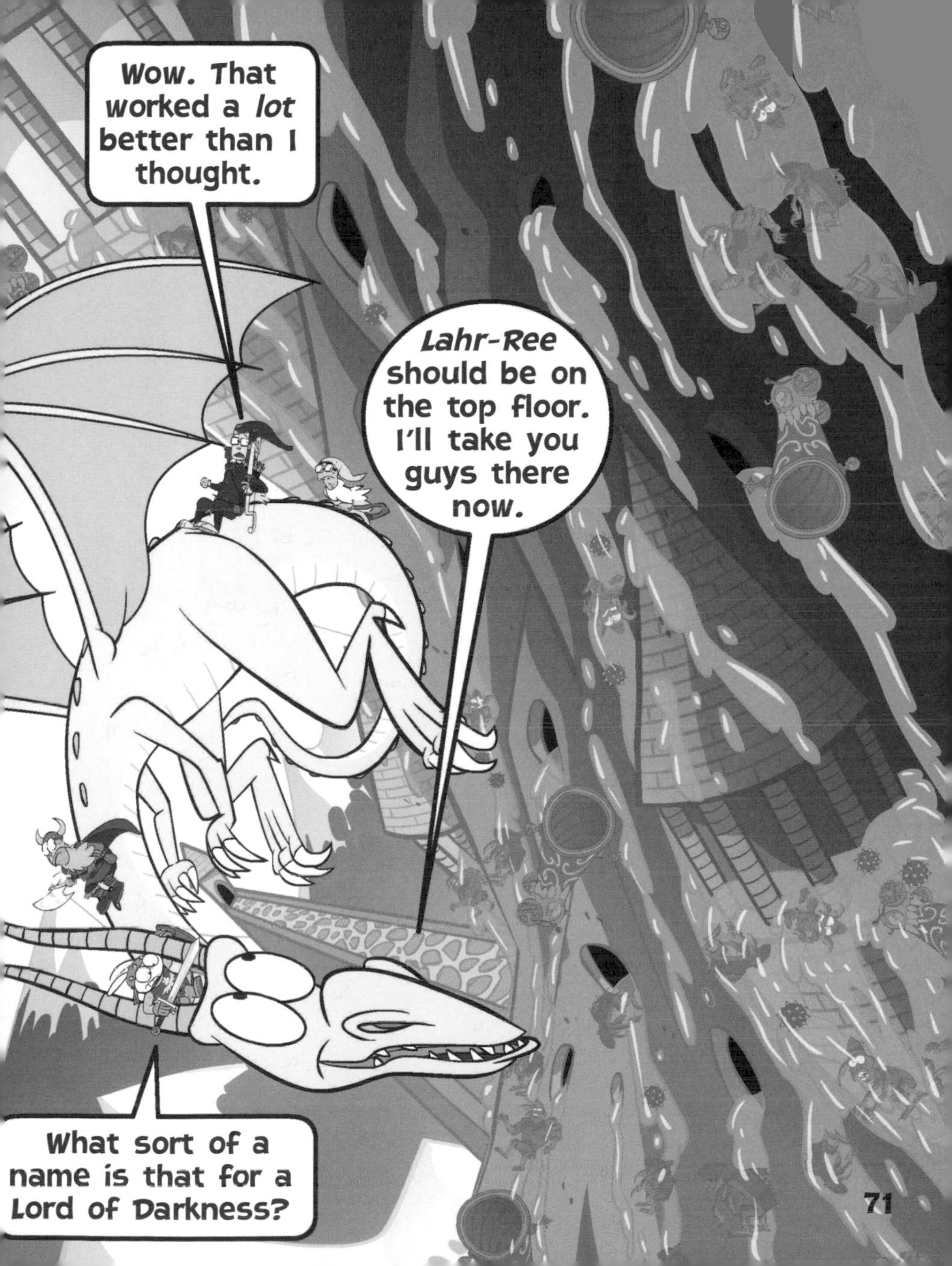
Wow. That worked a *lot* better than I thought.
Lahr-Ree should be on the top floor. I'll take you guys there now.
What sort of a name is that for a Lord of Darkness?

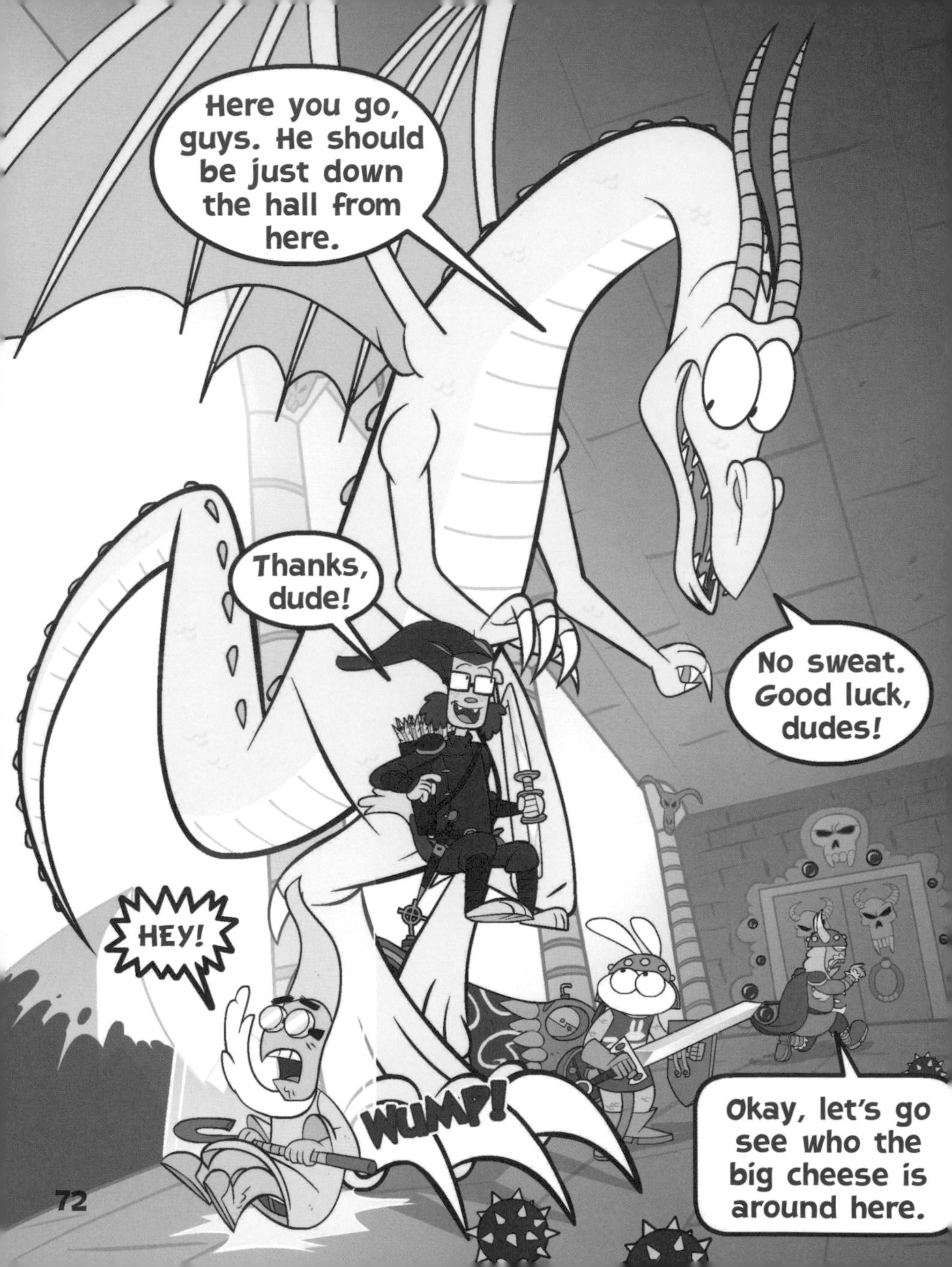
Here you go, guys. He should be just down the hall from here.
Thanks, dude!
No sweat. Good luck, dudes!
HEY!
WUMP!
Okay, let's go see who the big cheese is around here.

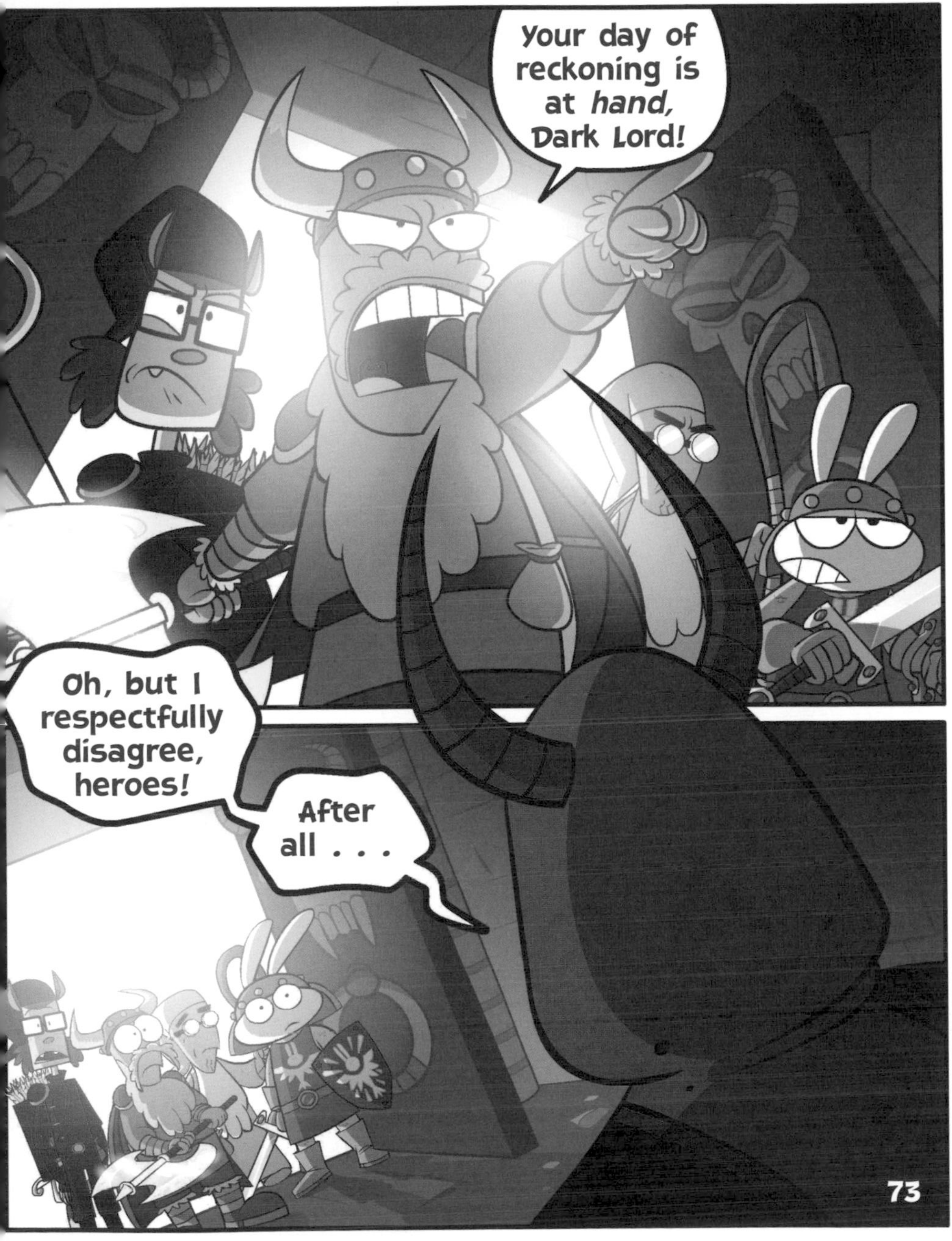
Your day of reckoning is at *hand,* Dark Lord!
Oh, but I respectfully disagree, heroes!
After all . . .

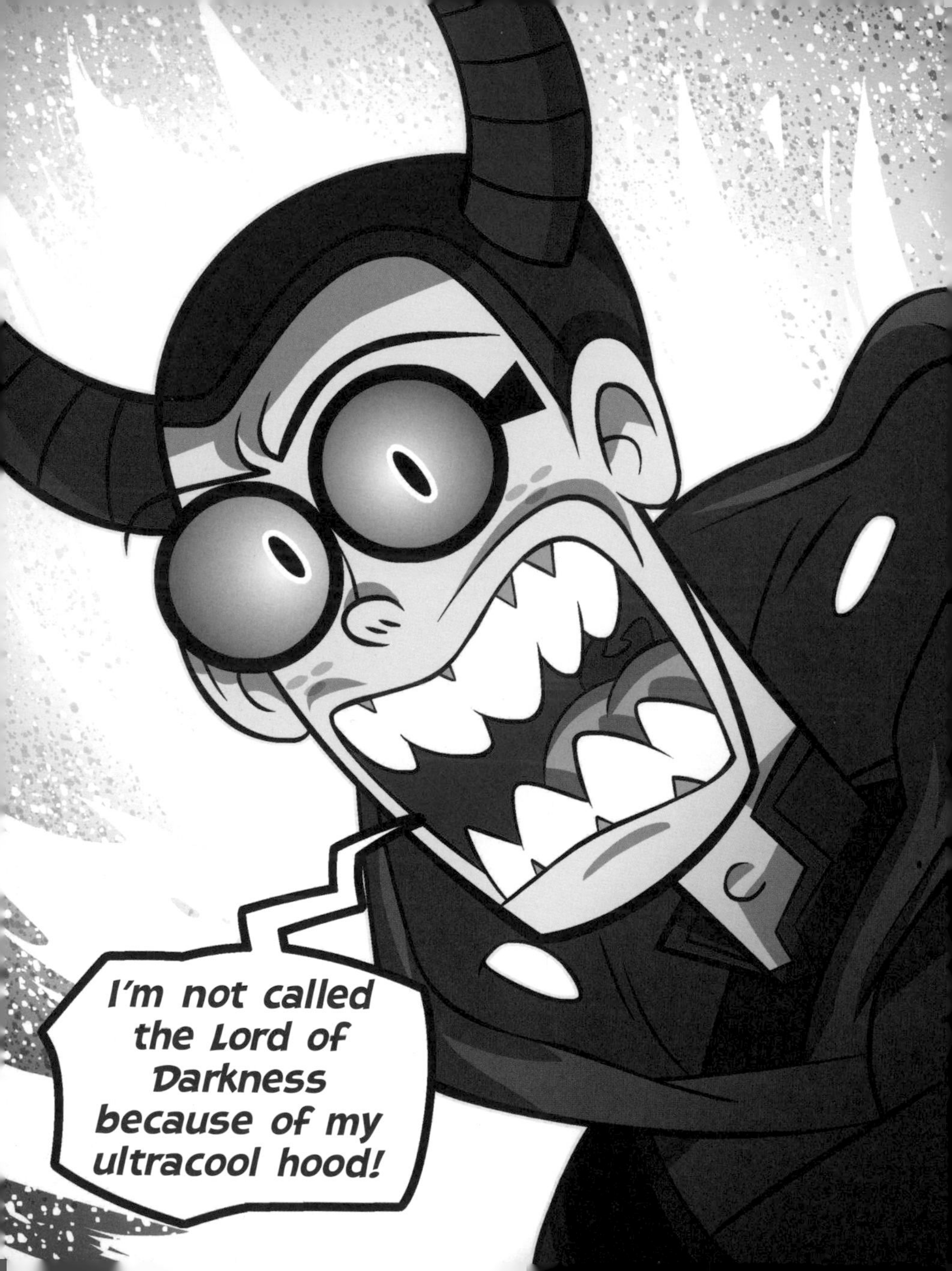
I'm not called the Lord of Darkness because of my ultracool hood!

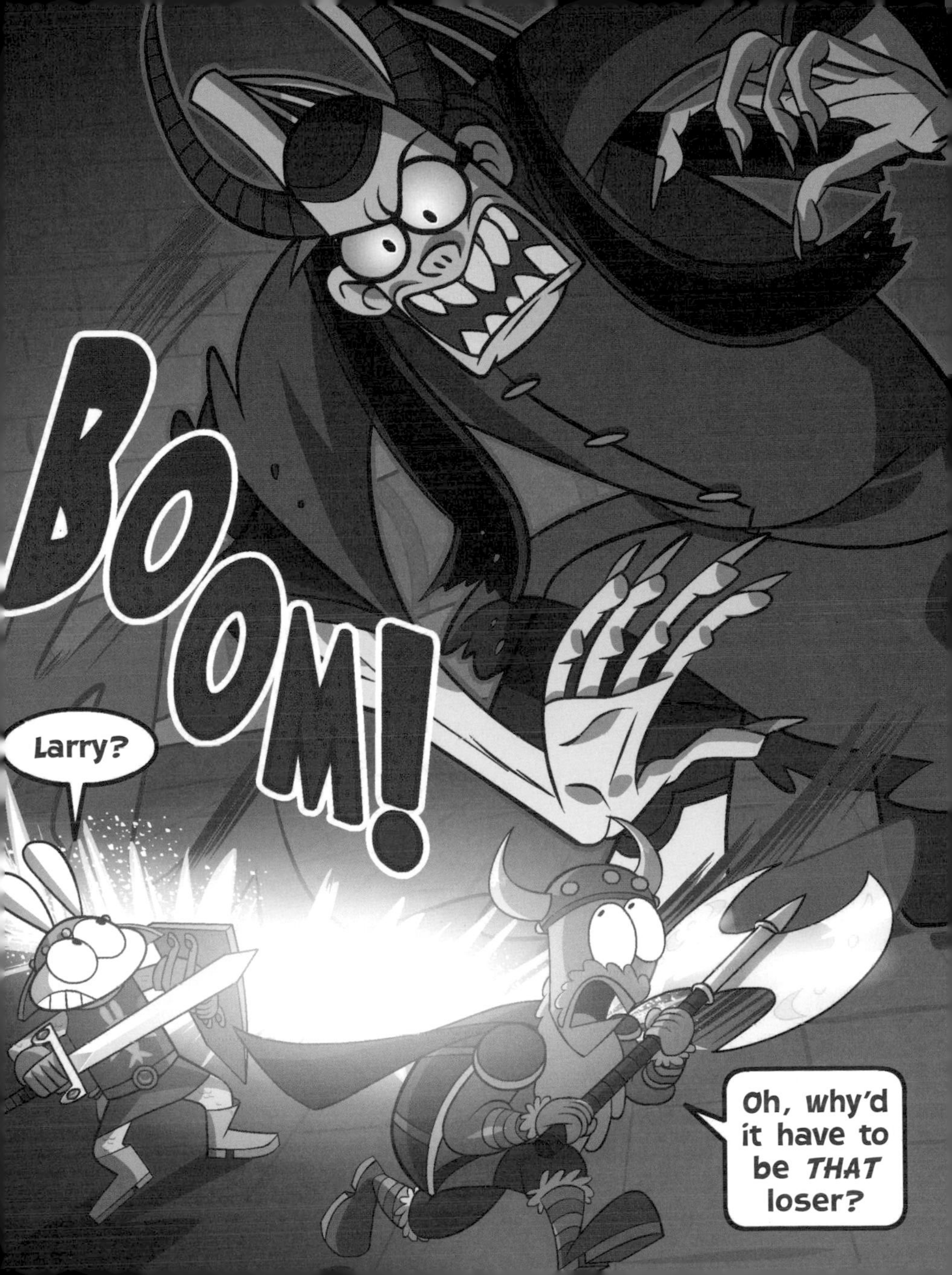
BOOM!
Larry?
Oh, why'd it have to be *THAT* loser?

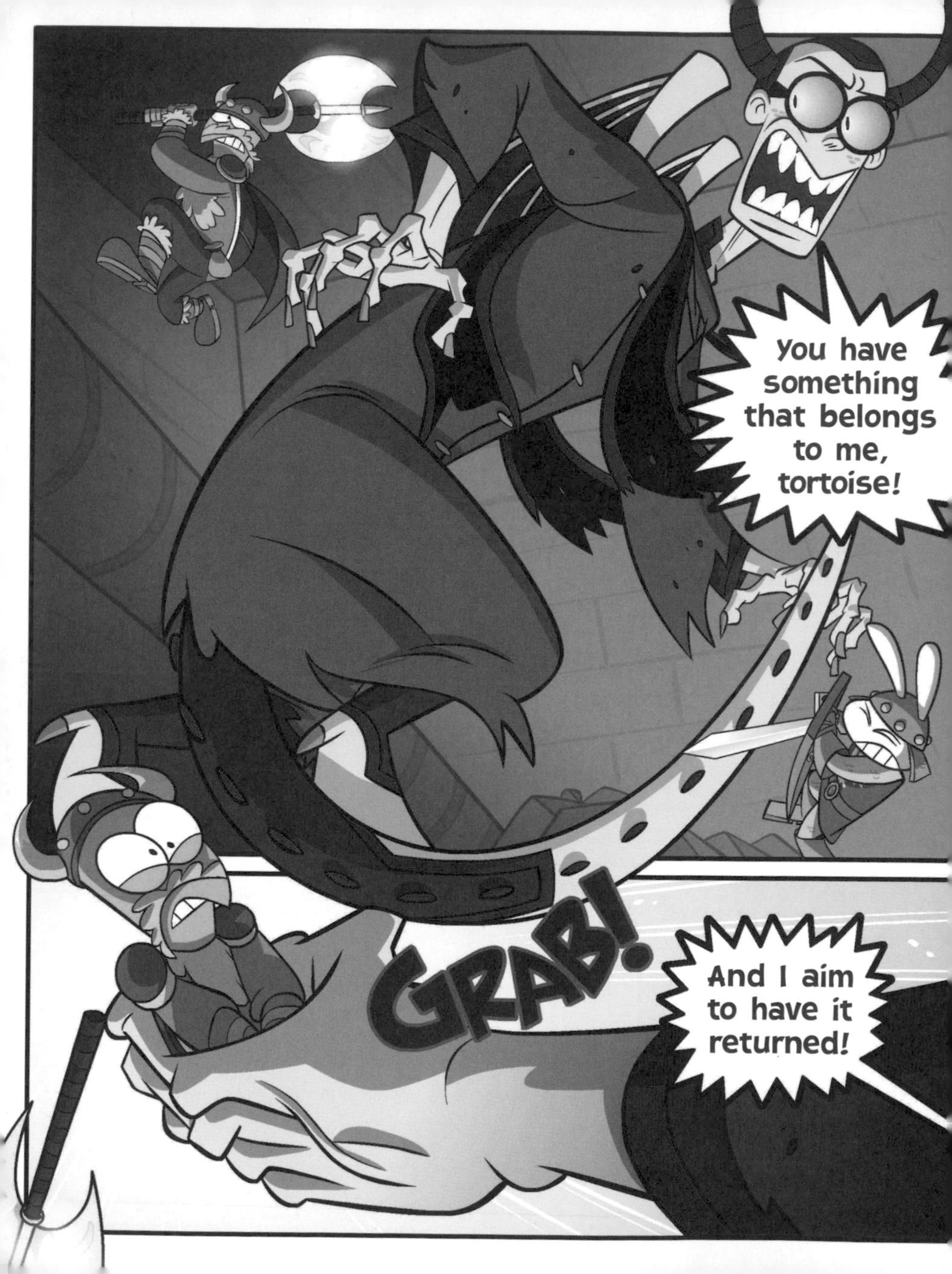

You have something that belongs to me, tortoise!
GRAB!
And I aim to have it returned!

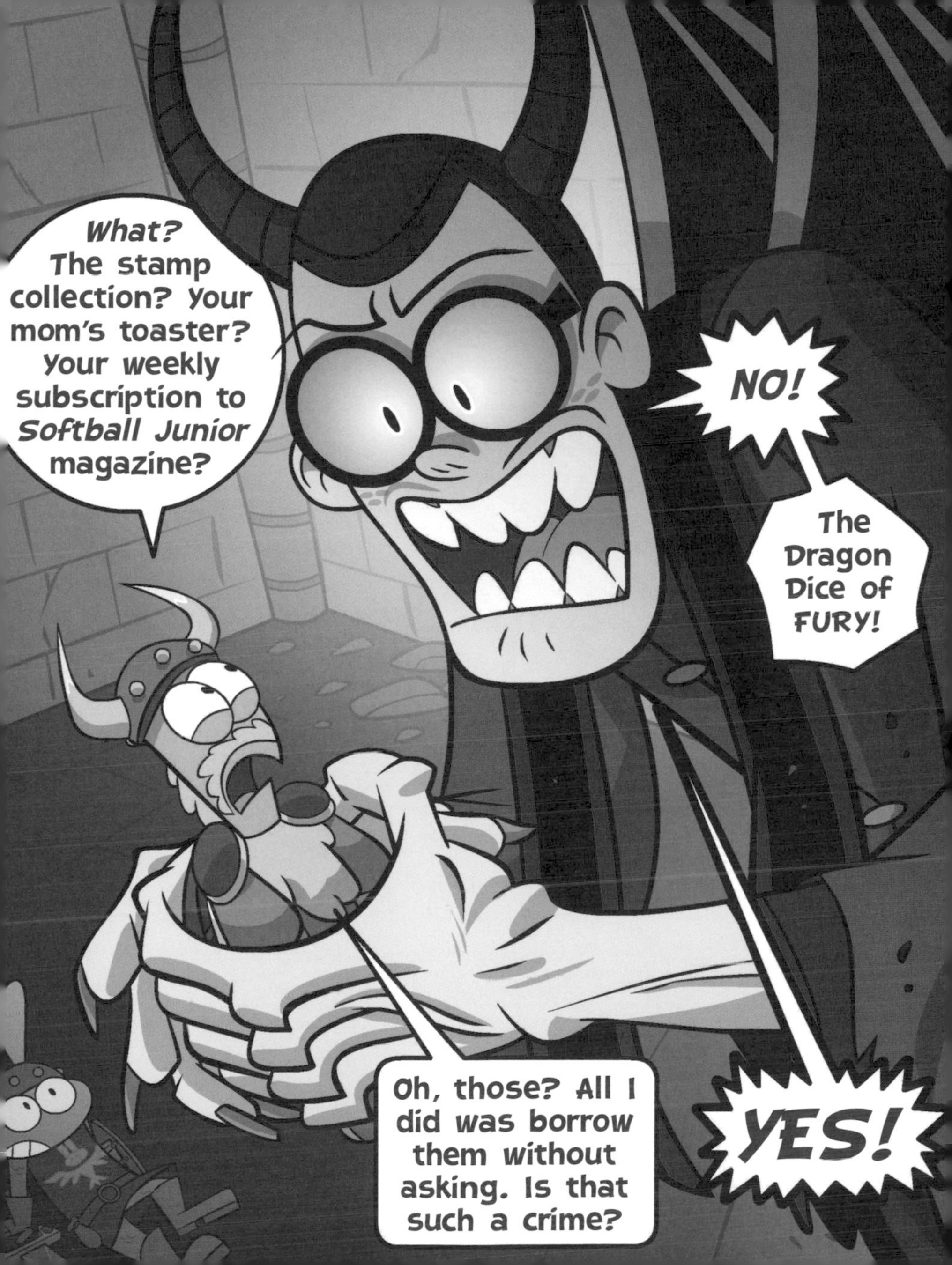
What? The stamp collection? Your mom's toaster? Your weekly subscription to *Softball Junior* magazine?
NO!
The Dragon Dice of FURY!
Oh, those? All I did was borrow them without asking. Is that such a crime?
YES!

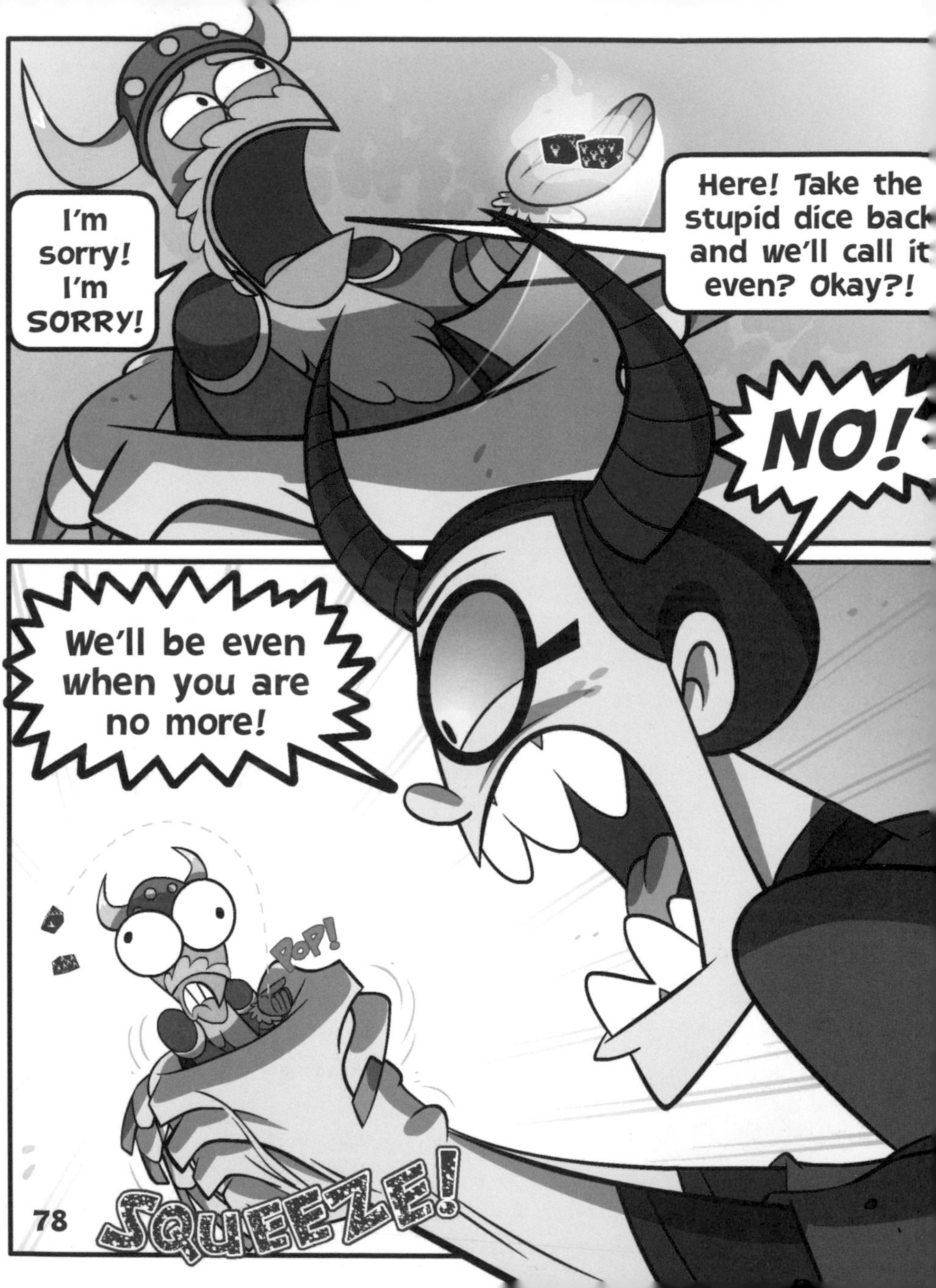

I'm sorry! I'm sorry! I'm SORRY!
Here! Take the stupid dice back and we'll call it even? Okay?!
NO!
We'll be even when you are no more!
POP!
SQUEEZE!

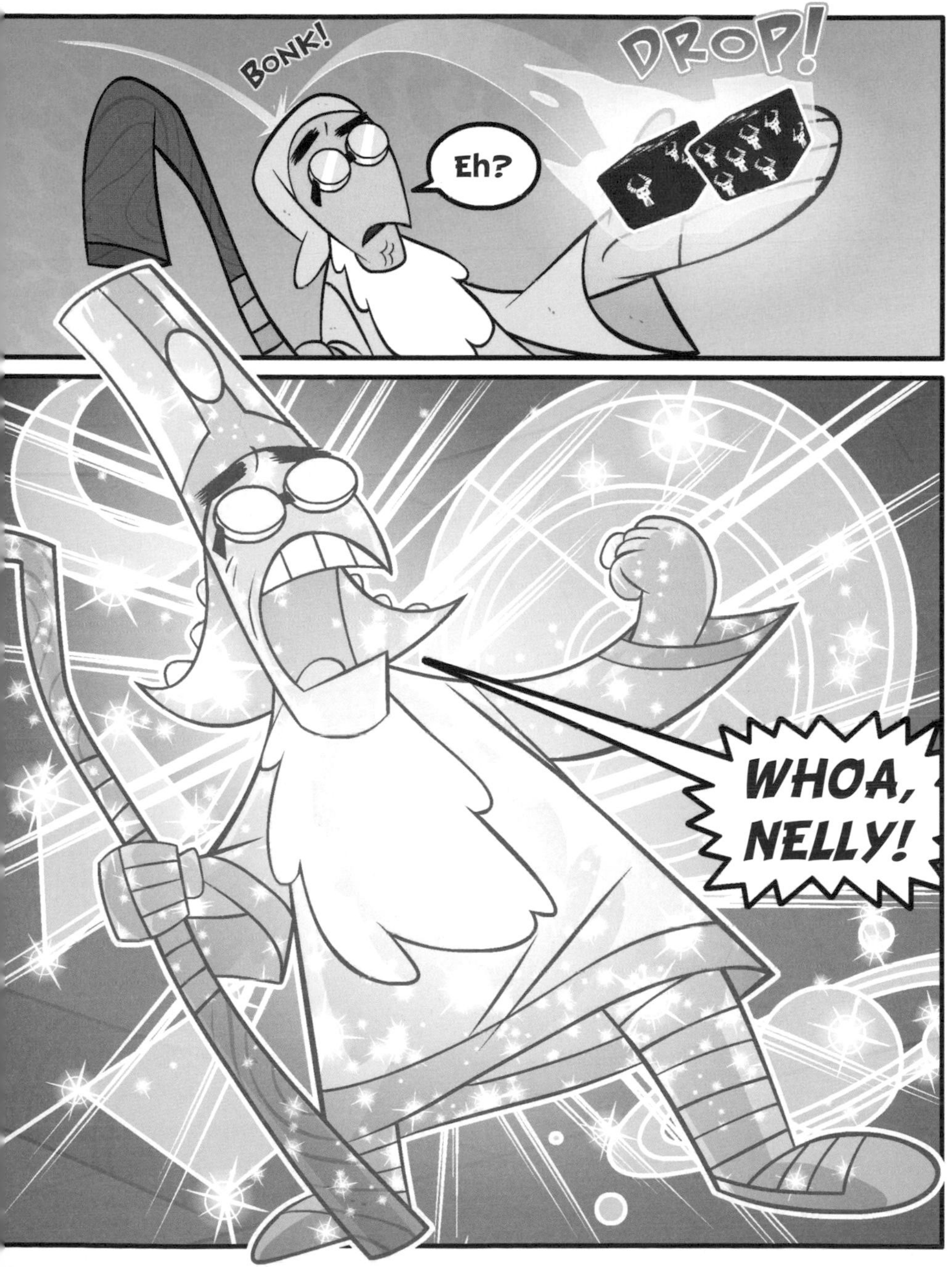
BONK!
DROP!
Eh?
WHOA, NELLY!

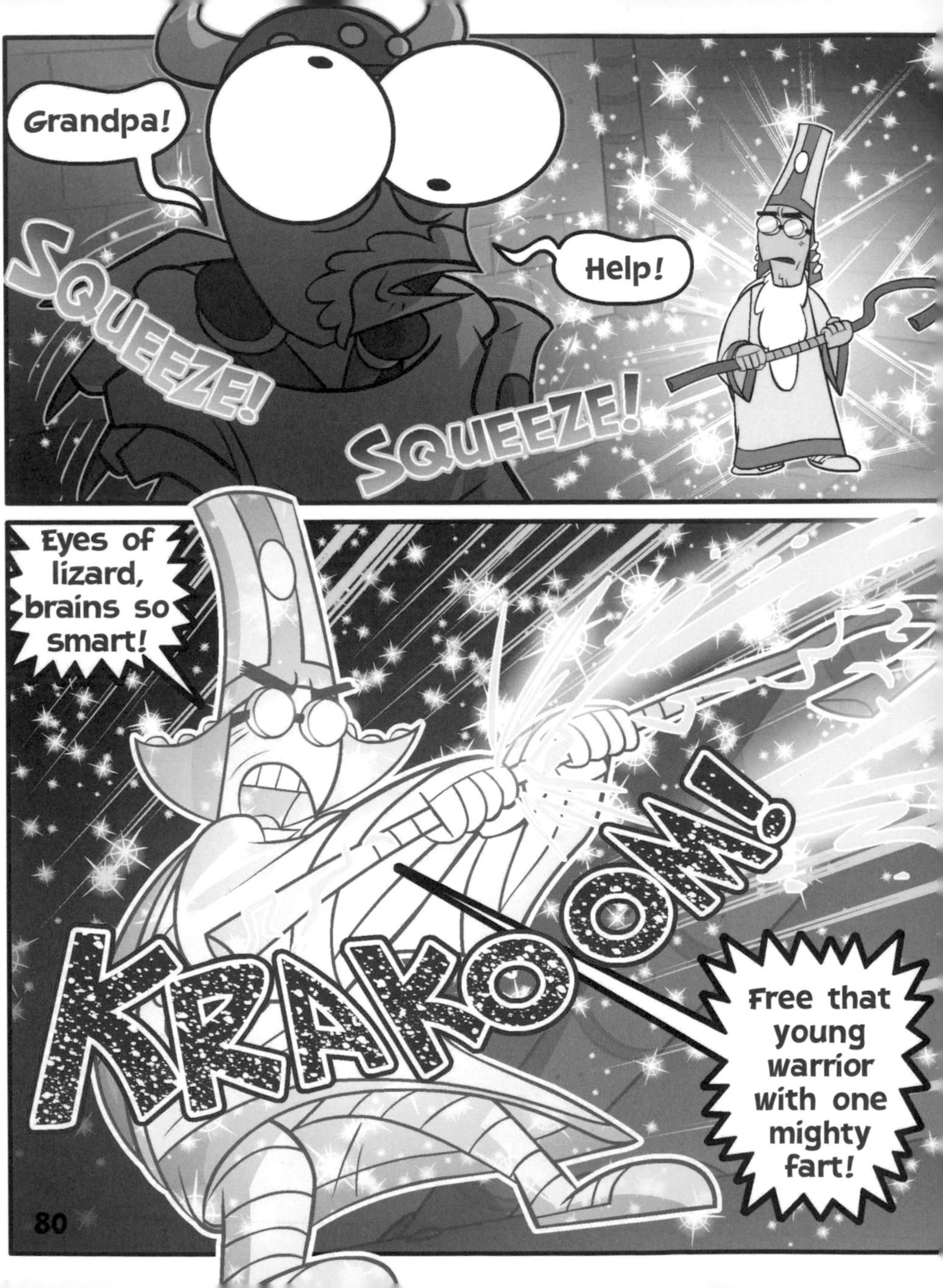
Grandpa!
SQUEEZE!
Help!
SQUEEZE!
Eyes of lizard, brains so smart!
KRAKOOM!
Free that young warrior with one mighty fart!

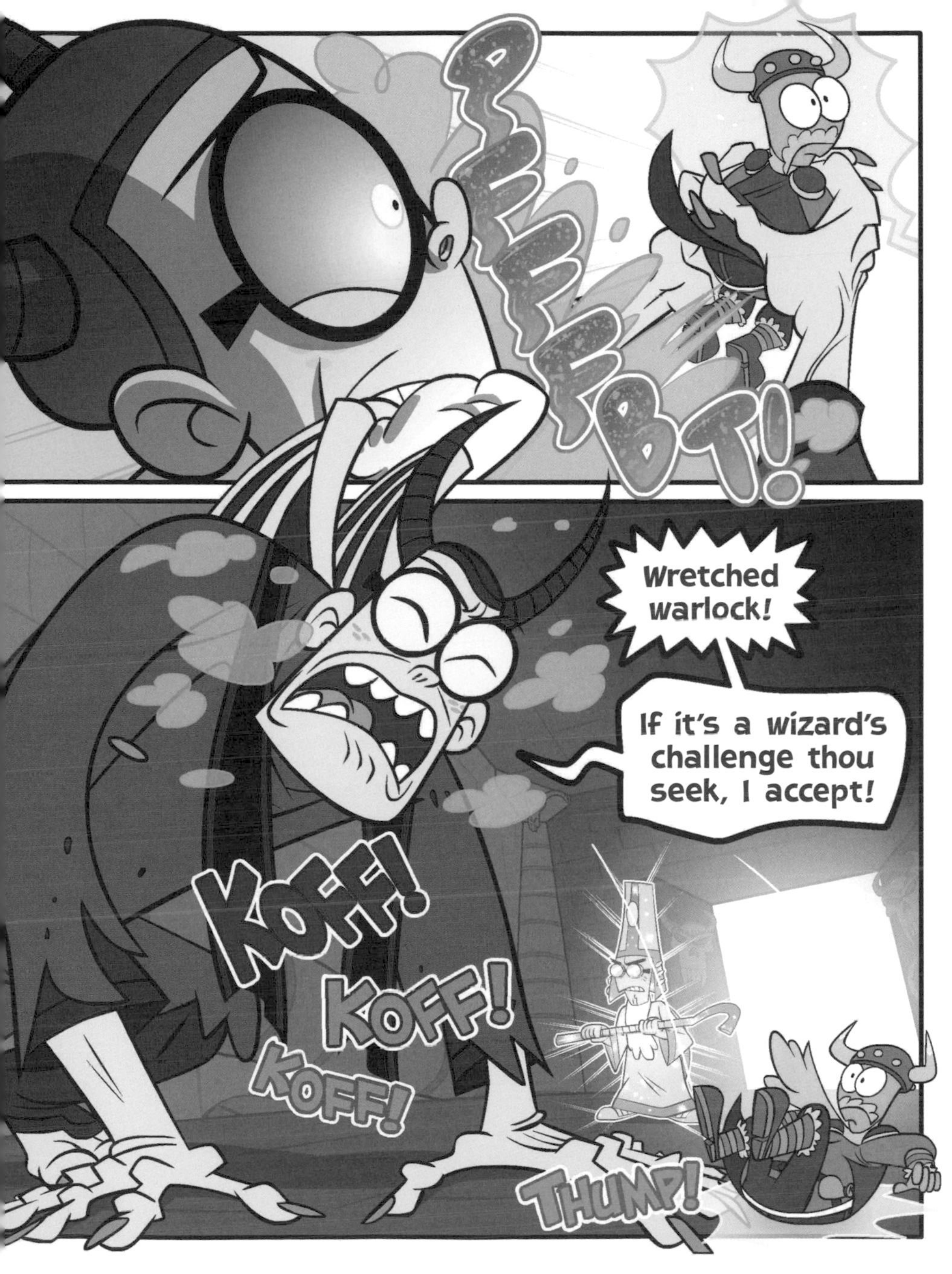
Wretched warlock!
If it's a wizard's challenge thou seek, I accept!
KOFF!
KOFF!
KOFF!
THUMP!

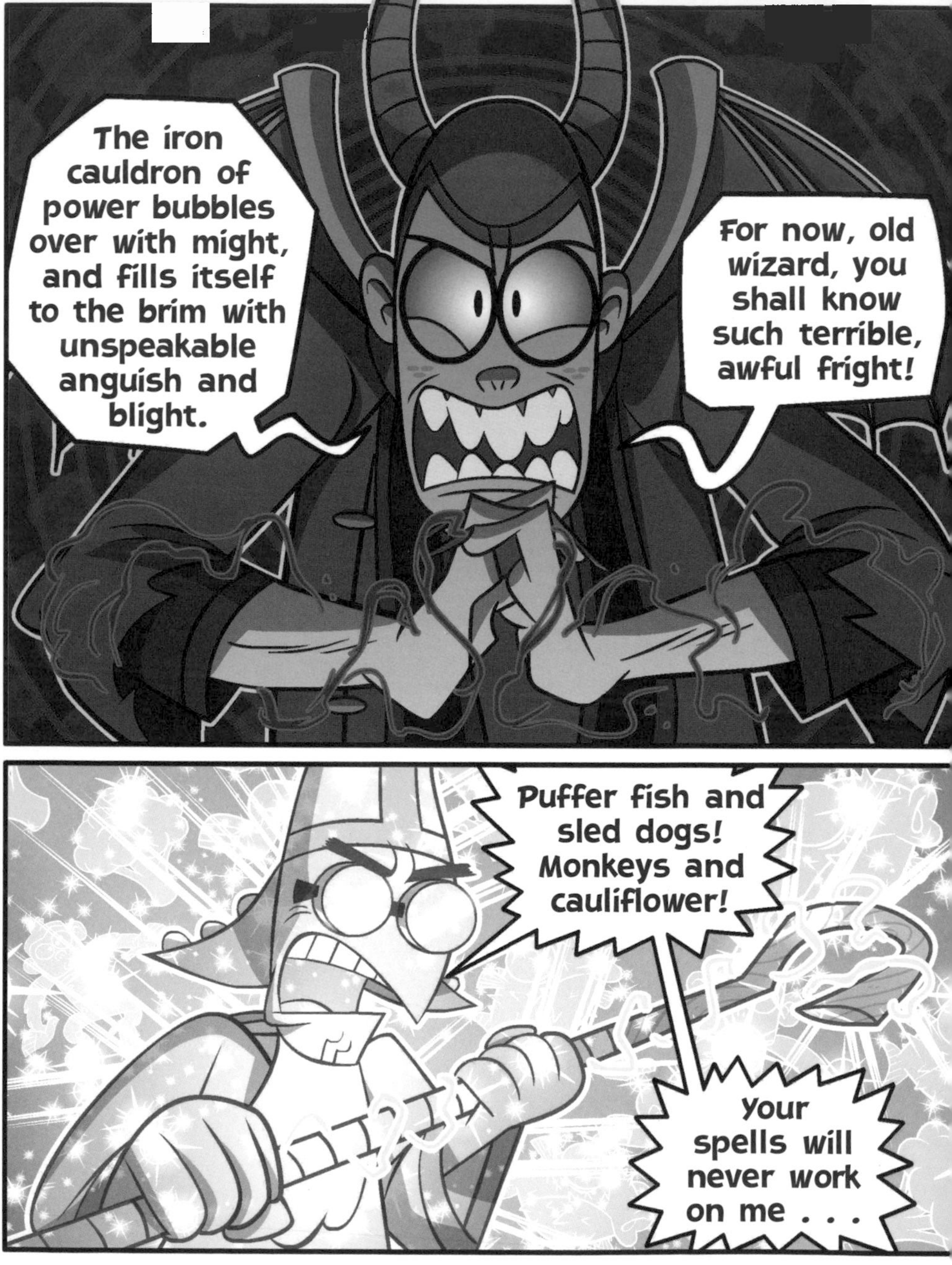
The iron cauldron of power bubbles over with might, and fills itself to the brim with unspeakable anguish and blight.
For now, old wizard, you shall know such terrible, awful fright!
Puffer fish and sled dogs! Monkeys and cauliflower!
Your spells will never work on me . . .

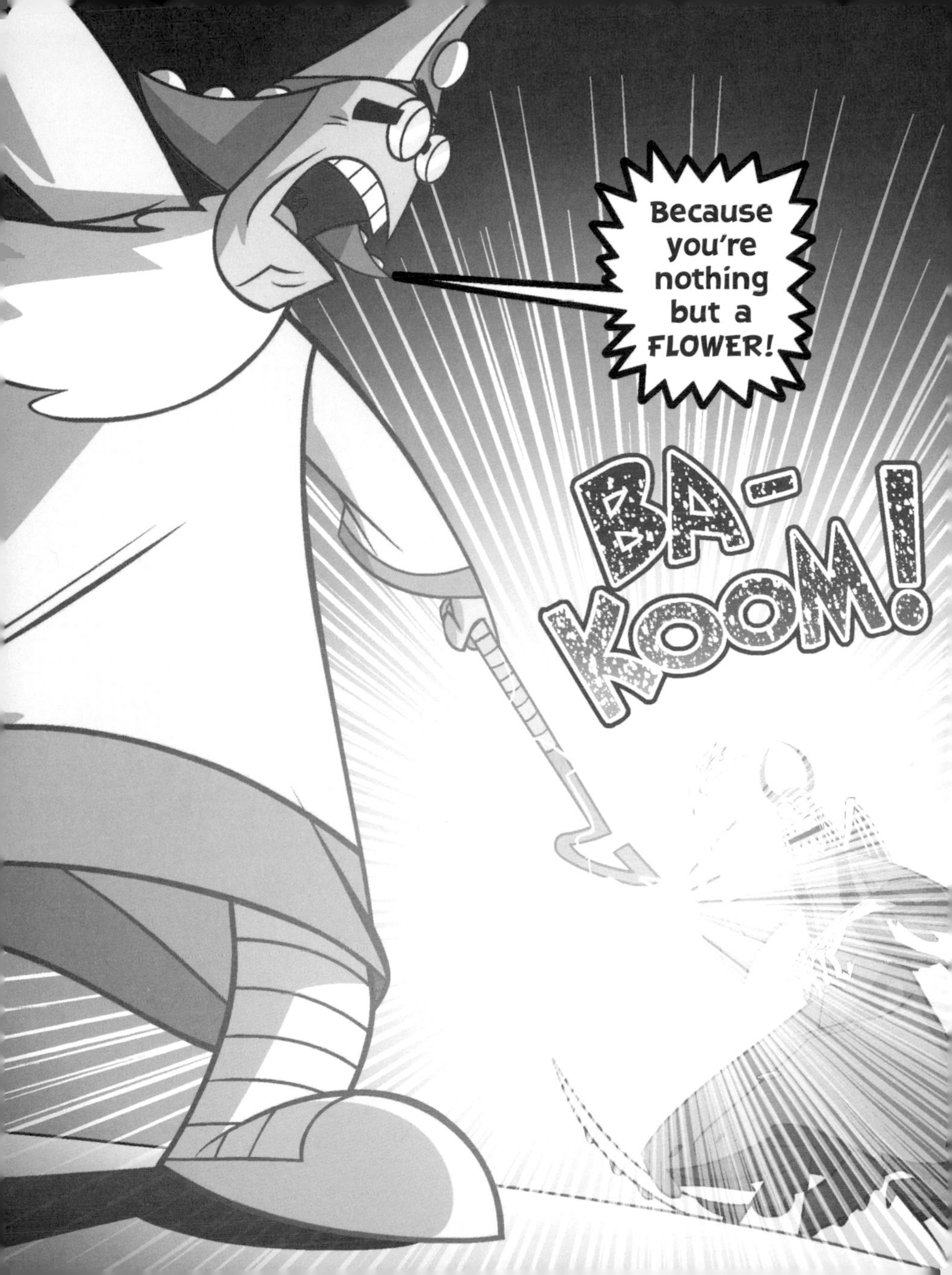
Because you're nothing but a FLOWER!
BA-KOOM!

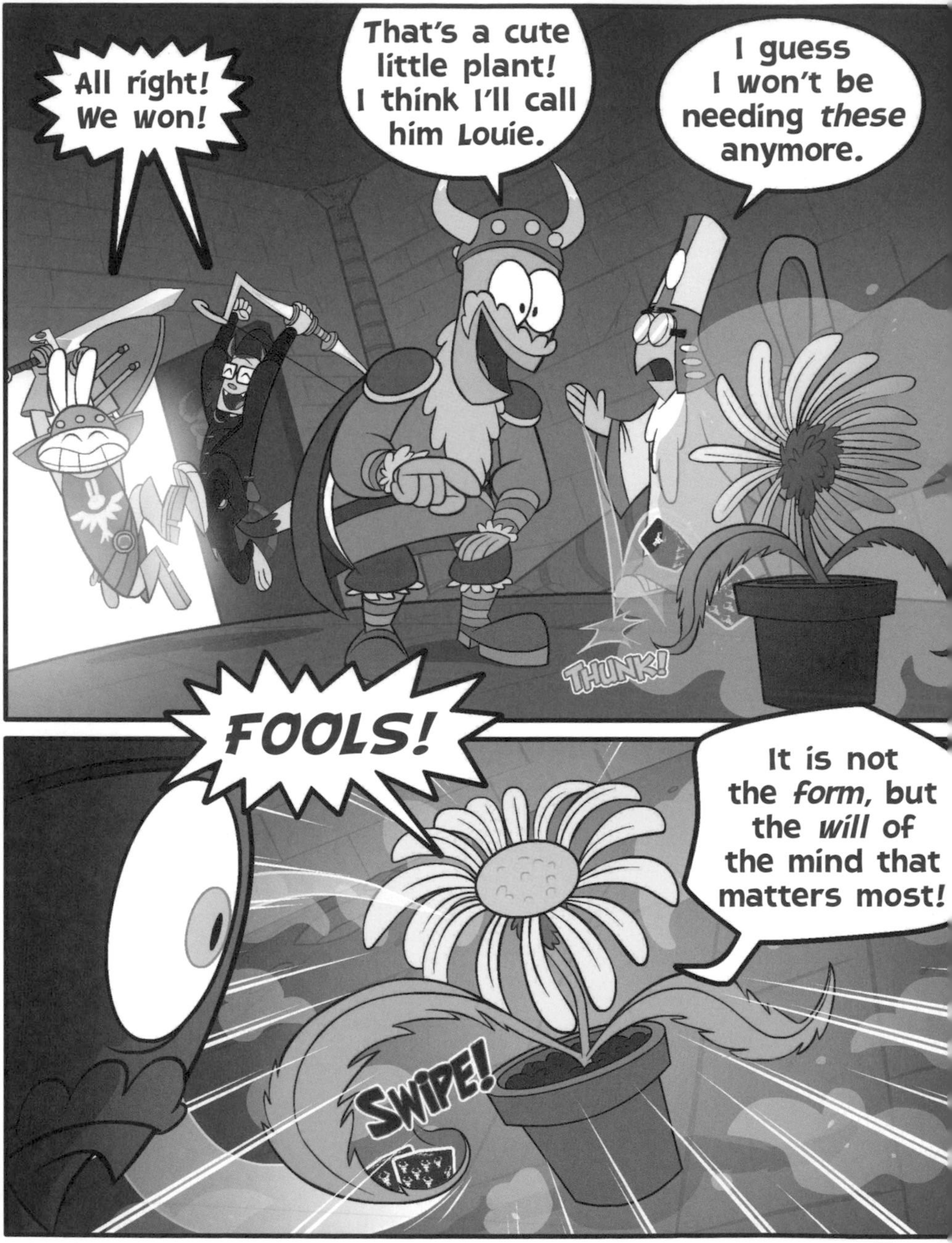
All right! We won!
That's a cute little plant! I think I'll call him Louie.
I guess I won't be needing *these* anymore.
THUNK!
FOOLS!
It is not the *form,* but the *will* of the mind that matters most!
SWIPE!

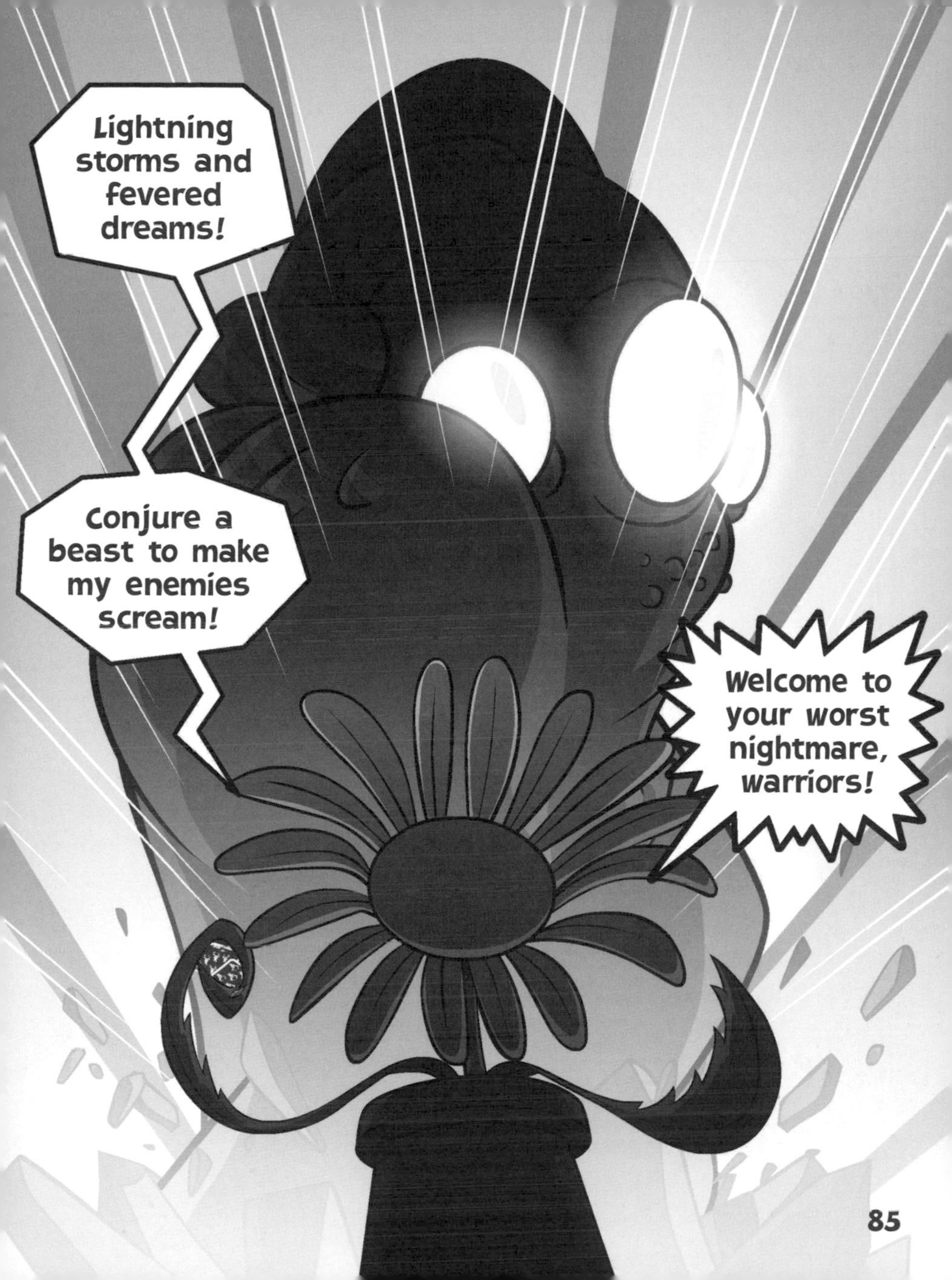
Lightning storms and fevered dreams!
Conjure a beast to make my enemies scream!
Welcome to your worst nightmare, warriors!

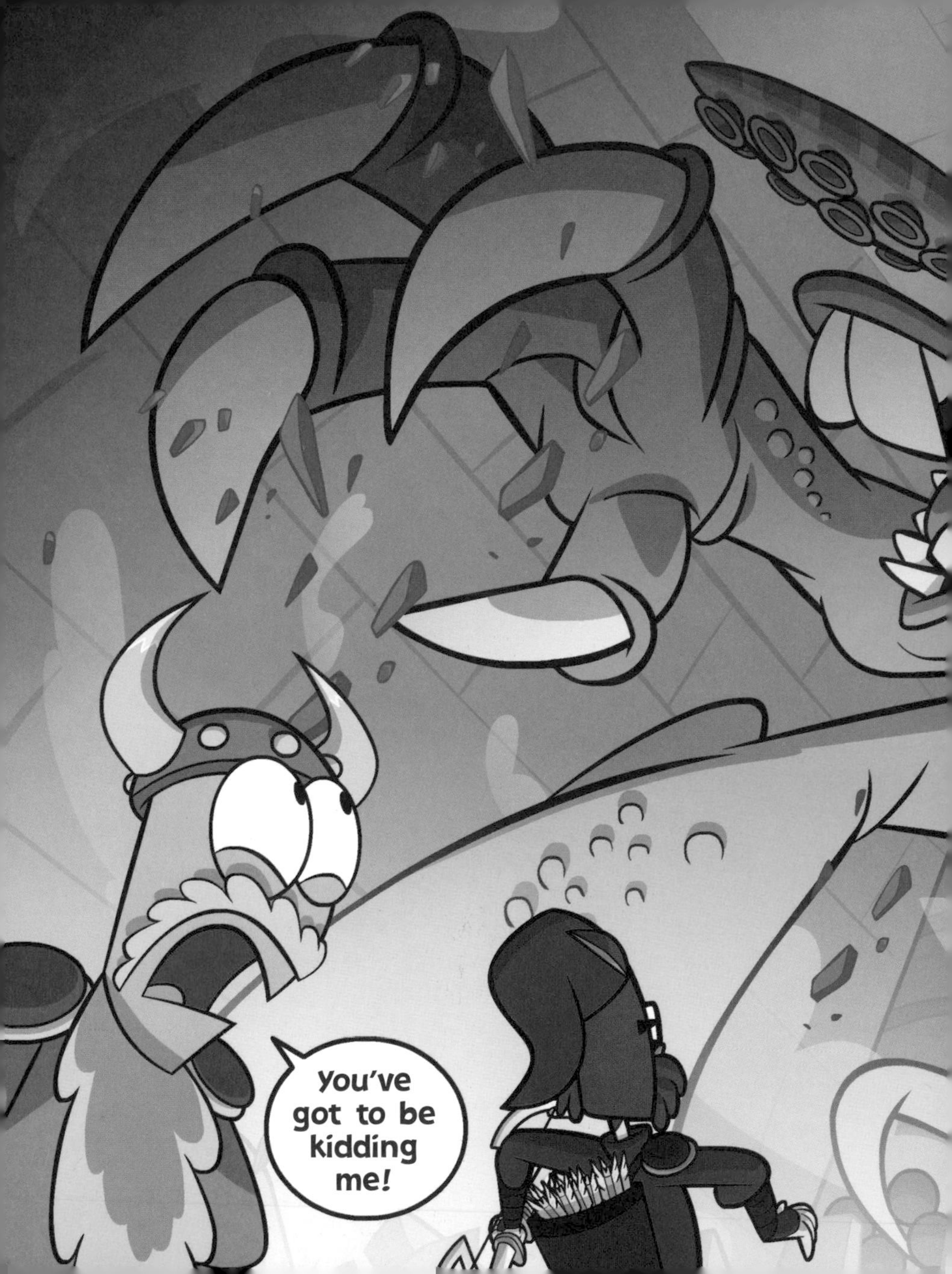
You've got to be kidding me!

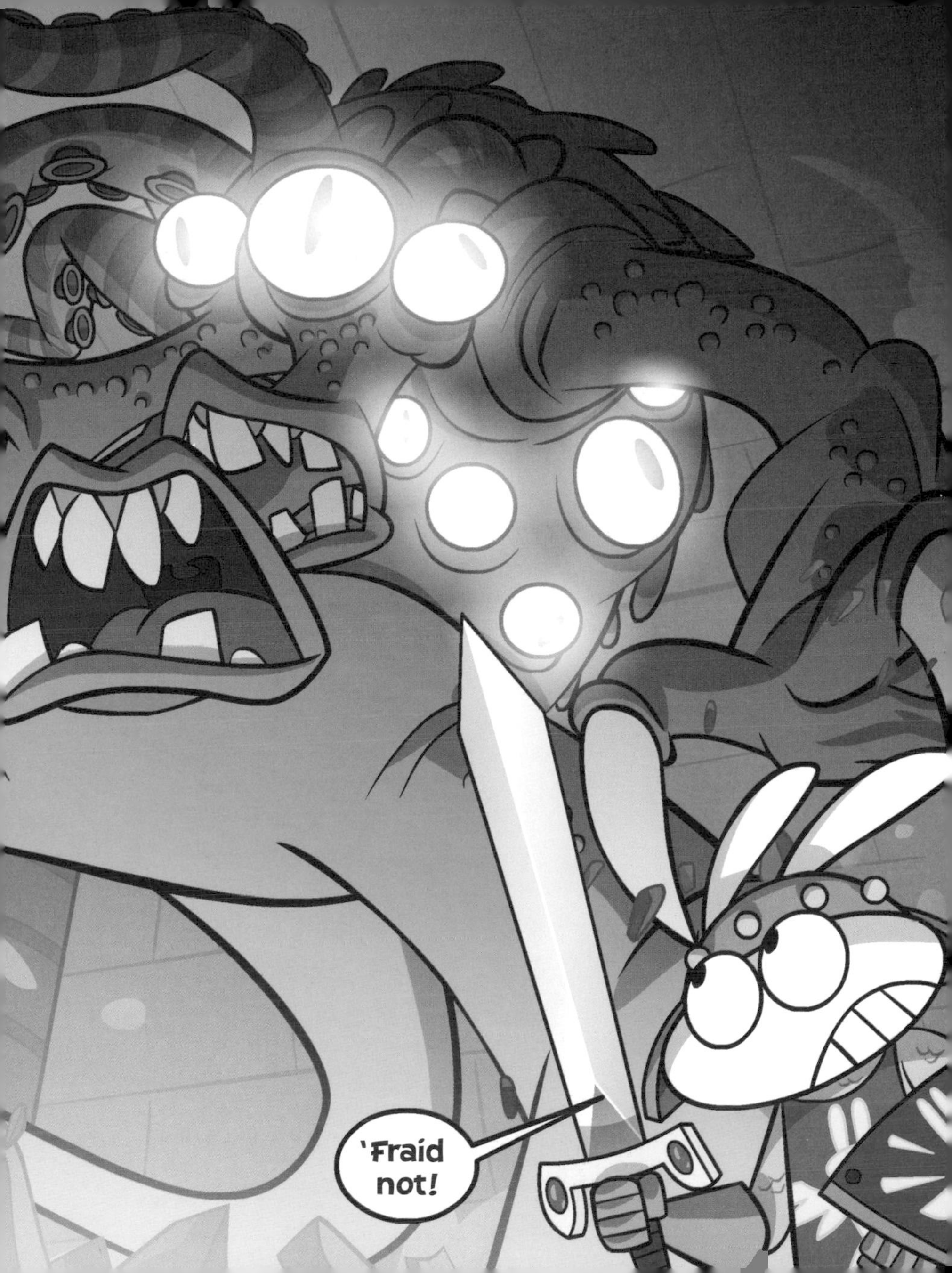
'Fraid not!

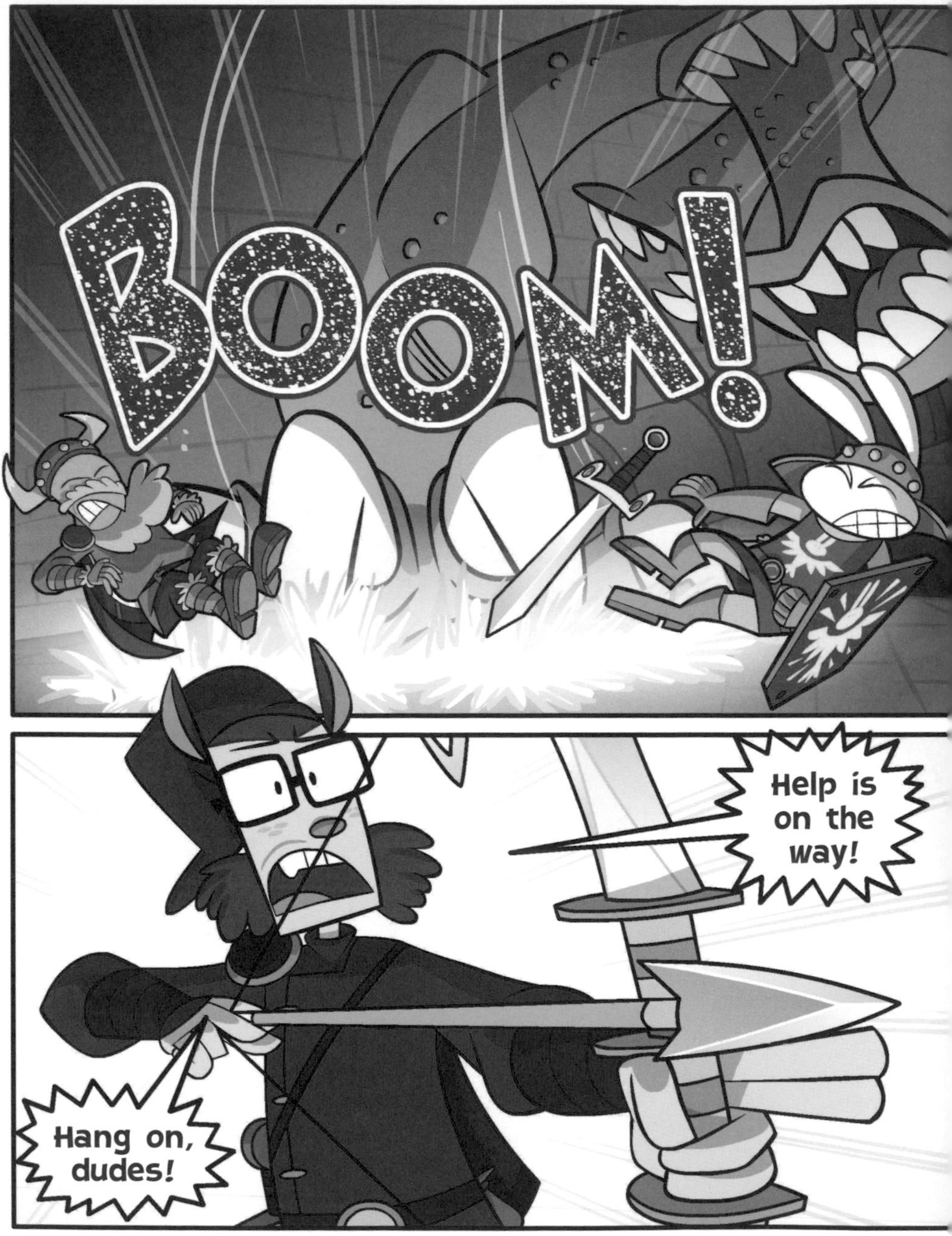
BOOM!
Help is on the way!
Hang on, dudes!

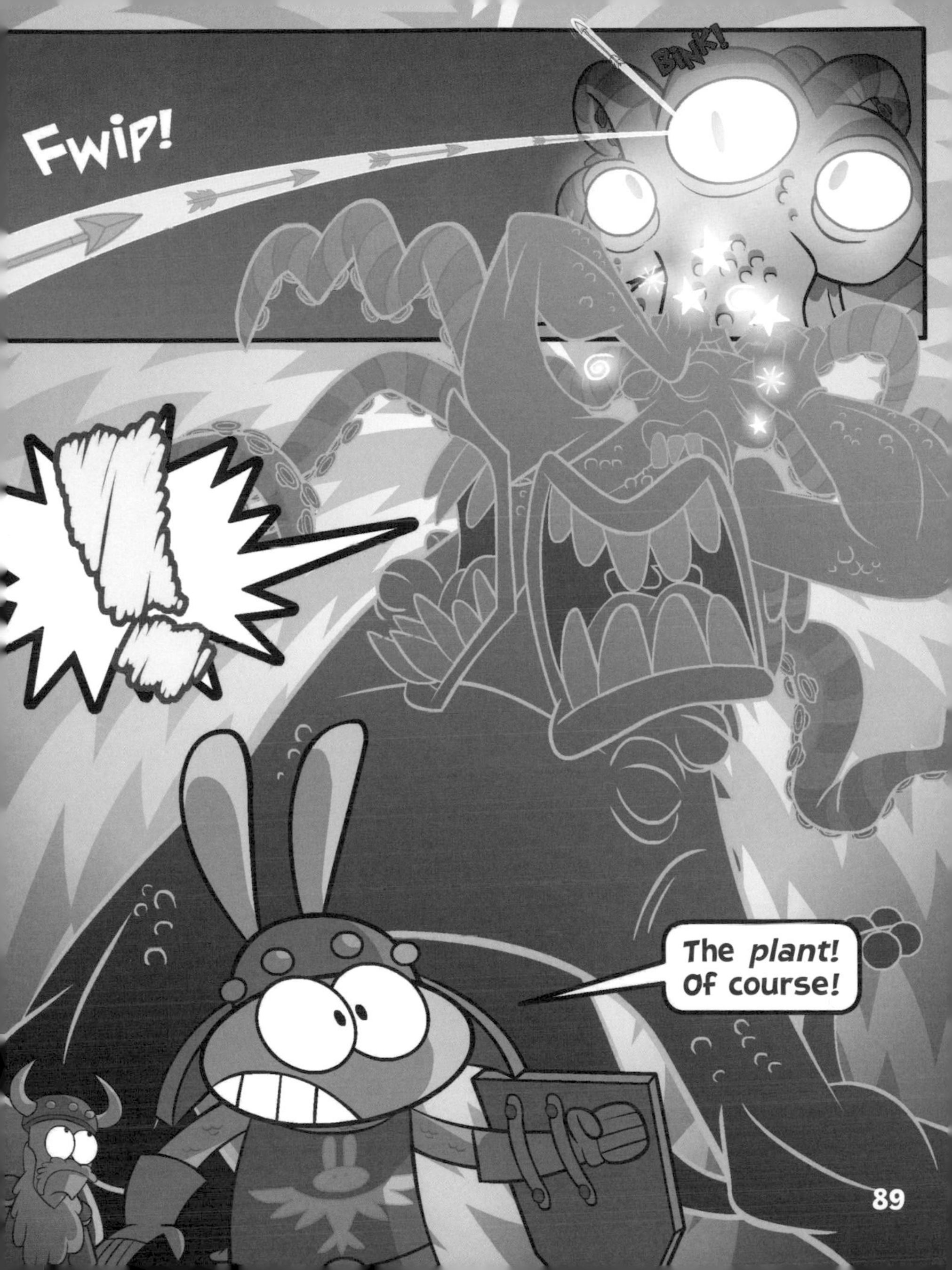

FWIP!
BINK!
!
The *plant*! Of course!

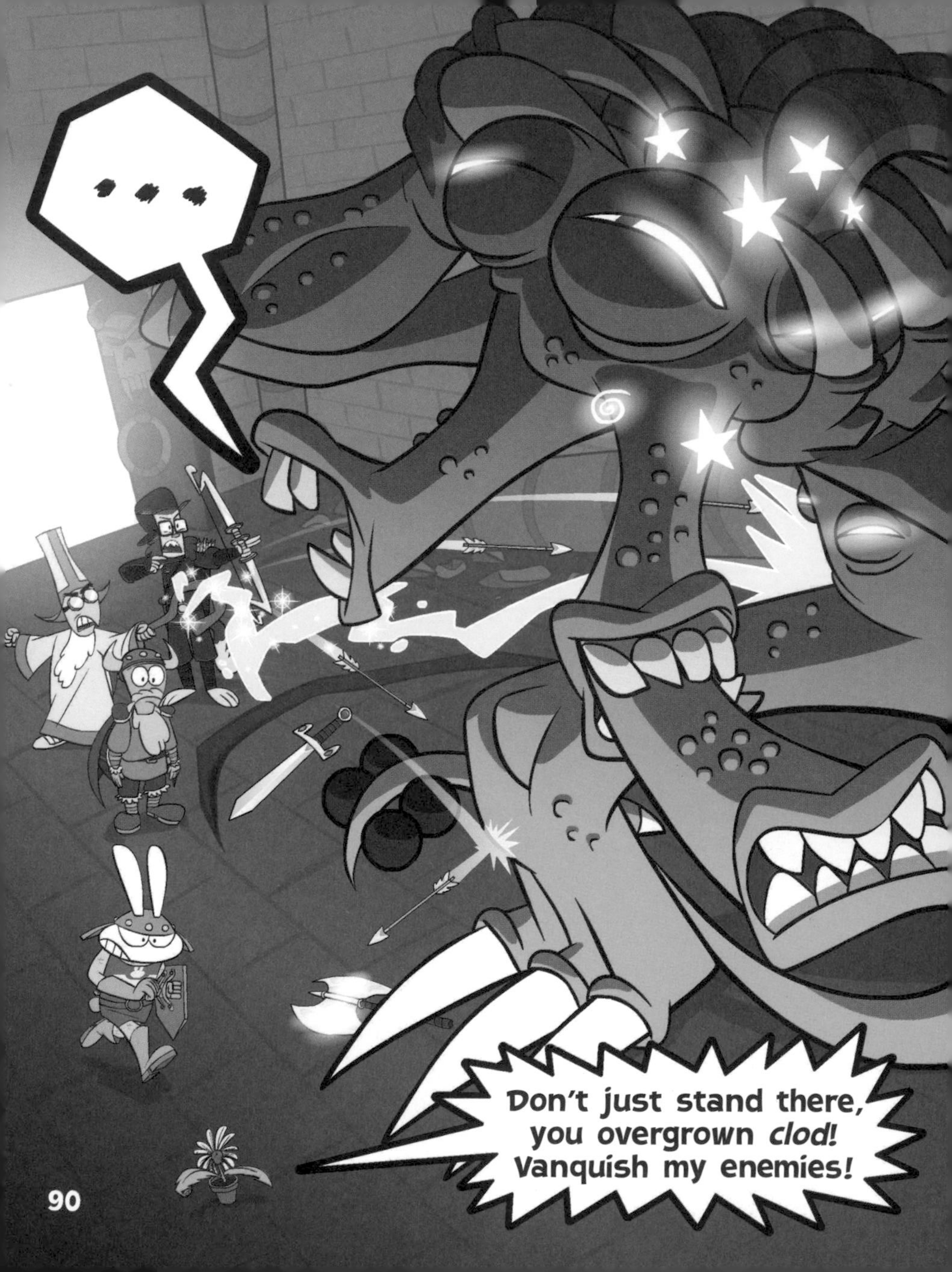
. . .
Don't just stand there, you overgrown *clod*! Vanquish my enemies!

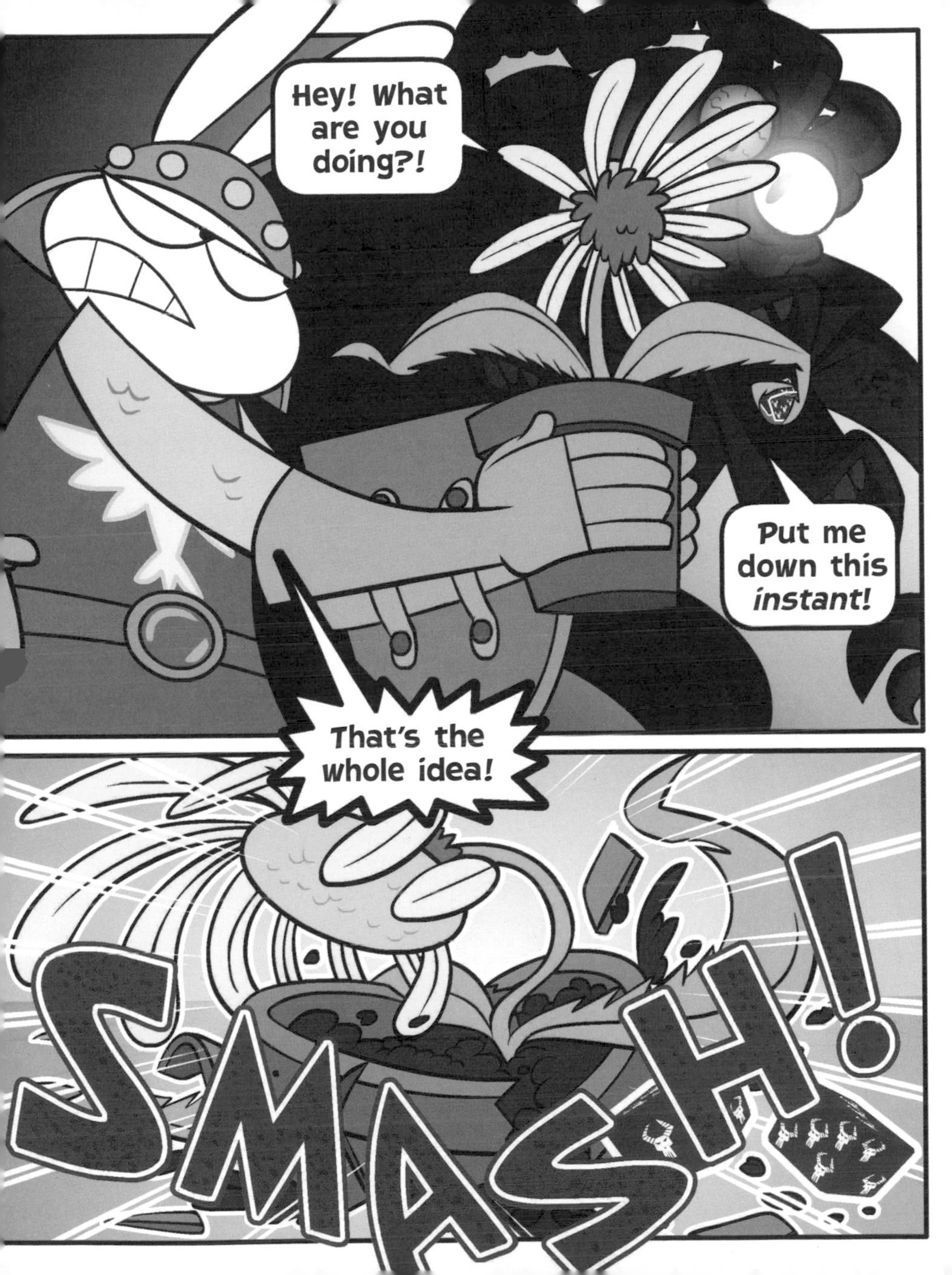

Hey! What are you doing?!
Put me down this *instant!*
That's the whole idea!
SMASH!

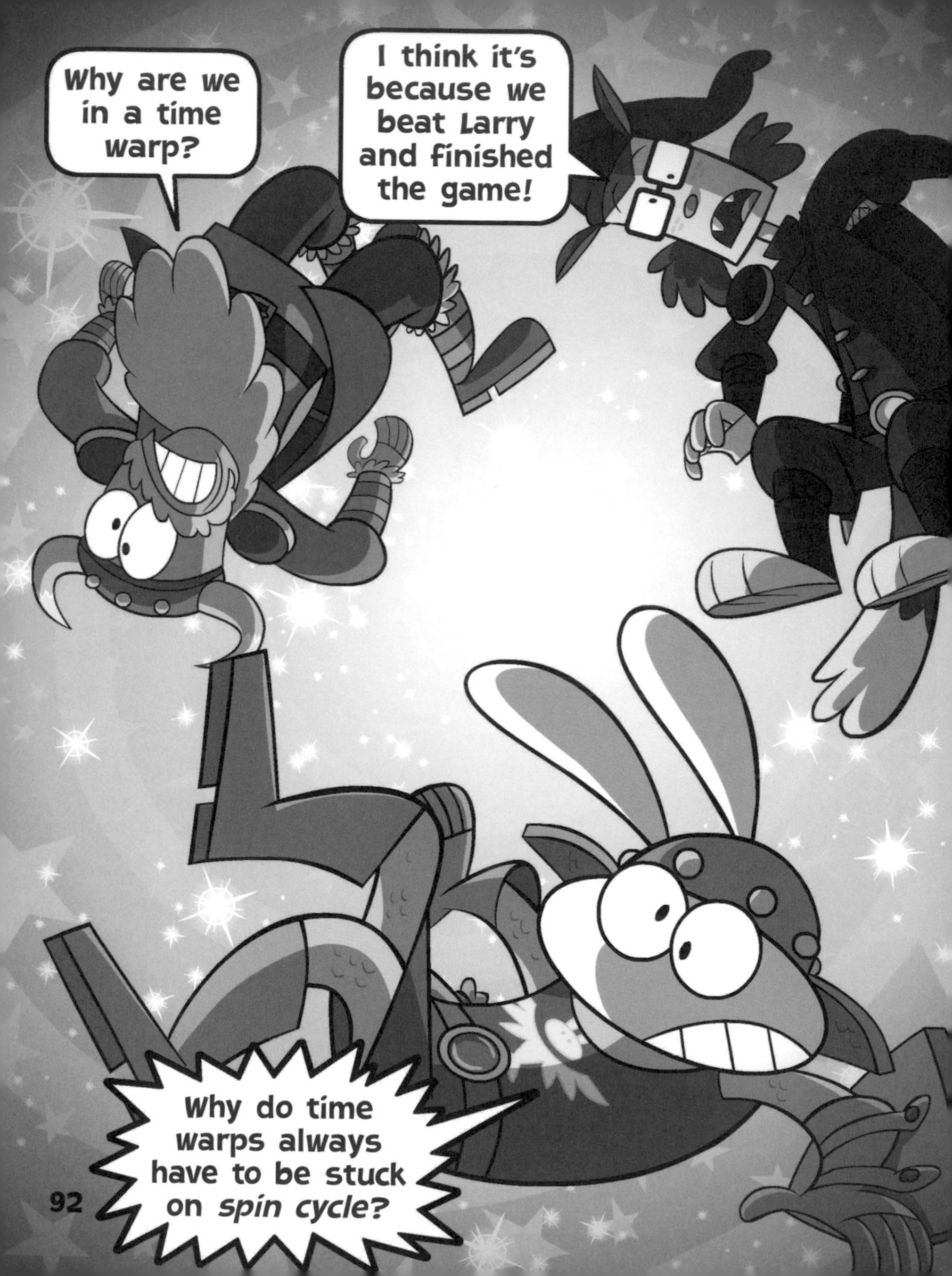
Why are we in a time warp?
I think it's because we beat Larry and finished the game!
Why do time warps always have to be stuck on *spin cycle*?

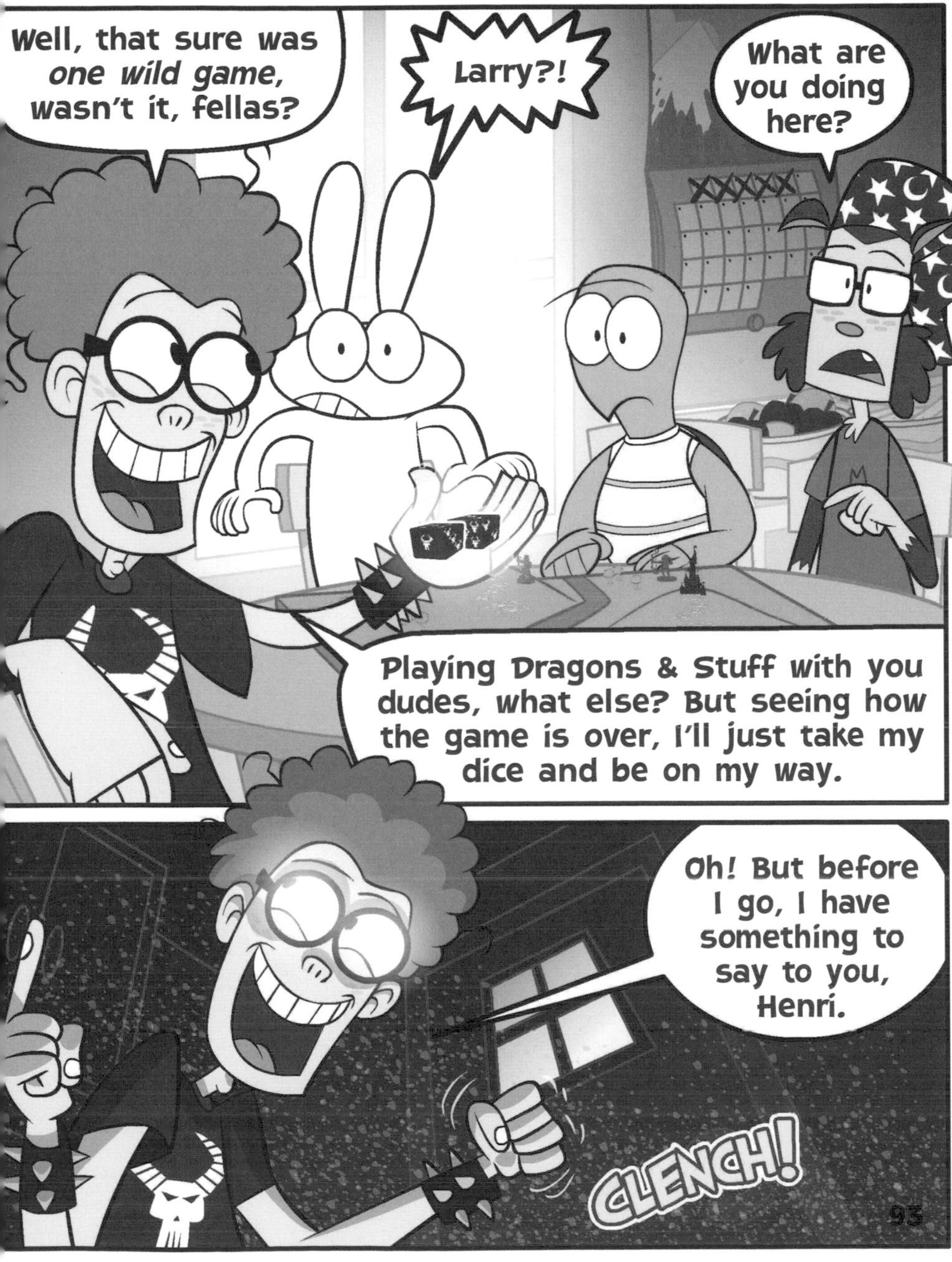
Well, that sure was one wild game, wasn't it, fellas?
Larry?!
What are you doing here?
Playing Dragons & Stuff with you dudes, what else? But seeing how the game is over, I'll just take my dice and be on my way.
Oh! But before I go, I have something to say to you, Henri.
CLENCH!

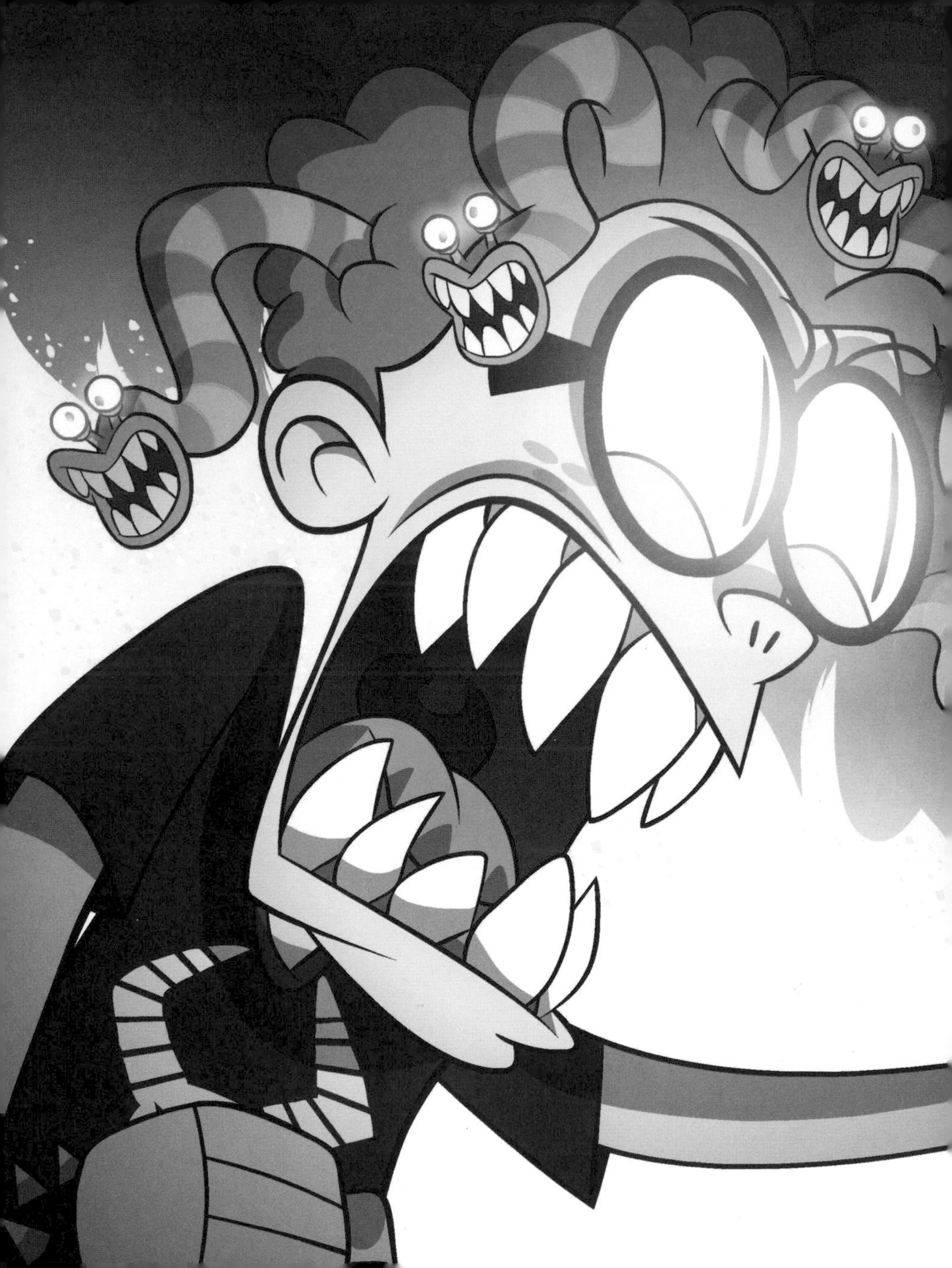

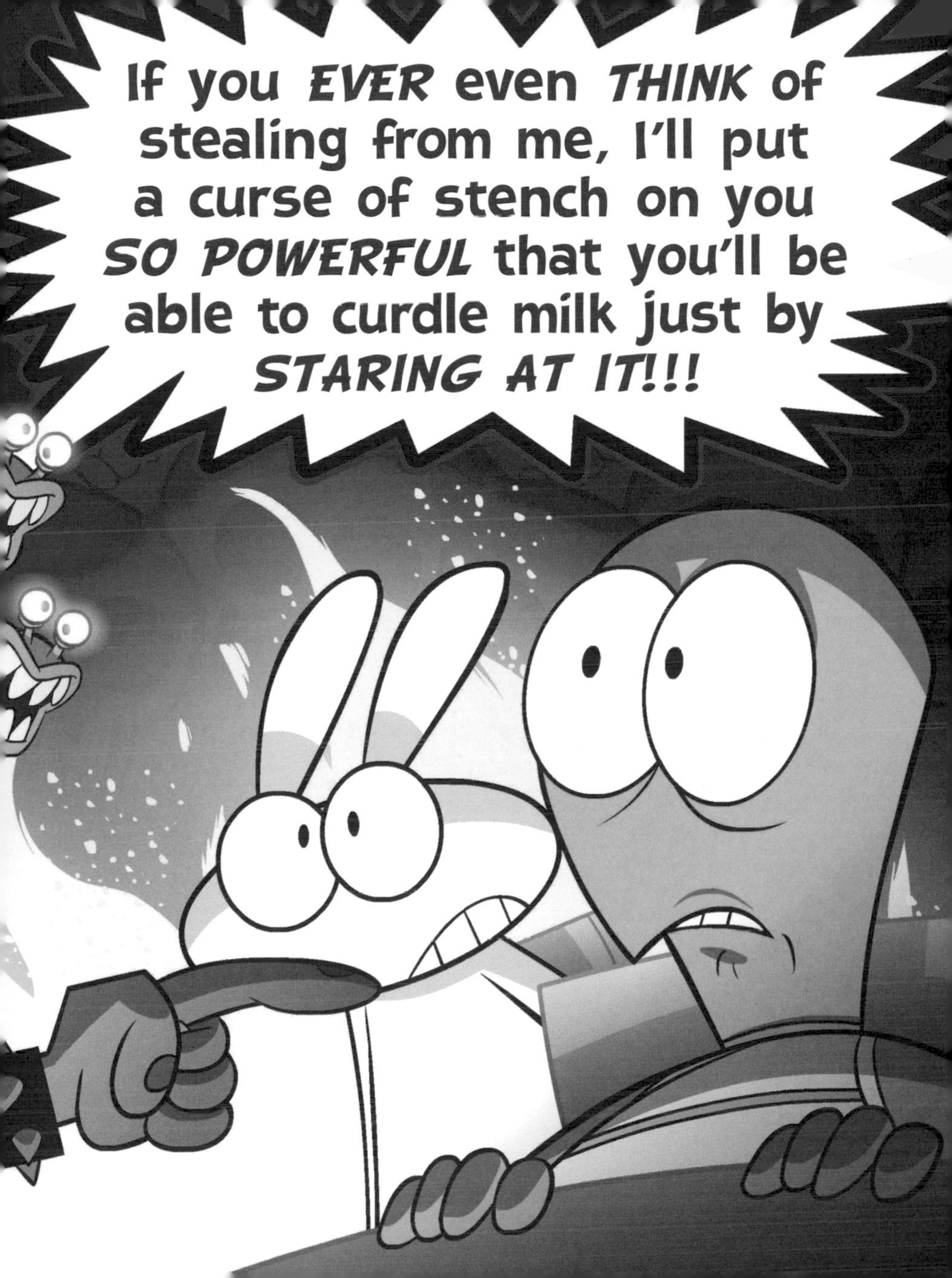
If you *EVER* even *THINK* of stealing from me, I'll put a curse of stench on you *SO POWERFUL* that you'll be able to curdle milk just by *STARING AT IT!!!*

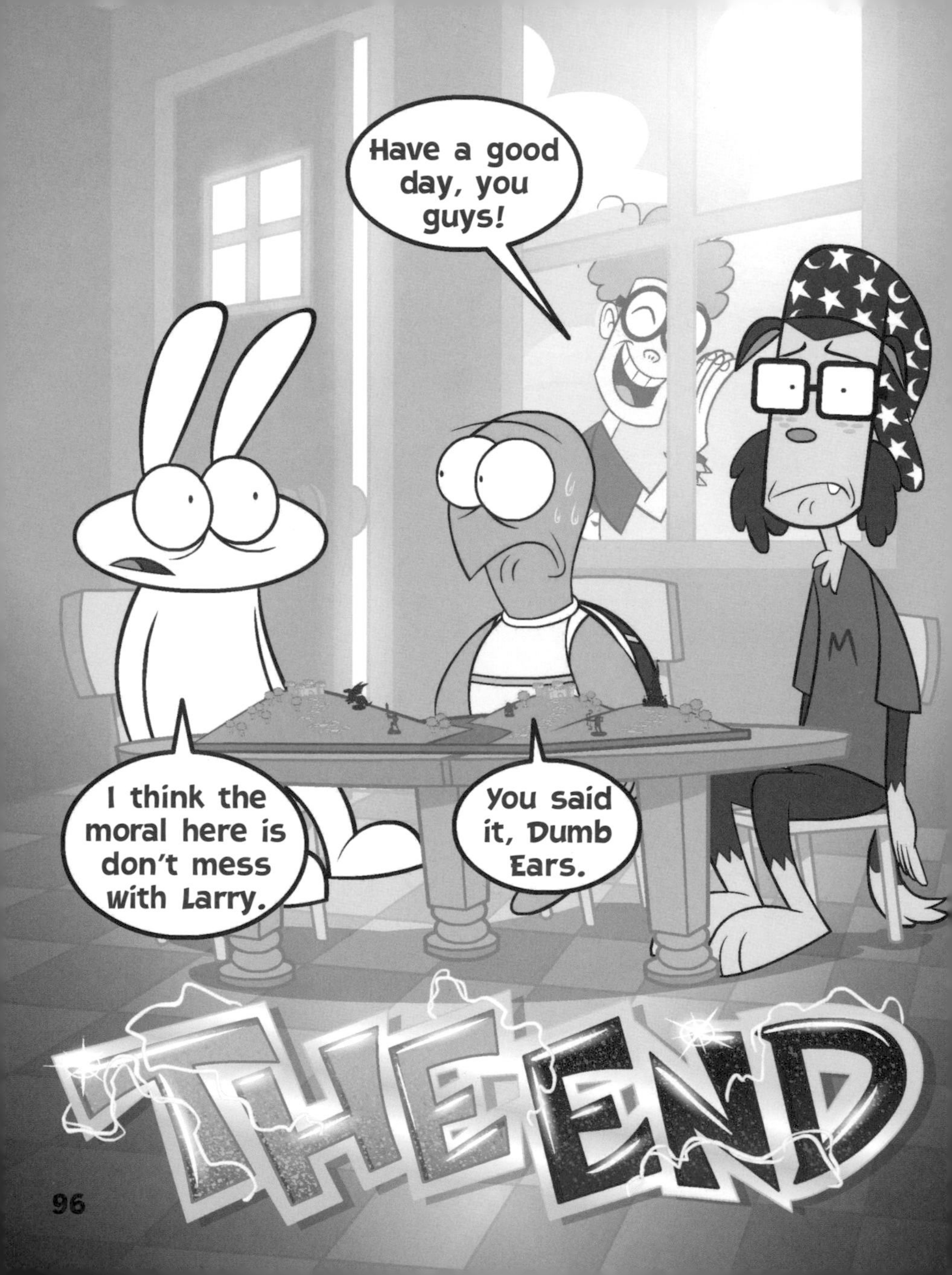

Have a good day, you guys!
I think the moral here is don't mess with Larry.
You said it, Dumb Ears.
THE END